PRAISE FOR
THE GRIMM LEGACY

"A fizzy confection . . . the story buzzes along at a delightful clip."
—*The New York Times Book Review*

"Captivating . . . a richly imagined adventure with easy appeal for Harry Potter fans."
—*Booklist*

★ "Fast-paced, filled with humor and peopled with characters who are either true to life or delightfully bizarre . . . fantasy lovers will feel very much at home in this tale that pulls out all the stops."
—*School Library Journal,* starred review

"Mixing tongue-in-cheek humor . . . with suspense, Shulman conjures an enticing slice of magic realism that fairy tale buffs should relish."
—*Publishers Weekly*

"It looks like Shulman, bestselling author of *Enthusiasm*, has another winner. Her gothic-tinged mystery/romance is well written, funny, teen-savvy, and virtually unputdownable."
—*Children's Literature*

"Appealing mix of fairy tale and romance—who can resist a trip on a flying carpet?"
—*VOYA*

"*The Grimm Legacy* is terrific fun for tweens and teens, and not to be missed."
—*BookPage*

Books by Polly Shulman

Enthusiasm

The Grimm Legacy

The Wells Bequest

the WELLS Bequest

POLLY SHULMAN

PUFFIN BOOKS
An Imprint of Penguin Group (USA)

PUFFIN BOOKS
Published by the Penguin Group
Penguin Group (USA) LLC
375 Hudson Street
New York, New York 10014

USA ★ Canada ★ UK ★ Ireland ★ Australia
New Zealand ★ India ★ South Africa ★ China

penguin.com
A Penguin Random House Company

First published in the United States of America by Nancy Paulsen Books,
an imprint of Penguin Young Readers Group, 2013
Published by Puffin Books, an imprint of Penguin Young Readers Group, 2014

THE LIBRARY OF CONGRESS HAS CATALOGED THE NANCY PAULSEN BOOKS EDITION AS FOLLOWS:
Shulman, Polly.
The Wells Bequest / Polly Shulman. pages cm
ISBN 978-0-399-25646-2(hc)
Summary: Two teenagers use H. G. Wells's famous time machine to race through time and stop
a dangerous enemy. [1. Time travel—Fiction. 2. Science fiction.] I. Title.
PZ7.S559474We 2013 [Fic]—dc23 2012036571

Puffin Books ISBN 978-0-14-751028-0

Printed in the United States of America

Chapter opener art © 2013 by iStockphoto.com/liseykina

1 3 5 7 9 10 8 6 4 2

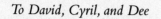

To David, Cyril, and Dee

CONTENTS

1. How a Six-Inch-Tall Me Appeared in My Bedroom 1

2. The New-York Circulating Material Repository 15

3. Jaya Rao 23

4. Five Automatons, One Wink 30

5. The Great Man's Assistant's Great-Great-Grandson 43

6. I Build a Very Strange Radio 51

7. A Stiletto, a Niddy Noddy, and a Serpent 63

8. Jaya Hits Me 72

9. The Wells Bequest 83

10. Simon's Sabotage 95

11. My Brilliant Idea 105

12. Chocolate at the Time Traveller's House 118

13. Jaya Stops Time 132

14. The Terror 140

15. The Death Ray..150

16. The Shrink Ray 157

17. Time Passes—Backward 166

18. A Steam Train in Manhattan 174

19. Her Royal Highness, the Rani of Chomalur 183

20. Two Geniuses and One Very Long Lecture 195

21. A Firefight on South Fifth Avenue 208

22. I Meet Myself Coming and Going 216

23. A World Without Simon 222

24. Jaya's Brilliant Idea 228

25. I Save the Life of the Most Awesome Girl in the Universe ...232

26. The Green Mouse Machine 239

Note to Readers 251

Librarian's Note 255

Acknowledgments 259

CHAPTER ONE

How a Six-Inch-Tall Me Appeared in My Bedroom

The Wednesday when the whole time-travel adventure began, I was fiddling with my game controller, trying to make the shoot button more sensitive.

Wednesdays are my intense days. It was a Wednesday back when I took the test for Cooper Tech, where my big sister, Sofia, goes, and a Wednesday when I found out I didn't get in. It was a Wednesday when I didn't get into any of the other schools I was hoping for either and learned I would be going to my current school, the Manhattan Polytechnic Academy. Which means it was also a Wednesday when Sofia stopped calling Poly "Tech for Dummies" and started telling everybody that Poly kids are really very creative.

It's not just bad things that happen to me on Wednesdays, though. I was born on a Wednesday. My family came to America on a Wednesday. And it was a Wednesday both times Jaya Rao and I first met—the Wednesday when I first met her, and the one when she first met me.

I had just figured out how to double the input speed on

my game controller. I was messing around with the wires with half my attention, while with the other half I tried to think of a good science fair project. Science fair projects are a big deal in my family. Dad is the chief technology officer at a big media software company downtown, Mom is a cognitive neuroscientist, my brother, Dmitri, is a physics major at MIT, and my sister, Sofia, can't seem to remember she's not actually an immuno-oncologist yet, just a high school junior interning in Franklin-Morse Hospital's immuno-oncology lab.

Me? I'm a student at Tech for Dummies, where the kids are really very creative.

I toyed with the idea of doing something really very creative involving rats. I like rats. They're jumpy and inquisitive, like me. But what, exactly? Something with mazes, or chemicals, or electric shocks? Everything I could think of sounded pretty unpleasant for the rats. Besides, rats have minds of their own. They were sure to make my project skitter off in surprising directions, with unusable results.

That's what usually happens to my experiments, even without rats. I'm great at coming up with clever fixes and mysterious surprises. Unfortunately, science fair judges aren't so crazy about mysterious surprises.

I reconnected the game controller to my computer and launched Gravity Force III. A space raider appeared at the upper left of my screen. I whipped the cursor down to the right, ducking my ship behind a dust cloud. My fix worked! The button moved twice as fast as before, and so did the blaster fire. This was great!

I heard a slither behind me, then a crash. I looked up, startled.

A blast of wind had come from nowhere. It had blown my new manga poster off the wall and knocked over my lamp. And— wait! Was something wrong with my eyes? Slowly, right in front of me, an object was appearing.

No, it wasn't my eyes. The thing had heft. It was a machine around the size of a football, made of glittering metal. It had gears and rods and knobs and a little saddle, with two tiny dolls sitting on it. They were moving like they were alive.

Not dolls—people.

But that wasn't even the weirdest part. The weirdest part was that one of the tiny people looked just like *me*.

"Hi, Leo! Bet you're surprised to see us," said the one who didn't look like me. She was sitting in front of him. The guy who looked like me—*exactly* like me, with my long face, brown eyes, that stupid curl falling down his forehead—was hugging her tightly around the waist so he wouldn't fall off the saddle.

I should have been too busy with surprise and confusion for anything else, but I felt a distinct jab of jealousy.

That surprised me even more. I never thought much about girls, but when I did, it was the action-graphic type, the kind of girl who wears skintight bodysuits and high-tech, thigh-high boots so she can kick the blaster out of the bad guy's hand while doing a backflip.

The tiny girl on the tiny machine looked nothing like that. She was wearing an old-fashioned dress like something out of an educational video about pioneers. Her knot of black hair had fallen over her left ear, and tufts were sticking out in all directions. Her dress was all muddy. She had soot on her face and a funny chin. She was the most beautiful girl I had ever seen.

"What . . . who . . . where did you come from?" I said. Wow, Leo. Real smooth talking.

"Hi, um, me," said the tiny guy. He was wearing a dorky old-fashioned suit. "It's me, Leo. I'm you. Wow, you're big. Listen, this is important. Read H. G. Wells—"

"What do you mean you're me?"

"I'm *you,* only later. Well, right now we're the same time, but I was later before. Then I was earlier. But from a linear point of view, I guess I'm always later. But it doesn't matter—"

"What? What are you talking about?"

"It's not important. The important thing is, read *The Time Machine.*"

"I don't understand. How did you get so small?"

"We used a shrink ray," said the girl impatiently, like it was obvious. "Listen, Leo, this is *important.* When you meet Simon FitzHenry, make sure you stop him from—"

"Jaya! Stop it!" Mini-me put his hand over her mouth. "You'll change history! Ow! Don't bite!"

She pulled his hand away. "I'm *trying* to change history! Save everybody a whole lot of trouble."

"*Cause* everybody a whole lot of trouble, you mean. Wow, you're impossible."

"Me? If we just tell him a few things that he's going to know anyway soon, we can stop Simon before he—"

The guy covered her mouth again. "Come on, Jaya. We don't have time to argue about this right now. Ow!"

She spat out his hand again. "Oh, so *you're* the impatient one now? What do you mean, we don't have time? Time is *exactly* what we have. We have all the time in the world."

"No, we don't! My sister's coming."

The girl—Jaya—ignored him. "Listen, Leo," she said to me. "You have to tell Simon not to—"

Mini-me leaned around her and pressed a lever. They started to fade, getting softer and more transparent. Jaya was still talking, but I couldn't hear her. The wind sprang up again, knocking my books over. Then they were gone, machine and all.

Not a moment too soon. My door burst open. "Jeez, Leo, what's all the banging?" It was my sister, Sofia.

"Just knocking things over." I picked up the lamp and the books and put them back on the desk. I turned my back, hoping she'd go away. I had a lot to think about.

"You know what the trouble with you is?" asked Sofia.

"Yeah. I better by now, because it's your favorite thing to tell me."

"The trouble with you," she said, "is you're growing so fast you don't know where your hands and feet are."

"That's not what you said yesterday. Yesterday the trouble with me was I didn't have the simple human decency to put the milk back in the fridge."

"Maybe the two things are connected," Sofia said, sitting down on my bed. She looked like she was planning to stay awhile.

I tried to make her leave by saying, "Well, I better get back to my project." I didn't think it would work, though.

It didn't. "What project?" she asked, looking pointedly at my computer screen, where my ship was lying in an ignominious heap of fragments. Schist! I'd almost made it to Level VIII before the tiny machine distracted me. That crash was going to poison my score.

I had to admit, it was a little crazy to worry about a game score being destroyed by impossible tiny people riding a science-fiction machine.

"Science fair," I said.

"What's the topic?"

I shrugged. "I was thinking about teleportation or maybe time travel. Maybe I could build like an anti-gravity device. Or a shrink ray."

Sofia waved her hand in the air, the way she does. "There's no such thing."

She was wrong. After what I'd just seen, I knew those things existed. That machine with the little people had to involve teleportation or anti-gravity or time travel. Or maybe all three. It definitely involved a shrink ray. I said, "Sure there is! Physicists can teleport subatomic particles. Just ask Dmitri. Or time travel—you told me yourself you could go back in time if you had a faster-than-light spaceship."

"So you're going to build a faster-than-light spaceship for your science fair project?"

"No, but . . ." Why did Sofia always make everything sound so impossible? "I thought I could work on the theoretical underpinnings. You know, like Dmitri did when he won the Randall Prize."

"Oh, well, listen, Cubby." That's her pet name for me—Leo, lion, cub, get it? She uses it when she's trying to be nice, which means when she's not saying what she's really thinking, which in this case was: *Dmitri's a genius, you idiot, and you're . . . not.*

See, I can read minds! Maybe I should do my project on telepathy.

"Until you get up to the Randall Prize level," Sofia continued gently, "the judges like to see a nice, clear demonstration of something hands-on. Why don't you try some genetics experiments breeding *Arabidopsis*?"

"Grow plants?" I knew how that would end: with thirty-two paper cups full of dead dirt.

"All right, *Drosophila*."

"You want me to breed fruit flies in the apartment? Mom's gonna love that."

"Fine, then. If you don't want my help, why'd you ask me?"

I hadn't, actually, but there was no advantage in pointing that out. "I'm sorry. Maybe Ms. Kang has ideas." Ms. Kang is my science teacher.

"Good plan, Cubby. Let me know what she says." Sofia ruffled my hair, just to rub in how much more mature she was than me, and left me alone with my thoughts.

Now that I had some privacy to think, my thoughts were pretty alarming. What had just happened? Either I'd been visited by a pair of kids straight out of a science-fiction story or I was losing my marbles.

Choice A—the science-fiction story—sounded much better than choice B: wacko Leo. But in my experience, unfortunately, sounding better rarely makes a thing true. That's one reason I never do as well on multiple-choice tests as other people who have the same "natural gifts," as my parents like to call them. I tend to pick the interesting choice.

I knew which possibility Sofia would pick here. There isn't a multiple-choice test known to man that Sofia couldn't ace. She wouldn't hesitate to go for choice B: Leo is loopy.

The truth is, I do sort of see visions sometimes. Sometimes when I'm thinking very hard about a gadget I'm trying to build or fix, I imagine it so clearly it seems real. I see it in front of me, with all its gears and wires. But it isn't *actually* real, and it certainly never talks. This vision was a whole different kind of freaky.

What if Sofia had seen the tiny people herself? Would she conclude *she* was crazy too?

Definitely, I decided—and she's so proud of being rational that considering herself crazy would drive her completely out of her mind. It was lucky my visitors had vanished before she came in.

Well, not lucky, exactly. I remembered what the one who told me he was me had said just before they disappeared: "My sister's coming."

That meant the little guy must really *have* been me! And he'd talked about a time machine and the danger of changing history. That's exactly what *I* would worry about if I found a time machine: going back to the past and changing something so that my parents never met or messing things up so that World War III started last Wednesday or my family never left Moscow. The little guy on the machine talked just like me.

Except, if he was me, how could he act that way with that amazing girl, Jaya? Calling her impossible! Sitting there calmly on a time machine with his arms around her waist!

Well, Future Me knew her better than I did. Maybe she *was*

impossible. I had no idea what she was really like. I only knew I wanted to find out.

But how could I find her? It's not like I could put an ad on Craigslist: *You: Six inches tall, dark complexion, messy hair, gorgeous. We met in my bedroom. You knocked over my lamp. You disappeared before I could get your digits.*

Where would I even begin to look for her?

Then it hit me. Maybe I didn't have to! My future self clearly knew her well. Maybe I just had to sit tight and wait until she appeared in my life. It would be pretty soon, too—Future Leo didn't look any older than I am now.

The idea made my insides do a happy little dance. Soon I would know that amazing girl well enough to tell her she was impossible.

Then a less cheerful thought struck me. Jaya and Future Me had a time machine. They were traveling back in time. What if they changed something in the past—or even in their past, my future? What if they snarled up the universe in a way that made me never meet the girl?

Unthinkable. Somehow—somehow!—I would have to stop that from happening.

I wished I had someone to discuss this with. Not my family, obviously. My best friend, Jake, was cool enough not to freak out, no matter what I told him. But he wouldn't be any help. He wasn't interested in thinking too hard about anything.

I would see what my science teacher, Ms. Kang, had to say. She has lots of interesting thoughts about things like whether the universe goes on and on forever or loops back around on itself or what cavemen talked about when they were falling asleep. I wouldn't tell her about the tiny, lamp-knocking-over time travelers, of course, but we could discuss general topics in time travel.

I found her the next day in the little room next to the library, which used to be a coatroom. She was grading tests, bent over in a student desk chair, the kind with a big flat arm for writing on. Ms. Kang gets cold easily, so she's always tugging the sleeves of her sweaters down over her hands. She has very dark, slightly purplish red hair, which is kind of strange—don't most Korean people have black hair? Maybe she dyes it. Her lips are the same color as her hair, but I'm pretty sure that's lipstick.

"Hi, Leo," she said, pushing aside the tests. "What's up?"

"Hi, Ms. Kang. I need to ask you something," I said.

"Okay, shoot."

I suddenly felt self-conscious, so instead of asking about time travel, I said, "Why do you hang out in this little room instead of the science office?"

"I miss being near the library." Ms. Kang used to be the school media specialist before she switched to teaching science. "And nobody knows where to find me here, so I can actually get my work done."

"Oh, I'm sorry! I didn't mean to interrupt you."

I started to leave, but she caught my sleeve. "Not *you*, silly! Sit down. Is that what you wanted to ask me—why I work here?"

I sat in the other chair. "No, not really. I wanted to ask . . . What do you know about time travel?"

"That's more like it." She rubbed her hands together. "Well,

I know that we're all traveling forward in time together, at a rate of one second per second. But that's probably not the kind of time travel you mean. Why do you ask?"

"I was thinking about my science project." That was true, anyway. "Has anyone ever made, you know, a real time machine? Like you could use to go backward and forward in time?"

"Not to my knowledge," said Ms. Kang. "But some physicists think it might be possible. If you could build a faster-than-light spaceship, theoretically you might be able to arrive before you left."

I nodded. "That's what my sister says."

"Or you could try to find a wormhole in the space-time continuum."

"A wormhole! Where would I look?"

"Nobody knows for sure, but I have some books that you could start with. There's a good one by Stephen Hawking. The thing is, nobody knows for sure whether time travel is possible. Like Hawking pointed out, if there really are time machines, why haven't we ever met any time travelers?"

"Yeah, but . . ." *Yeah, but I have!!* I wanted to say. *I met two of them yesterday! And one of them was ME!* If I said that, Ms. Kang would think I was crazy. "Maybe this isn't where they want to come," I said. "I mean *when* they want to come. Or maybe there just aren't that many of them. I've never met any travelers from Iceland, but that doesn't mean the Icelanders don't have airplanes."

"True," said Ms. Kang.

"So do you think I should . . . I don't know, try and make a time machine myself?"

"You mean for the science fair?"

I nodded.

Ms. Kang tilted her head. "No harm in trying. I wouldn't count on getting it done for the fair, though. The deadline's at the end of the semester."

"If it took longer, I could use the time machine to go back in time and show myself how to finish," I said. "I could even make an extra time machine and carry it back in time to my present-day self."

Hey! Was that what I had been doing yesterday?

No, probably not—in fact, I'd seemed to be trying very hard *not* to tell myself anything about time machines.

Ms. Kang shook her head. "Wouldn't that be cheating? The other kids only get a few weeks to work on their projects."

She was right. Plus, that would be changing the past, and the one thing Future Me seemed completely certain about was that I/he shouldn't change the past.

But wait. If the only reason I wasn't changing the past was that Future Me was dead set against it, then by influencing *me* to not change the past, Future Me was doing exactly what he didn't want to do: changing the past. So in order to save Future Me from changing the past, did I have to change the past myself?

"You okay there, Leo? Your face is all scrunched up."

"Sorry. I was just trying to think the whole time-travel thing through," I said. It's all right, I told myself. I hadn't needed Future Leo to tell me changing the past was dangerous. I knew that already, all by myself. "So if I can't build a time machine, got any other suggestions?"

"But Leo, you're usually so full of ideas! Remember that

time you used mirrors and fiber-optic cables to project the view from the roof into the auditorium? Or when you and Jake tuned the toilets to play chords when they flushed? Why don't you do something like that?"

"For my *science fair* project? But those things weren't real science! They didn't discover anything new or test any theories. They were just . . . fun." That was one great thing about Poly. It may not be as rigorous as my siblings' schools, but the administration can be surprisingly tolerant. Any other school would kick you out for messing with the plumbing.

"The science fair is supposed to be fun too," Ms. Kang pointed out.

I shook my head. "Not if you come from *my* family. Science fairs are deadly serious. If I do some silly gag project, my brother and sister'll disown me."

"Wow, that sounds like a lot of pressure," said Ms. Kang. "You're not your brother and sister, you know. You have your own unique talents and interests."

"I know," I said. "That's the problem."

"I can't see it as a problem. But if you really don't want to build one of your fun inventions, have you considered submitting something in the History of Science category?"

"History of Science? Is that even a category?"

She nodded, tugging down her sleeves. "Sure. It's not as popular as some of the more hands-on ones, but it's on the list. You'd look at how some aspect of science or technology developed over time."

"Like, write a library research paper instead of doing an experiment?" I liked that idea. No plants or mice to die on me.

Ms. Kang nodded again. "It could be book research, or you could do some hands-on history. You could look at how scientific tools changed over time and how that affected the science. Like telescopes or clocks. Maybe you could build a model."

"The library has lots of books about science and history. But where would I find a bunch of antique telescopes and clocks?" I asked.

Ms. Kang said, "Have you ever heard of the New-York Circulating Material Repository?"

CHAPTER TWO

The New-York
Circulating Material Repository

Before I did anything else, I had to follow Future Me's advice. That afternoon I hunted down *The Time Machine* and found a nice sunny corner in the public library with a beat-up chair to sprawl in.

It's a good book. The hero, an inventor, builds a time machine and uses it to travel to the distant future, where humans have evolved into two separate species—the happy, peaceful Eloi and the downtrodden, apelike Morlocks. The Morlocks catch him and he almost doesn't escape. The story gets pretty exciting, but what excited me most was the time machine. The description sounded a lot like the one I'd seen.

I read it carefully, looking for hints about how to build it, but the book didn't really give any. While I was at the library, I also checked out books about science to get ideas for my project.

On Wednesday, I found myself walking through misty drizzle to the address Ms. Kang had given me. I'd finally decided to do my project on the history of robots. Maybe I could use some ideas from old technology to build a new model—that might be more fun than just writing a paper. As long as my model didn't go crazy and decide to kill all humans.

The building was a row house on the Upper East Side with a brass plaque beside the door that read *The New-York Circulating Material Repository*. I pulled open the heavy doors. Inside was a big room, way wider than the house itself.

I stood in the entryway staring around me, trying to figure out how the inside could be bigger than the outside. It bothered me so much, the feeling seemed almost physical. It felt like an itch.

A girl a little older than me was sitting behind a big wooden desk reading a book. She looked up. "You look lost," she said. "Can I help you?"

"I hope so," I said. "I'm doing a history-of-science project, and my teacher said there were old scientific instruments here?"

"You'd better ask the reference librarian. Go up to the top floor and follow the signs for the catalog room. Elevator's that way."

"Thanks."

"Sure." She went back to her book.

I took the creaky old elevator and walked down a long hallway to a door marked *Catalog Room*. It opened onto a wide room with high, arched skylights. The sky was bright blue with fluffy white clouds bouncing around it—the kind of clouds angels sit on in Christmas cards.

But wait—wasn't it raining outside? I hadn't seen any sign of the rain letting up. Was my mind playing tricks on me—was this more evidence of Loopy Leo?

A broad beam of sunlight shot through the skylight and fell

on a desk where a man was filing cards in a box. It looked almost on purpose, like a spotlight aimed at the desk.

Rows and rows of wooden drawers lined the walls, with big, thick books on shelves above them. One man had pulled out a drawer and was flicking through the cards inside it. A woman was standing on a ladder, reaching for one of the big books. I didn't see any computers anywhere.

I paused in the doorway. Which of the people was the reference librarian?

I randomly picked the one in the sun. "Excuse me," I asked, keeping my voice down, the way librarians like. "Are you . . . is there a reference librarian here?"

"That's me," he said. "What can I do for you?" He was short, with broad shoulders and crinkly eyes. He had a slight Spanish accent. He looked like he'd just finished laughing and might start again any second.

"I'm doing a history-of-science project, and my teacher told me I could find historic robots here," I said.

"Nice," he said. "Did your teacher explain about the repository?"

"She said it was like a library, only with objects instead of books. She said you would have different robots I could compare."

"That's right. We have plenty of robots."

"So where do you keep them?" Clearly not in this room. The drawers were way too small.

"Downstairs on Stack 5, mostly, but the public's not allowed in the stacks."

"What are stacks?" I asked.

"The rooms where we store the objects. You have to look

up your objects in the catalog and write down the call numbers on call slips. Then you'll give the call slips to a page in the Main Exam Room and someone will go get your items for you."

"Oh, okay. How do I find the call numbers? I don't see any computers."

"No, we use traditional card files. Here, I'll show you." He shut the box he'd been using and came out from behind his desk. As he did, the beam of sun faded away. I looked up at the skylight. It was still filled with blue sky and fluffy clouds, but the sun had gone behind one of the clouds, turning it gold at the edges.

Where was the rain? Had it stopped?

That was the obvious explanation, but as I looked up at the sky I got the distinct feeling it wasn't the correct one. It felt almost like I was looking up at a different sky—the sky of some other world.

"Wasn't it raining?" I said. "The sun . . ." I stopped. I didn't want him to think I was crazy.

The reference librarian looked at me closely. After a moment, he said, "The card files are this way. Come."

I followed him to the left-hand wall of drawers.

"*R* for 'robot'—here." He pulled out a drawer labeled *R–Rom*. "See? *Ringbolt . . . ripsaw . . . ritual object . . . road map . . .* There you go." He flicked through the cards until he came to one labeled *robot,* then stood aside so I could look through the drawer myself.

"Thanks," I said, sticking my finger in the spot to hold my place and flicking ahead past robot after robot.

"Here, you'll need these." The librarian handed me a bunch of small, blank forms, along with a stubby little pencil. "Fill out a separate call slip for each object. When you're done, take them to the Main Exam Room and give them to the page on duty. Down the hall to the left." He went back to his desk. As he sat down, the sun came out from behind its cloud and fell in bright squares on his desk.

A card catalog may not sound all that exciting, but as I flipped slowly through the robot section, my heart started to pound. I couldn't believe what I was reading! They had working models of three Mars rovers. The deep-sea robot that found the *Titanic*. The first robotic vacuum cleaner. These things were robot superstars!

But everything listed under *robot* in the catalog was from the twentieth century or later. For my history-of-science project, I was going to need to study earlier ones too. Where were all the older robots?

I was about to go ask the reference librarian when I noticed a card at the beginning of the section that said *See also: android, automaton, cyborg.*

I pulled out the *A–Ap* drawer. Most of the androids were fairly recent too. Then I pulled out *Aq–Az* and flipped to *automaton*. Bingo! Some of these automatons were thousands of years old.

I couldn't believe people had invented robots so long ago— and I couldn't believe such fragile machines had made it through all those centuries. My own stuff usually breaks in a matter of months.

Not that it matters—I can always fix it.

The earliest automaton in the repository's collection was from ancient China, made by a man called Yan Shi. I copied its description and call number onto one of the paper slips. I chose four others to start with: a steam-powered bird from ancient Greece, a hand-washing maidservant made by a twelfth-century Kurdish inventor, a mechanical knight designed by Leonardo da Vinci, and John Dee's wooden flying beetle from the sixteenth century. I copied out their call numbers and info onto call slips and took them down the hall to the Main Examination Room.

Once again, I was blown away. It was like walking into a landscape made of light.

All four sides of the Main Examination Room up to the ceiling were filled with brilliant stained glass. But that doesn't even begin to describe it. They didn't look frilly or churchy. They hardly even looked like windows. The scenes were so vivid they seemed alive.

I turned around slowly to take it all in. On one side, the window showed a rain forest. Brightly colored birds peeped through the branches. At least, they looked like birds—but some of them had very strange shapes, with four wings or spiky crests and skin like lizards. Not birds—maybe . . . dinosaurs!

I felt like I had one foot in a library and the other in a primordial forest. Or like I'd walked into the paleontology room at the natural history museum and the dinosaurs had suddenly come to life. Why had I never heard of this place before?

In the next window, snow was falling across a wide white valley. A herd of shaggy mammoths with lumpy foreheads was crossing the valley. I felt a wisp of cold air, as if a distant breeze were blowing toward me from the faraway tundra.

On the third side, a horse and two foals stood on a carpet of glowing autumn leaves, frozen like deer when you startle them. I got the strangest feeling they would leap away as soon as I turned my back.

No, not horses. Horses don't have spotted stripes, and these animals were too small. When I looked carefully, I saw they had toes.

The last window showed a rocky orange desert. There were dunes, canyons, and craters, crisscrossed by riverbeds that looked like they had been dry for eons. Something about that landscape felt creepily alien. I stared at it, trying to decide where it was supposed to be. Arizona? Africa? It could be anywhere. . . .

Or could it? Something about it bothered me intensely. What a freaky place this library was! I stared at the window, trying to figure out why it felt so *off.* Was it the shadows? In the picture, the sun was setting and the moon was rising.

No, not *the* moon. *A* moon.

The scene in the window couldn't have been anywhere on Earth. In the sky there were two moons. I was looking at a landscape on another planet.

I shook myself slightly. Come on, Leo, I told myself. It's not an actual planet, just a picture. Why should stained-glass windows always show boring, terrestrial scenes? Why not dinosaurs and alien planets sometimes? And the horse looked pretty normal, anyway. Except for the toes.

I turned back to the horse and her foals. They were still there, frozen. But I was pretty sure the left-hand foal had had his head down, just a minute ago. Now he was looking right at me.

A shiver went straight through me, from my scalp to my own toes. This was *crazy*! Animals in stained glass windows don't *move*. I had to have been mistaken. I *had* to.

I pulled my eyes away from the glowing scenes in the windows and looked around. The rest of the room looked like any fancy library reading room, with rows of long tables and carved wooden chairs. People were sitting here and there, examining objects and writing in notebooks.

It didn't sound like a library, though. In the background I heard a quiet whooshing, gurgling sound, like a stream. Every so often something would rustle and thump, like an animal in the bushes. Were the noises coming from the *windows*?

Get a grip, Leo! I told myself. The noises weren't coming from the windows—they were coming from an area in the center of the room, a sort of big wooden booth where a guy and a couple of girls were filing papers and handing objects to the patrons.

That must be where I was supposed to give my call slips to what the reference librarian had called "the page on duty."

I went up to the big window in the front of the booth. The page on duty was a girl. Once again, I was in for a surprise. Not *a* girl—*the* girl.

Jaya, the girl from the time machine.

The girl from the time machine was real!

CHAPTER THREE

Jaya Rao

In real life she was tall, as tall as me, and skinny, with long arms and legs. She wasn't exactly beautiful—at least, she wasn't what I would have called "beautiful" a month ago. (I must have been an idiot a month ago.) She was wearing ordinary clothes, jeans and a cotton sweater, instead of the long dress she'd worn the first time I saw her. She had big black eyes and smooth, light tan skin. Her wavy black hair looked like a lion's mane. It made you want to touch it with your fingers.

For some reason I found it painfully embarrassing to be standing in front of her, seeing her life-size and real enough to touch. I realized I hadn't completely believed she existed outside of my brain. It was like I'd invented her. Somehow, that felt like something I had no right to do, like spying on her.

"Do I have mustard on my nose?" she asked.

"What? No. Did you just eat lunch?"

"No. You're staring."

"Oh! I'm sorry." Even more embarrassing! "I just—I think we've met before."

"No, I don't think so," she said. "You don't look familiar."

"You're Jaya, aren't you?"

"Yes, I am." She sounded surprised. "Why don't I remember *you*?"

"Do you usually remember people?"

"No, not everybody, but . . . I would definitely remember *you*. Where did we meet? Was it here at the repository?"

"No, in—" What was I going to say? *In my bedroom, the other evening. We were riding on a time machine. You were six inches tall.* "I'm not sure. Maybe in . . ." I shrugged. Go, Leo! Way to make a first impression.

On the other hand, she had said she would definitely remember me. That was flattering, right?

Unless she meant she would definitely remember a weirdo like me.

Someone cleared his throat behind me, and I saw a short line had formed. "Sorry," I said. I gave Jaya two slips from the top of my pile.

"You forgot to put your name," she said, handing me a pencil.

"Oh, sorry." Sorry, sorry, sorry. Stop saying *sorry,* Leo! "You must think I'm a total boson."

"A total what?"

"A boson. It's a subatomic particle."

"I know what a boson is. But why are you calling yourself a subatomic particle?"

"Oh, right—I keep forgetting other people don't call each other bosons. It's what my family says when someone's being, like, a jerk or an idiot. Because my brother studies physics."

"That *is* a good word," she said. "Thanks! I'll definitely start using it. Here, sign your slips in the corner."

I scribbled my name and gave her back the call slips. She jotted something on them, rolled them up, and stuffed them into a little plastic tube like a skinny, transparent soda can. Then she opened a little trapdoor in a pipe that wound around the booth and disappeared down the floor. The whooshing sound got louder—so this was where it was coming from.

She stuck the tube into the pipe and let the door snap shut. I could hear it thumping as it was sucked into the pipe and traveled through it.

The part of my brain that gets caught up in how stuff works started doing its thing. I wondered where the tube was going and how it was sucked in. Did the pipe branch, or was it a straight shot to wherever the tube was going? If it did branch, was there any way to route the tube to one branch or another? How did the tube come out the other end? I started building a whole network of tubes in my head.

"Here you go, Leo Novikov," Jaya said, breaking my train of thought. She handed me a wooden disk with the number 17 stenciled on it.

"Thanks. Um . . . what do I do with this?"

"Watch the board." She pointed overhead to an array of glass numbers. Some of them were glowing. "When your number lights up, come back and get your items." She flashed me a smile. She had straight white teeth, with one crooked canine. I had never seen anything as perfect as that one crooked tooth.

Get a grip, Leo, I told myself again. I thanked her and sat down at a nearby library table where I would have a good view of the board—and of Jaya.

I tried not to stare as she moved around the booth talking to the other patrons, putting plastic tubes into the pipes, and taking things out of a small elevator in the wall. I couldn't keep my eyes off her. Her quickness. Her big, dark eyes.

She was real! The girl in my impossible dream wasn't a dream after all. And I'd found her without even looking!

How could that have happened? It was the kind of coincidence that drove my sister crazy. Sofia hated what she called "crucial coincidences." When they happened on a TV show, she would throw pillows at the screen, yelling, "Bosons! Bosons!"

Of course, if you thought about it, my finding Jaya wasn't really a coincidence. It just looked like one because I didn't know the future yet—but Future Leo did. My meeting her today was always going to happen. You could call it fate.

Did Jaya know about the time machine? Should I tell her? No, she probably didn't know yet. She hadn't recognized me. If I told her, maybe she would freak out and think I was scary nuts.

But Future Jaya seemed perfectly comfortable with flying around on a tiny time machine. So if she didn't know already, sometime between now and whenever that was, she would find out about it. If it freaked her out, she would get over it.

A light flashed above the wall elevator. Jaya took two robots out of it and carried them to the counter. She flicked a switch and the number 17 lit up on the board.

I went up to the window.

"Here you go," said Jaya.

I sat down at a table with my two robots: Leonardo da Vinci's knight and the wooden beetle from sixteenth-century England.

The knight was about the size of a desk lamp. It moved when

you wound a crank. It was wearing armor, but you could open it up to see the insides and adjust the movement, which worked by pulleys and cables. Da Vinci had done an especially impressive job designing the neck mechanism—the knight could move its head just like a real person. I could see why everybody thought the guy was a genius.

As I put the knight through its paces, my mechanical-vision thing kicked in. I saw the knight's patterns of motion traced like glowing lines in the air. I looked back and forth between my own arms and the knight's arms. I could see how my own muscles worked like cables stretching and pulleys tightening too. For a moment I wondered if I were just an automaton myself. Had some genius built *me*?

I got out my notebook and started to draw the knight.

"Leo Novikov?" I looked up, startled. It was Jaya. "Are you almost done with those items?" she asked. "We're closing soon."

The room had an orange glow. The sun was setting in the stained glass above me. I must have been working for ages. "Schist! How did it get so late?"

Jaya laughed. "Schist?" she said. "Is that another of your family expressions?"

I nodded. "It was on our science vocabulary list last year. It's a kind of rock. It's what happens to hot sandstone when it gets squished really hard for a few million years."

"I know," said Jaya. "But I've never heard anybody use it as a curse before. It sounds really bad—in a good way."

"Yeah, it's one of my favorites. Even strict teachers can't object to a word from a vocabulary list, right?"

"Quark, no!" said Jaya.

"Good one!" I grinned at her.

"I'm a quick study," she said, grinning back. "So, are you done with these robots?"

I'd barely even looked at the wooden beetle. "Not yet. Is there any way I could reserve them for later?"

"Sure. Or I could sign them out to you. Then you can take them home."

"Really? You'd let me check them out?"

"Sure! We're a circulating repository—you can borrow pretty much any of our holdings. Just give me your member number."

"But I'm not a member," I said.

"You should join, then. Here, bring those robots up to the desk and I'll give you an application."

She slipped behind the counter and handed me a form. "Fill this out."

"Thanks." I ran my eye down it. It asked some pretty strange questions: my kindergarten teacher's hair color, my favorite kind of mushroom, the year I first saw snow.

I started writing. "What do I put here, where it says 'submitted by'?"

"Oh, that's me," she said.

"I don't think I know your last name," I said.

"Rao. And it's Jaya, not Jaia." She spelled it for me.

I finished filling out the form and handed it to her.

"Good. I'll give this to Dr. Rust, the head repositorian. You should get your card in the mail soon."

"Thanks."

Jaya scribbled her signature on the line above where I'd

written her name. "Your robots will be on the reserve shelf over here, under *N* for *Novikov.* Just ask the page at the window."

"Thanks again, Jaya," I said. "See you tomorrow."

"Oh, I don't work tomorrow."

"Really? When do you work?"

"Tuesdays, Wednesdays, and Saturdays," said Jaya.

"Okay, then I'll see you Saturday." It wasn't how I'd planned to spend my Saturday, but playing Gravity Force III with Jake no longer sounded nearly as fun.

CHAPTER FOUR

Five Automatons, One Wink

When I told Jake I was planning to spend Saturday at the library working on my science project, he groaned. "Schist, Leo! You're turning into a real Novikov."

"What are you talking about? I was born a Novikov."

"You used to be Novikov lite. You're turning into a homework-all-the-time, rah-rah-science, Dmitri-and-Sofia Novikov."

"But I always liked science. So do you! You loved that Jules Verne book I gave you for your birthday."

"Sure, I like science fiction. That's different from spending Saturday at the library when you don't have to. When am I going to get a chance to beat you at Gravity Force III?"

"Sunday," I said.

I woke up early on Saturday feeling excited and nervous. A time machine—maybe I'd find it today! And Jaya! I would definitely see *her*.

I put on all clean clothes, even my jeans. I examined myself in the mirror. The dopey curl that's always falling down on my forehead was falling down on my forehead. Couldn't it take a day off? I finally got it to stay back by wetting it and holding it up until it dried.

I went to the kitchen to get some breakfast. Sofia was there making coffee. She's fussy about her coffee. "Isn't it a little early for you?" she said.

I shrugged.

"Where are you going all dressed up like that?" she asked.

"Dressed up like what?"

"Clean clothes."

"Library. My science project." I grabbed a bagel and started to leave.

She stopped me. "Hang on, your hair's funny." She pulled at the front of my hair. I felt the curl fall down on my forehead again. "There," she said.

"SoFEEEa!!"

"What? Now you look normal."

After all that, Jaya wasn't even on duty at the Main Exam Room. The girl who'd been downstairs last time was sitting on a stool moving plastic tubes around. A guy I hadn't seen before was standing at the desk where Jaya had been. He had reddish-blond hair, shallow eyes, and a tiny mouth that made him look like an angry doll.

"May I help you?" he asked.

Make that reddish-blond hair and an English accent.

"Yeah, I wanted to know . . . um . . . where's Jaya Rao?" I asked.

"Downstairs on Stack 5. Why?" He didn't sound too friendly.

"Nothing, really, it's just . . . she put some objects on reserve for me."

"I can get those for you. Last name?"

"Novikov."

"Be right back." He pushed a wooden cart over to the reserve shelves, loaded it with my robots, and started pushing it back to the window.

"Thanks," I said. "So how do I get to Stack 5?"

"You don't. The public isn't allowed in the stacks."

"Oh well. I just wanted to say hi to Jaya."

The guy shrugged unhelpfully, but the girl said, "Are you a friend of hers? I can send down a message if you like."

"Cool. Just tell her Leo says hi," I said. Would she even remember me?

"Here, why don't you write her a note?" The girl handed me a blank call slip and one of the stubby little pencils.

"Okay, thanks." What to write? I bit the end of the pencil.

"Abigail, the pneums are piling up," said the English guy. He sounded like we were wasting his valuable time.

"All right," said the girl—Abigail. "Just give it to me when you're finished," she told me.

I took the robots over to one of the library tables, where I stared at the blank slip for a while. Finally I wrote *Schist, you're not here! I'm upstairs in the Main Exam Room. I just wanted to say hi. Leo N. (The guy with the robots.)* I folded it over, wrote *Jaya Rao* on the flap, and went back to the desk.

"Yes?" said the guy.

"My note," I explained, waving it at Abigail, who came over

and took it. I watched her tuck the message into a plastic can and stuff the can into one of the pipes.

"What are those things?" I asked the guy.

"What things?"

"Those plastic cans that Abigail put my note in."

"You've never seen pneumatic tubes?" His voice dripped with disdain, like I'd never heard of an airplane.

"Obviously not," I said. "What are they?"

"The pneumatic tubes carry papers and small objects around the building from floor to floor."

"I figured that's what they did. But how do they work?"

"I'm sorry, I would love to talk some more, but there are people waiting," he said.

Maybe he didn't want to admit he didn't know.

I decided I was done with the DaVinci knight, so I put it on the returns cart and gave the rest of my call slips to the snobby English page. Then I turned my attention to John Dee's mechanical beetle.

I'd looked Dr. Dee up the night before. He sounded really cool. He was an English alchemist, mathematician, and spy in the sixteenth century, back when nobody quite knew the difference between science and sorcery.

I kind of wish I could have been a scientist then. My sister is always calling my experiments "alchemy," and she doesn't mean it as a compliment. But I think I would have had a better time with science back when nobody objected if your invention had extra powers that nobody asked for or if you couldn't always explain exactly how you'd gotten them to work.

Dr. Dee's beetle was the size of my fist, made of carved wood crammed with incredibly complicated clockwork. It kept doing things that shouldn't have been physically possible—like flying. The wings should be way too small for that heavy body. When I wound it up, though, it leapt out of my hands. I had to throw my sweater over it to stop it.

It lay there rattling and trying to get loose until I was afraid it would flap holes in my sweater.

It was still flapping lethargically when my next batch of automatons arrived at the circulation window. I started with al-Jazari's hand-washing automaton. It operated by hydraulics, not gears. Basically, it used the same principle as a flush toilet. You pressed a lever and water would drain out of a basin, making the robot maidservant pour you a fresh bowl for your hands.

Should I build a hydraulic robot for my science project?

No, definitely not. If I did, I would probably flood the auditorium.

By far the most interesting automaton was the oldest: the life-size Chinese mechanical man by the ancient artificer Yan Shi. It was made of leather, wood, glue, and lacquer, according to the label. The thing was huge. How would I get it to my table?

It solved the problem itself by starting to walk when I touched its shoulder. Its wooden shoes clicked on the stone floor and its silk court robes rustled. When we reached my table, it stood there nodding like it was humoring me. The ends of its long mustache brushed its silk robes.

I touched its chin to steady it and stop the nodding. Bad idea. The automaton started to sing. It had a nicer voice than mine, but that's not saying much.

A man at a nearby table turned to glare at me.

"Sorry!" I touched the automaton's chin again, hoping that would stop it. But the mechanical man just sang a new tune— something more lively.

A woman at the table beyond the angry man frowned at me and said, "There are soundproof exam rooms you can use, you know."

"Sorry, sorry! I don't know how to stop it!" I put my hand over the automaton's mouth, but that only muffled it slightly. I tried shaking its arm. That made it start beating time with its fan.

A librarian was glaring at me too. Was I going to get kicked out on my second day at the repository?

I grabbed the mechanical man by both cheeks in panic, frantically trying to hold its head still.

That did it. It clapped its mouth shut like it had swallowed a fly.

"So that's how you shut that thing up! I had no idea you could make it stop—I always just let it run through all its songs. Simon should have warned you to use a soundproof room."

I spun around. When I saw who it was, my heart started pounding. Jaya!

She was wearing a thick sweater and a ridiculous hat. It had a cone-shaped knitted part and earflaps. A long felt zigzag stuck out of the top of the cone, with a pom-pom at the end. It was the dumbest hat I had ever seen. It looked great on her.

Apparently the robot thought so too. It winked at her.

"Did the robot just *wink* at you?" I asked, remembering to keep my voice low.

She laughed softly. "It winks at all the girls. Apparently that almost got its inventor killed. The emperor he made it for didn't like having his concubines winked at. Come have lunch with me. It's my lunch break."

"All right." I could hardly believe it.

I walked the Chinese robot back to the reserve desk, and Jaya pushed the others on a cart.

"Are you taking lunch now?" the English guy asked Jaya. "If you give me a minute, I'll come with you—we need to discuss your guest page application."

"Sorry, Simon, I can't today," said Jaya. "I'm eating with Leo. Anyway, I'm not sure yet if I'm applying."

"Oh, you really should! It's a fantastic opportunity—the Burton doesn't take many guest pages."

"I'm sure it would be fascinating," said Jaya. "London's great. The thing is, Francis wants the job so badly. I'd hate to stand in his way."

"You're terribly unselfish, Jaya. You ought to think of yourself sometimes. It would be brilliant to have you in London."

"Well, I'll think about it," said Jaya. "Leo and I need to get going now. I'll talk to you later, okay?"

"Right. Another time, then," said the English guy. He glared at me. His eyes might have been the death rays in Gravity Force III.

I walked to the elevator with Jaya, fizzing with happiness.

I tried to think of something to say while the elevator went slowly downstairs and while Jaya said hi to the page at the front desk today—an Asian guy with longish hair—and held the door open for me.

At last, when we stepped out into sunshine, I thought of a topic. "Where are we going?" I asked.

"Central Park. It's not that cold. Did you bring lunch?" She held up a bag. "You can share mine, or we can stop and get you a sandwich."

"There's that deli on Madison," I said.

More silence as we walked to the deli.

I found another topic. "So who is that guy?" I asked, just as Jaya started to speak.

She'd been saying, "So how's the research," but she stopped and said instead, "Who, Francis Chu? He's one of the repository pages. You'd like him. He plays all these crazy instruments. He can play like three at once."

"That sounds cool. But I meant the guy upstairs—the snooty one with the English accent who's always glaring at me."

Jaya laughed. "Oh, that's Simon. He's not *that* bad! He's a guest page from the Burton Repository in London. I guess he does sound a little snooty, but that's mostly the accent. He's perfectly friendly . . . if anything, too friendly. That accent is really cute!"

The name rang a bell, but I couldn't place it. "He's friendly to *you*, maybe," I said. "I'm pretty sure he doesn't like me."

"Well, he doesn't know you yet."

We reached the deli and I held the door open for her. Abigail was there, buying a yogurt. "Oh, good, you found each other," she said.

"Yeah, we're heading to the park to eat lunch," said Jaya. "Want to join us?"

"Sure," said Abigail.

Yow! The pleasure went pouring out of me. I felt like a little kid who drops his ice-cream cone. Had I bored Jaya so much already that she regretted asking me to lunch?

I bought a smoked turkey sandwich, orange juice, and an apple and followed the girls out of the deli.

We sat on a bench near the edge of the park, with Jaya in the middle. It was warm for October, but windy.

"So you guys work at the repository, right? What do you do there?" I asked.

"We're pages," said Abigail. "At least, I'm a page. Jaya's the head page."

"What do pages do?" I asked.

"A little of everything," said Jaya. "When you request something from the stacks, we go find it. When you're done with it, we pack it up and reshelve it. If you break it, we fix it. And if you fall asleep in the Main Exam Room, we wake you up at closing time."

"The head page has the hardest job," said Abigail. "She tells all us other pages we're doing everything wrong."

"I do not!" said Jaya.

"You do so, Miss Bossypants."

"Are you talking about that time with the ice-cream spoons? Because if you don't wrap them up all the way, they tarnish."

"Yes, and the time with the aardvark cage, and the time with the quetzal feathers, and the time with the zither . . ."

"All right, all right! Maybe I do. Do I really? Am I too hard on you guys?"

"It's okay, Jaya—I'm just teasing. I *want* you to tell me when I'm messing up. I would hate to ruin a perfectly good zither."

Silence fell again, broken only by chewing. This is way too awkward, I thought. She'll never want to have lunch with me again. Better start a more interesting conversation.

"If you had a time machine, where would you go?" I asked. "I mean when? Where and when?"

"Is this an essay question?" Abigail asked.

"No, I was thinking about time travel for my science fair project."

"I thought you were doing your project on robots," said Jaya. She sounded suspicious. Did she know about the time machine after all?

"I am," I said. "I decided time travel would be too hard. But I'm still interested. What do you know about time travel?"

Jaya shrugged. Her hat bobbed. "That it shows up in a lot of cheesy movies about knights trying to joust with trucks."

"I would totally kill for a time machine," said Abigail. "I'd use it to go forward a few millennia and see how they end up solving the climate-change problem."

"What if they don't solve it?" I asked. "What if the whole planet's a post-nuclear wasteland?"

"Why would it be? Global warming isn't the same thing as nuclear war," objected Jaya.

"Oh, there'll be plenty of war. When the oil starts running out, they'll fight over what's left. And food and land and clean water. Maybe they'll fight over your time machine so they can go back to the past before all the wars start," I said.

"Okay, so where would *you* go?"

I chewed my sandwich and thought about it. "I'd like to meet Leonardo da Vinci," I said.

"Me too," said Jaya. "Leonardo rocks. Or dinosaurs. Don't you want to see what colors they were?"

"Sure, from a distance," I said. Could that be how the stained-glass designer figured out what colors to make the dinosaurs in the Main Exam Room windows? Did they use a time machine?

"Shakespeare," said Abigail. "I'd go see the premiere of *Hamlet*. No, I know—I'd go hear Jesus preach."

"That would be awesome," said Jaya. "I bet he was a great speaker. But would you understand him? Do you know Hebrew?"

"Not Hebrew, Aramaic. That's what he spoke. I would learn it before I went."

"Would you warn him about Judas?" Jaya asked.

Abigail shook her head. "Don't you think he already knew?"

"Yeah, you're probably right," said Jaya.

I got out my multi-utility tool and used the medium blade to core my apple and slice it into eighths. I held out the slices.

"Fancy knifework! Thanks," said Jaya, taking one. "I would go meet Marie Curie. I'd warn her about radiation sickness."

"You can't!" I said. "That would change the past, and who knows what would happen? Maybe if she hadn't died young, they would have invented nuclear weapons decades sooner."

"Yeah, and maybe France would have used them to stop Hitler and World War II would never have happened," said Jaya. "That would have been a good thing."

"Maybe. Or maybe Hitler would have used them on New York and you would never have been born."

"Or maybe I'd be born Indian. My family lived in India back then. Maybe they'd still be there."

"But you wouldn't be *you*. Your parents might never have met. Or even if they did meet, what if they had a baby a year sooner or a week later? You could have been somebody else. You could have been a boson. You could have been a boy. Who knows *who* you would have been!"

"Maybe I would be somebody way better. Maybe I would be just like me, except with perfect teeth."

"I like your teeth," I said.

"You wouldn't if you were the one wearing the retainer. Anyway, maybe I would have liked being a boy."

"Don't you like being *you*?"

"Of course I do! That's the point," said Jaya. "I love being me. Whoever I was, I bet I would love being that person too."

"Well, I like you the way you are now," I said.

"Aww," said Abigail.

"You're sweet, Leo," said Jaya. "But how do you know the you in the world where I'm not me isn't saying the exact same thing to the not-me me right now?"

"I don't. But I don't care what he's saying because he's not me. He's just some other guy saying something to some other girl, who isn't you. Or maybe he's a girl and you're a guy, in which case he's some other girl saying something to some other guy who isn't you," I said. "It has nothing to do with *us*."

Jaya laughed. "Well, okay! I'm glad we got that cleared up," she said. "I wish I could see it. You'd make an adorable girl, with that curl." She reached out and tugged at the curl on my forehead. I had never hated that thing so much in my life.

Abigail laughed too. "So how long have you guys been going out?" she asked.

"What?" I found myself squeezing my orange juice carton so hard it crumpled. Juice spilled out the straw. "Going out? With Jaya?"

"Well, you don't need to sound so horrified about it!" Jaya laughed. She said to Abigail, "We're not going out. We only met this week."

"Oh, sorry," said Abigail. "I just thought, you know, with the whole lunch thing and how you guys talk to each other."

"I'm not horrified! Why would I be horrified? Jaya's amazing!" I said. I shook the juice off my hands and wiped them on my jeans. So much for clean jeans.

"That's okay, Leo." She patted my arm. "You didn't hurt my feelings. I know I'm an acquired taste."

"That's for sure," said Abigail. "But most of us acquire you sooner or later. Come on, let's go back. My shift starts in a few minutes."

CHAPTER FIVE

The Great Man's Assistant's Great-Great-Grandson

On Sunday night I beat Jake at Gravity Force III four games out of six. "Schist, Leo! What did you do to your controller?" he asked.

"I just fixed it a little."

"Will you fix mine a little too, then?"

"Sure, as long as you promise not to complain if it makes all your ships fly backward."

I couldn't go to the repository on Tuesday because I had a history test the next morning. I had to ask Sofia to turn down her music so I could study. The trouble with me, she told me, was that I didn't appreciate the brilliance of a well-made fugue.

I thought about all the alternate worlds in which I was actually good at tests. According to some physicists, there are zillions and zillions and infinite zillions of universes branching off from each other. Every time anything happens—a leaf falls, say, or a hurricane strikes, or you choose A instead of C as the answer to question 7 on your history test—that causes new worlds to branch off the old one.

If the physicists are right, there's a world somewhere in which the Leo passed the Cooper Tech entrance exam. That Leo is probably doing his science fair project on particle physics like Dmitri. Maybe he'll even win first place with his project—if he's good at tests, he's probably good at science projects too. But he never met Ms. Kang, and she never told him about the repository.

There's another world in which my dad took that job he was offered five years ago out in Silicon Valley. The Leo in that world is the son of a zillionaire now. He has his own workshop in the family compound, with lemon trees out his window. But he never set foot in the repository either, and he never met Jaya.

There's another world where Leo doesn't get visions like I do. He can't fix things or invent stuff. I don't know what that Leo likes to do instead—maybe he plays hockey. Hockey Leo is probably more popular than me, especially if he makes a lot of goals. But he didn't even try to enter the science fair, and he never saw the time machine.

Okay, so I probably didn't do as well on my history test as some of the other Leos in other universes. But it isn't actually so bad being this Leo, in this universe.

I went back to the repository after school on Wednesday. I decided to check out the later robots—the ones listed under *robot* in the catalog. I copied out the call number for the earliest one I could find: a 1921 robotic servant from a Czech company called Rossum's Universal Robots.

In the Main Exam Room, under those glowing windows, Jaya was working with the pneumatic tubes. She waved at me.

Simon was at the desk. I handed him my call slips. He put the first two in a tube and passed it to Jaya, but he gave me back the call slip for the Czech robot.

"Sorry," he said, not actually sounding very sorry at all. "This item is in one of the Special Collections. You need permission from a supervisor to examine it."

"Okay. How do I get permission?"

He sighed, like I was asking him to do a huge favor instead of his job. "I'll have to send a request to a supervisor."

"Can you do that, then, please?"

"Can I see your card?"

"It hasn't arrived yet," I said. "I just applied for it last week."

"Well, come back when you've got it. Next, please." And he turned to the person behind me on line.

"Hang on, Simon," said Jaya. "Leo, can I see that call slip?"

I handed it to her and she scrutinized it. "I'll take it down-stairs to Dr. Rust when the shifts change," she said.

An hour later she came over to the table where I was working.

"I'm sorry, Leo," Jaya said. "That Rossum's robot is restricted access and Dr. Rust isn't willing to make an exception. You can try again after you get your card. Doc will want to talk to you first, though."

"Okay. Thanks for trying. But how come . . ."

"How come what?"

"Well, what's so special about that particular robot? They let me handle the Leonardo da Vinci knight. That one must be incredibly rare! Why is this one restricted when that one isn't?"

"Oh, well, the Rossum's robot . . ." Jaya paused, as if trying to decide what to say. "It's in a Special Collection, that's all. Some of the collections have restrictions because . . . because of the way the repository categorizes things."

"I see," I said, although I didn't. "Well, thanks for asking."

On Saturday, I took my lunch with me to the repository. When my stomach started growling, I put my robots on the reserve shelf and went to the park to look for Jaya.

She was sitting on the same bench, this time with Simon and the page I'd seen at the front desk. "Leo!" she called when she saw me. "Come join us!" She scooted over to make room.

"Hi, Jaya," I said, sitting down. It was exciting to be so close to her. Our arms touched.

"You know Simon and Francis, right? No? This is Leo. He's doing a project on robots. Leo, this is Simon FitzHenry and Francis Chu. So how's it going with the robots?" asked Jaya.

"It's interesting. The repository has a great collection. Some of them are thousands of years old! But most of the old ones aren't exactly what I would call robots."

"What do you mean?" asked Francis.

"Well, a lot of them are really just hyped-up windup toys. I mean, the mechanisms are amazingly clever sometimes, but they only do one thing. Once you wind them up or get the hydraulics going, they just do whatever they were built to do—pour out soup or wash the floor or whatever."

"What's wrong with that? Shouldn't they do what they're built to do?" said Simon.

"Yes, but a real robot would do more."

"Like what?" asked Francis.

"Respond to directions, at least. Ideally, it would be able to make some decisions for itself," I answered.

"I see what you mean," said Jaya. "If a windup floor washer counts as a robot, then your dishwasher is a robot too."

"I wish our dishwasher *was* a robot," said Francis. "Our dishwasher is *me*."

Jaya laughed. "I always thought there was something a little robotic about your eyebrows."

Francis wiggled his eyebrows rhythmically.

Simon said, "The repository has the earliest remote-controlled robot ever made. That should fit your definition. My great-great-grandfather helped to invent it."

"What? Really?" said Jaya. "Was your great-great-grandfather an inventor?"

"Yes. He worked in Nikola Tesla's lab."

"Nikola Tesla? The guy who invented AC electric engines and the radio?" asked Jaya.

"That's right," said Simon.

"So your great-great-grandfather invented a remote-controlled robot?" I asked.

"Yes," said Simon. "That is, Tesla always gets the credit for inventing it, but my great-great-grandfather did most of the heavy lifting."

"But wasn't Tesla from Eastern Europe?" objected Francis. "I thought your family was English. Didn't you tell us you were descended from some king of England?"

"That's on my father's side," said Simon. "Tesla had a lab in New York. My mother's great-grandfather worked there. My father's family is descended from Henry VIII—hence our name, FitzHenry."

"That's the one who kept beheading all his wives, right?" asked Jaya.

Francis snorted. "You do look a little like Henry VIII, Simon, except much thinner and without the turkey leg," he said.

Simon clenched his jaw and glared. I could easily imagine him beheading wives.

"So if your great-great-great-grandfather or whatever was Henry VIII, why aren't you the king of England?" I asked him.

"That's the Fitz part of FitzHenry," explained Francis. "It means Simon's really-great-grandmother wasn't the queen, just one of King Henry's girlfriends. Maybe she was one of the serving wenches with the turkey legs."

Simon had gone pale. "My family is descended from the Tudors," he said. "Who is *your* family descended from?" He sounded furious.

"Sorry, Simon, no offense meant," said Francis.

Simon didn't answer.

I tried to change the subject. "Tell me more about the remote-controlled robot," I said.

"I'm afraid I'd better be getting back," said Simon. He got up and walked quickly out of the park.

"Francis, you shouldn't tease him," said Jaya. "You know how sensitive he is."

"*Sensitive* isn't how I would put it. He's a royal psycho," said Francis. "He thinks he's such a hotshot because his family are big patrons at the Burton Repository in London. But your family's just as important here, and *you're* not stuck-up."

"Well, he's a long way from home. And you did give him a hard time about his ancestors."

"You're right. Maybe that was mean. But he does look exactly like that painting of Henry VIII," said Francis, starting to laugh again.

I'd heard of Nikola Tesla, but I didn't know much about him. I checked out his autobiography and a few histories of early electrical technology.

Tesla's remote-controlled robot was actually a robotic submarine that he controlled with a radio device. It was the first time anybody had done that. Tesla invented lots of amazing things. He had a pretty sad life, though. He worked for Thomas Edison when he was young, but after Edison refused to pay Tesla some money he'd promised, they ended up becoming bitter rivals. They had a long fight—called the War of the Currents—over whose kind of electricity would control the world's standards: Edison's direct current or Tesla's alternating current. Tesla's AC won, but he didn't get the money or credit for it. His boss, George Westinghouse, did.

Some people say Tesla was a way better inventor than Edison, but he was never anywhere near as successful. People like Edison and Westinghouse kept taking credit for his work. Then there were the crazy things he claimed to have invented but could never get to actually work, like a death ray that he thought would end war.

He died poor and alone instead of rich and famous. He went nuts at the end, too. His best friend was a pigeon.

What amazed me most, though, were Tesla's visions.

In his autobiography, Tesla described how, as a kid, he sometimes had such vivid memories that he didn't know if he was remembering something or actually seeing it. Later on, the same thing happened with his inventions. While he was thinking about an idea for a new machine, he would see it in front of him. He described seeing his first great invention that way, a new kind of electric motor. "The images were wonderfully sharp and clear and had the solidity of metal," he wrote.

When I read that, my jaw dropped. That's exactly what happens to *me*. Did that mean I was a genius—or crazy?

CHAPTER SIX

I Build a Very Strange Radio

I had been coming to the repository for a few weeks. Simon hadn't gotten any friendlier, but Francis and Abigail always waved and smiled when they saw me in the Main Exam Room. The reference librarian, Mr. Reyes, knew my name. I'd gotten used to the library's weird ways: the changing pictures in the stained-glass windows, the beams of sunlight on rainy days, the big rooms that shouldn't fit inside that small building. I'd even gotten used to seeing Jaya, though my heart still beat faster when I did.

But what about the time machine? Shouldn't it have appeared by now? Every time I went to the repository, some part of me expected to see it. But I never did.

Then one Wednesday, I had an idea. What if the time machine was somewhere in the stacks? They had wild things here like Leonardo da Vinci's knight and Tesla's remote-controlled submarine. If a time machine existed anywhere, wouldn't the repository be the perfect place for it? Maybe it even had a call number!

I looked around the Catalog Room, daunted. Where should I look for time machines?

Might as well start with the obvious, I thought. I pulled out the drawer marked *Tel–Tin* and started flipping through cards. *Tiger beetle, tilbury, timber hitch* . . . It couldn't really be that simple, could it? Would they actually file their time machines under *time machine*?

I continued to flip cards. *Time bomb* (they had one of those?), *time clock, time lock, timepiece (see clock), time sheet, timetable, timpani, tintype* . . .

That's where it should have been: between *time lock* and *timepiece.* It wasn't there.

Of course it wasn't. I felt like an idiot.

Could they be keeping the time machine in one of those mysterious Special Collections, then—the ones I still wasn't allowed to borrow stuff from? Or was it just not here at all?

Wherever it was, I knew I was going to find it soon, before I was too much older. I would have to look harder.

I wished I could get into the stacks to look for the time machine. But only staff were allowed in there.

I had a sudden thought: What if I worked at the repository?

As soon as it occurred to me, I knew how much I wanted it. Not just for the time machine, but for the repository itself. I wanted to understand how the library worked. I wanted to explore its corners and its strange geometry. I wanted to learn its secrets.

Jaya's shift was due to start in a few minutes, so I went downstairs to catch her arriving. I had gotten very good at running into Jaya.

She came around the corner with Abigail. "Hi, you guys," I said, hurrying up to them as if I were just arriving too. "Hey, I've been wondering. How do you get a job at the repository?"

"You want to work here? That's a great idea, Leo!" said Jaya.

"So are there openings? How do you get a job?"

"My social studies teacher recommended me," said Abigail.

"Me too, my sewing teacher," said Jaya.

"Really? You take sewing?" asked Abigail.

Jaya nodded. She was wearing her funny hat, and the pom-pom bounced around. "Everybody does at Miss Wharton's School. It's an old school tradition. Miss Bender is the best. I made this hat."

"Wow, that's impressive!" said Abigail.

I said, "So I would need to get a recommendation from a teacher?" I could ask Ms. Kang. "Anything else? Do I fill out an application or something?"

"I don't know," said Abigail. "There's a test we all had to take, but I've never heard of anybody *asking* for a job. Everybody I know got recommended by someone connected to the repository. Like my teacher—he was a page when he was our age."

"There's always a first time," said Jaya. "Come on." She opened the repository door and pushed me through. "Let's go talk to Dr. Rust."

I followed Jaya upstairs. I felt a surge of excitement when we walked through the Staff Only door into the repository's forbidden depths.

The back areas were plainer than the public rooms. We went down white-painted corridors with lamps hanging from the ceilings. At last we came to a door with a brass nameplate that said *Lee Rust, Head Repositorian*.

Jaya knocked. "Dr. Rust? Are you busy?"

"Always. But come in," said someone inside.

"This is Leo Novikov. He wants to ask you something," said Jaya, pushing me into the room.

There were massive bookcases overflowing with leather-bound books, file cabinets with drawers of all sizes, and a big oak desk with faces carved at the corners and paws at the bottoms of the legs.

One of the faces was grinning. The other had a very, very serious expression, like my sister when she's trying not to laugh.

"Nice to meet you, Leo," said Dr. Rust, a medium-size person with reddish-brown hair and a zillion freckles. "You're the young man who's studying robots, aren't you? Rick Reyes mentioned you. He says you're very perceptive. What can I do for you?"

As we shook hands, I thought I saw a slight movement at the corner of the desk. It looked almost like the serious carved face had winked at me. Stop imagining things, I told myself.

"Jaya says—that is, I was wondering . . . would it be possible for me to work here?" I said.

"Possible? Perhaps. Customary? Definitely not." Dr. Rust waved at the chair nearest the face that couldn't possibly have winked (could it?). "Have a seat. What school do you go to?"

"Poly—the Manhattan Polytechnic Academy." I sat down and waited for the usual look of disapproval.

It didn't come. "Poly," said Dr. Rust thoughtfully. "I don't think I know anyone there. Did a teacher recommend you?"

"No," I said. "But I'm sure my science teacher would, if I asked her. She's the one who told me about the repository."

"What's her name?"

"Ms. Kang."

"Aha! Would that be Emma Kang?" asked Dr. Rust. "She was one of our best pages."

"No—Lisa."

"Oh, too bad. I don't know her. The recommendation really needs to come from someone connected to the repository."

That didn't sound good. "I don't think I know anyone connected with here."

"Well, we'll come back to that," said Dr. Rust. "What sort of toaster do you use?"

"What sort of *what*?"

"Toaster. For making toast."

"A classic Sunbeam. The automatic kind. Only—my sister likes her toast pale and limp, and Dad likes it almost burnt, so I rewired it with a voice-recognition sensor so it knows who it's toasting for."

"I see." Dr. Rust looked pleased. "And what's your email security password?"

I hesitated. I didn't want to ruin my chances for the job, but my password was private. "I don't feel comfortable saying," I said at last.

Dr. Rust nodded. "Quite right. What do you like about the repository?"

"Well, obviously, the amazing objects you have here. I mean, Leonardo da Vinci's robot! But the whole place is awesome. I like the pneumatic tubes and the stained-glass windows in the

Main Exam Room, and everybody here is so cool, especially—"

I was going to say "especially Jaya," but I stopped myself before I could embarrass myself like that. I finished lamely, "Especially everybody," and blushed.

"I see. Describe the windows in the Main Exam Room, please."

"They're made of stained glass," I said. "They're stained-glass pictures."

"Pictures of what?"

"Well, there's the jungle with the dinosaurs, and the frozen tundra with the mammoths, and the forest with the ancient horses—they have toes—and the Mars landscape."

"You see *dinosaurs* in the summer window?" said Jaya. "I know everybody sees the windows differently, but I've never heard of dinosaurs!"

"What do you mean, sees them differently?"

Dr. Rust frowned at Jaya and said, "The repository operates on principles of subjective anomaly."

"I don't understand," I said.

"That's okay—don't worry about it."

I didn't pursue it. If this was a job interview, I didn't want to blow it by annoying the head repositorian with too many questions.

"You saw Mars, did you say?" continued Dr. Rust.

"Well, it *could* be Mars. Definitely not Earth because there are two moons. Mars has Phobos and Deimos. They might be too small, though. Maybe it's some other planet."

Dr. Rust nodded. "So this Lisa Kang told you to come here. Why?"

"To research my science project. She said you have a great collection of robots. Which you do."

Jaya jumped in. "Leo would be awesome on Stack 5—he has a real feel for scientific instruments. We're going to need a new page when Simon goes back to London. I was hoping maybe you could waive the recommendation thing this time."

"No, I'm afraid that's not possible," said Dr. Rust.

The disappointment stung. It's not like I wasn't used to being turned down for stuff, but I wanted this way more than I ever wanted to go to Cooper Tech or play in some stupid orchestra. "Is there anything I can do? Can I ask someone else for a recommendation?" I asked.

"I'm sorry. The recommendation really needs to be the person's own idea."

"Please, Doc!" said Jaya. I was flattered at how she was sticking up for me—it made my disappointment feel both better and far worse. "Leo would be perfect. Can't you make an exception this one time?"

"No, I can't," said Dr. Rust. "Fortunately, it seems I don't need to. He has a perfectly valid recommendation."

"From who? He just said he doesn't know anyone!"

"From you, of course. Don't you think the recommendation of our head page counts for anything? Really, Jaya, it's not like you to be so modest. Run along now—your shift is about to start, and I have a task for this young man." Dr. Rust walked over to one of the file cabinets and opened a medium-size drawer.

"Thank you! Thank you *so much*!" I said.

Jaya made no move to go. "Oh, right, the button test. Don't worry, Leo, you'll do great."

"What's the button test?"

"Dr. Rust asks all the pages to sort buttons when they're

applying for the job. It's like an entrance exam. Which ones are you going to give him, Doc?"

"Enough, Jaya. This is Leo's test, not yours, and it doesn't involve buttons," said Dr. Rust, taking a clock and a radio out of the drawer. "Go run some call slips or something." Dr. Rust waved her out the heavy, carved door and shut it firmly behind her.

"Let's get you set up, Leo," said Dr. Rust, putting the clock and the radio on the desk in front of me. "Do you need any tools?"

I took my multi-utility tool out of my pocket. "I have this. What am I doing with it?"

"You're disassembling these machines and using the parts."

"Using them for what?" I asked.

"That's up to you, isn't it?"

I turned the radio over and unscrewed the case. It was an old-fashioned FM radio, the kind with vacuum tubes. I disassembled it carefully, lining all the parts up on the desk.

The clock was mechanical, not electrical—the kind driven by, well, clockwork. Gears with interlocking teeth. I went at it with my multi-utility tool, unscrewing screws and un-interlocking teeth and lining up the parts under the ones from the radio.

I tugged at my hair while I thought about what to make. I do that a lot when I'm thinking—it's one of the things Sofia's always saying is wrong with me. It might partly explain that stupid curl.

A plan started to form in my mind. I saw all the parts clicking together. Then I started putting them together in real life. I assembled a radio where the position of the minute hand would control the station and the position of the second hand would control the volume. I reassembled the clockwork, rejiggered the radio, found some extra copper wire at the bottom of my backpack, and assembled my device. I tightened the last screw, wound it up, plugged it in, and turned it on.

It was horrible. That lady on the weather station began with a whisper that rose over the course of sixty seconds into a screech about *clouds* GIVING WAY TO **SUNSHINE** *on* **FRIDAY!!!** Then abruptly she turned into that irritating song about rivers, the one with all the cellos. At first it was so quiet it tickled my ears, but then it swelled and swelled until I felt like I was standing at the edge of a waterfall with the backup vocals and the strings screaming because they were being swept *away* OVER *the* **EDGE**! Then came a second of silence that turned into that guy my parents hate, ranting in a rising voice about an evil senator who doesn't *understand the* **AMERICAN PEOPLE**!!!

Dr. Rust switched it off. "Okay, that's very . . . um . . . interesting. Now reassemble it. Make something new."

I tugged at my hair. What could I make with vacuum tubes? One time at a science museum I saw old vacuum tubes made into one of those machines that shoot lightning around the room—a Tesla coil. But I didn't have all the necessary parts, and besides, it might start a fire. Burning down the repository probably wouldn't get me a job.

I wished one of my visions would start. Why couldn't I have them when I needed them?

Then it came to me: A theremin! I love theremins, not just because of the eerie, whoopy sounds they make but because they're the only musical instrument you can play without touching. You wave your hands over them and they wail like a ghost.

It was a little tricky, and I had to ask Dr. Rust for a few spare parts, but I did it. I turned the clock into a metronome and played "Twinkle, Twinkle, Little Star" on the theremin. It sounded like a spirit from beyond the grave recalling better days.

"Nice! Okay, one more time," said Dr. Rust, handing me a new object. It had an outlet on one end and a wire on the other. In between was a solid black box the size of a matchbox. "This time, use this."

"What is it?"

"It's a conceptual coupler."

"I've never heard of a conceptual coupler. What does it do?"

"That really depends on you."

I poked at the box with my tools, but I couldn't get it open. Dr. Rust watched me, smiling faintly. What should I do with the thing—what on earth does a coupler do? Connect things?

I decided to start simple and see what happened. I reassembled the radio and the clock. I plugged the radio into the coupler's outlet and connected the coupler's wire to the clock's hands. Then I wound the clock, plugged in the coupler, and switched the radio on.

It sounded like a normal radio.

I fiddled with the radio controls. Nothing unusual, just different stations.

But the black box must do *something*—otherwise, why would Dr. Rust tell me to use it? Maybe if I adjusted the clock. I moved the minute hand back an hour.

Yes! The music changed. It was that hit song from last year, the one about the guy who passes the girl the escalator when he's going down and she's going up.

That wasn't particularly surprising. They still play that song all the time. But as I kept turning the clock's hands backward, the songs got older and older. After a few turns of the hour hand they were playing oldies, then jazz, then scratchy ragtime and opera.

Then I turned the hand counterclockwise one more circle of the dial and the music stopped dead. Nothing but static.

Could it—no, that was crazy. Was it really . . . ? Impossible!

When I attached the radio to the clock with the conceptual coupler, did I really make a time-travel radio? The static would make sense then—it would mean I'd gone back so far in time that they hadn't invented the radio yet.

Did Dr. Rust know I'd built a *time-travel radio*? Why was I the only one freaking out?

If this really was a time-travel radio, it should play the future, too. I started spinning the clock's hands forward.

Dr. Rust stopped me hurriedly, picking up the radio and unplugging it from the coupler. "Thanks, Leo. You clearly have the touch, but I think that's enough for now."

"Wait! I want to see what happens when it goes far enough forward," I said.

"Another time, perhaps. Let's not get ahead of ourselves. To-morrow is another day. Now, when can you start? Monday? Wednesday?"

"But—" A time-travel radio was a huge big deal! If I tuned

it to a news station in the future, could I find out tomorrow's winning lottery numbers? Could I predict the next earthquake and save lives?

Then my mind processed what Dr. Rust had just said. "Wait—do you mean I got the job?"

"Exactly."

"Oh! Thank you!" I would be working at the repository with Jaya! Maybe soon I would find the time machine!

"So when can you start?" asked Dr. Rust again, patiently.

I thought about Jaya's hours. "I could come Tuesdays, Wednesdays, and Saturdays," I said.

"Good," said Dr. Rust. "Come in Tuesday after school—does three thirty suit? Ask for Ms. Callender."

CHAPTER SEVEN

A Stiletto, a Niddy Noddy, and a Serpent

My parents were pleased when I told them about my new job, even though it wasn't in a lab. "Are you working in the science collections, Lyonya?" asked Dad. "They're pretty famous."

"I'm not sure yet. Probably," I said.

Sofia wasn't impressed, though. "That's that weird place on the Upper East Side where they keep all those old flowerpots, right?" she said. "Why would you want to work there?"

"Have you ever actually been inside, So-So?" I used to call her that when I was a baby. She pretends not to mind—she thinks I won't use the name so much if I don't know how much she hates it. I save it for when she's really bugging me; I don't want it to lose its power through overuse.

"No, but the theater geeks always go there to borrow their props and stuff," she said. "And believe me, there's nothing geekier than Cooper Tech theater geeks."

"Really? Is that why you were so upset when you didn't get that part in *West Side Story* last year?"

She sighed elaborately. "You know what the trouble with you is, Leo?"

I left the room before she could tell me.

My first day on the job, I went up to Stack 6 to look for Ms. Callender. I got that quiver of excitement again when I went through the Staff Only door. It opened into the middle of a long room with rows and rows of shelves and cabinets stretching away in both directions.

Three librarians sat at large carved oak desks, only a little less elaborate than Dr. Rust's. Simon was putting objects on a cart.

"Ms. Callender?"

"Yes?" said one of the librarians. She had round cheeks that bunched up into apples when she smiled at me.

"I'm Leo Novikov, the new page. Dr. Rust said to come find you."

"It's good to have you here, Leo." She introduced me to the pages and the other librarians—Rick Reyes, who I already knew, and a thin, unsmiling woman named Lucy Minnian. "Here's Jaya, our head page," she said. "She can show you what to do."

"New blood! I love breaking in pages!" said Jaya, grinning. Her crooked canine tooth looked razor sharp.

"Be nice," said Ms. Callender.

"Me? I'm always nice."

All three librarians laughed, even stern Ms. Minnian.

"Jaya's our pet dragon," Ms. Callender told me. "Don't let her burn you to a crisp."

"Oh, Leo and I are old friends," said Jaya.

"Great. Off you go, then."

I couldn't quite believe my luck. A whole afternoon with Jaya! I followed her downstairs to Stack 5.

She led me to a clearing in the middle of the floor, where the cabinets and shelves stopped. There were little elevators, a sink, a cabinet full of boxes, gloves, and cleaning and packing materials, and a few chairs and tables. Pneumatic tube pipes snaked across the ceiling.

"When a call slip arrives in a pneum, you go find the item on the shelf. Check the call numbers—it's not hard."

We sat down to wait for call slips.

"So how long have you been working here?" I asked. "The librarians all seem to treat you like family."

"I guess they do. Well, in a way I *am* family. My big sister used to be a page here when she was my age, and my dad's on the board of directors. I've been coming to the repository since I was tiny. I've been here longer than some of the librarians. I've only been a page for a couple years, though."

"Do you think you would want to work here when you grow up?"

"I'm not sure. I love this place, but it's all about preserving old stuff. I think I might want to work with new stuff instead."

"Like doing what?"

She shrugged. "Maybe I'll be an angel investor, like my aunt."

"Your aunt's an angel?" It wouldn't completely surprise me.

"An angel *investor*. She funds start-up companies in England. Or maybe I'll start a think tank. I like to be in charge. I'm very bossy."

I laughed. "You think?"

"Admit it!" she ordered.

"Okay, okay, I admit it! Don't fire me!"

"I won't, as long as you always do exactly what I say."

"Yes, boss. I know—you're the next Thomas Edison. You'll found a new Menlo Park."

She shook her head. "Didn't Edison invent the lightbulb and the phonograph? I'm not really an inventor myself."

"Actually, there already was a lightbulb—Edison just improved it. His big thing was hiring other inventors and telling them what to do—like Tesla."

"Oh, okay. I'll start an idea incubator. What about you—what do you want to do?"

"I don't know. Everybody in my family is a scientist, but I don't think I have the patience and discipline for it, and I don't have the grades, either. I'm much better at coming up with crazy, out-there ideas."

"That's perfect," said Jaya. "You can come work for me in my idea incubator."

"Okay. What ideas are we incubating?"

She considered. "I'll hire the best engineer in the country to come up with a way to stop earbud wires from tying themselves in knots. That would be a real service to humanity."

"Oh, that's easy," I said. "Make them wireless."

"Okay. Then I'll hire the best engineer in the country to find lost wireless earbuds."

"I see your point," I said.

"You know what else I'd like? A hands-free umbrella. It's pretty much impossible to hold an umbrella and open a door at the same time without dropping your cell phone. Sticking the umbrella under your chin just dumps water down your shoulder."

"I've seen umbrella hats," I said. "Like a sunshade, only bigger."

She shook her head. "No good. You'd poke out people's eyes. Everybody would have to wear goggles. And goggles would get all steamed up in the rain. No, the solution has to involve some kind of force field."

"I wonder if you could repel the raindrops ultrasonically?" I mused, tugging at my hair. "Or break them up before they hit you."

"Now you're thinking," she said.

Something banged in the pneumatic pipes. With a scudding thump, a pneum fell into the basket.

Jaya jumped up. "Here, want to run your first slip?" She pulled it out of the pneum and handed it to me.

I unfolded it and read, "*VT 746.12 S53. Niddy noddy. Oak. Massachusetts, 1780s.* What the quark is a niddy noddy?"

Jaya laughed. "It's a handheld spinner's weasel. Don't you even know *that*?"

"Now I do," I said. "What's a spinner's weasel? And don't say an un-handheld niddy noddy."

"Okay, I won't. Go fetch! The 740s are that way." Jaya pointed to the left. She got a book out of her backpack and started to read.

I walked past rows of closed cabinets and open shelves, scanning the numbers on the ends.

The niddy noddy turned out to be a wooden stick the length of my forearm, with two shorter sticks attached at the ends at right angles. The wood was smooth and dark, as if generations of hands had worn it down.

"Found it?" asked Jaya when I got back.

"I think so. But I still don't know what it is."

"I'll show you." She took it and waved it around in front of her.

"It's for rowing boats?" I asked.

"No, silly, it's for winding yarn."

"Oh! Obviously," I said. "Why is someone borrowing it?"

"To wind yarn, I would think," said Jaya, handing it back. "Initial the call slip and send it upstairs."

I ran three more call slips—a stereoscope viewer, a lathe, and an embroidery stiletto—while Jaya sat with her legs out in front of her, reading.

"It's fun having a new kid to train," she said when I came back with the stiletto. It was a thick needle as long as my pinky finger.

"Is that what you're doing? Training me? Wow, training people looks a lot like reading a book."

"Is it my fault you're a quick study?"

"That's because I have such a good teacher. What are you reading, anyway?" I asked.

"Jules Verne. *Le tour du monde en quatre-vingts jours,*" she said, with a perfect French accent, waving the book at me. Show-off! It was an old paperback with a picture of a hot-air balloon on the cover.

"*Around the World in Eighty Days,* right? I read that," I said.

"How is it in English?"

She wasn't the only one who could show off. "I wouldn't know. I read it in Russian."

"Really? Why Russian?"

"It was my dad's copy."

"Is your dad Russian?"

I nodded. "He's from Moscow. What about you—where are your parents from?"

"Chomalur, in southern India."

The pneum basket thudded again. Instead of a single call slip, the plastic tube held a whole sheaf of them, all canceled with pages' initials, including the four I'd run myself. "What do I do with these?" I asked.

"Those get filed. I'll show you," said Jaya.

The call slip file was a big wooden box with compartments. I watched Jaya's long, dark fingers dancing through the papers. Her fingers were just a little too long—they looked a little sticklike. They fascinated me. I wondered what it would feel like to hold her hand.

"And now it's time for my break—I'll be back in twenty minutes." She pulled on her ridiculous hat.

The stair door opened a few minutes after she left. It was Francis. "Hi, Leo," he said. "Ms. Callender sent me downstairs while Jaya's on break in case you run into trouble. This stack's usually pretty quiet, though." He sat in Jaya's chair.

"What are the other stacks like?" I asked.

"Oh, not that different from this, mostly. My favorite's Stack 4, musical instruments," he said. "Except for . . . no . . . well, yeah, Stack 4. I like to play the instruments."

"You're allowed to do that? Use the objects in the stacks?"

"We're not really supposed to, but the librarians don't mind if you're careful," he said. "And nobody minds how loudly I play in the stacks. Except Simon FitzHenry—he always tells me to 'lower the volume a touch, if you wouldn't mind.'" Francis imitated Simon's accent.

"What a grudgebucket," I said.

"I don't think he likes me very much," said Francis.

"Does he like anyone?"

"He likes Jaya. He likes her a *lot*."

I felt a twinge of jealousy. I changed the subject. "What instrument do you play?"

"Lots of things, a little. I'm teaching myself the serpent."

"What's that?"

"It's a medieval wind instrument. It has a great sound."

"Do you like the theremin? I made one the other day," I said. "When Dr. Rust gave me my page test."

"Oh, nice! Do you play anything?"

I shook my head. "I used to—violin—but I sucked so bad my parents let me stop. Which if you knew my parents, you'd be impressed with my suckitude."

He laughed. "Really? Are they musicians?"

"No, scientists. But they're big on persistence and success."

"Maybe violin just isn't your instrument. Maybe you'd be better at the serpent. Or the krummhorn, or the guiro, or the African thumb piano."

"Possibly," I said. "I don't think my parents would be too happy, though. They think if you're not playing the violin or the piano, you might as well be banging on a toy xylophone."

"Hey, I love banging on a toy xylophone! Have you ever heard the band Flashcube? They have a great song for toy xylophone and bass guitar. And the lead singer is totally hot."

The door opened as he was speaking. "Who's totally hot?" asked Jaya, coming in.

"You, of course."

She laughed and hit him on the shoulder. "It's okay, Francis, I know I'm not your taste."

I didn't think it was possible to be jealous of someone for getting hit on the shoulder.

"It's only because my heart belongs to the lead singer of Flashcube," said Francis. "Later, guys. Gotta go practice my serpent."

CHAPTER EIGHT

Jaya Hits Me

I was getting impatient to find the time machine. The next day at lunchtime I went to talk to Ms. Kang. She was in the school library. "So, you used to be a librarian. Can you give me some advice?" I asked.

"Once a librarian, always a librarian," said Ms. Kang, tugging on her sleeves. "What do you need to know?"

"Well, there's some stuff that I think should be in the repository, but I can't find it in the card catalog. Is there someplace else I could look?"

"There might be. Sometimes separate divisions have their own catalogs. The other thing you could try is looking for a special-subject thesaurus."

"What's that?"

"It's a book of synonyms that tells you how the librarians decided to catalog their holdings. Say you're looking for books about cooking. Should you look under *food preparation* or *cookbooks* or *cooking* or *culinary arts*? Most libraries use the Library of

Congress Subject Headings, but sometimes they have their own way of categorizing things."

"Thanks, Ms. Kang. That's really helpful."

"Hey, Jaya," I said next time I saw her. "Is everything in the repository here in the stacks, or are there other storage areas? And do they have separate card catalogs?"

"Well, some of the collections have special storage requirements, like the living material, so we keep them in special areas. But there's only one card catalog."

"Wow, you have living things here? Where?"

"Most of them are downstairs in . . . I guess you could call it sort of an interior garden."

"I would love to see that!"

She looked uncomfortable. "It's one of the Special Collections. They're restricted access."

"Is that where they keep the stuff I'm not allowed to borrow yet, like that Czech robot from Rossum's?"

Jaya nodded. "That's in one of the Special Collections."

"Are the Special Collections in this building?"

"Yes, down in the basement on Stack 1."

"I see." If there really was a time machine in the repository, I bet that's where they kept it. I would have to figure out some way to get down there.

The problem, it turned out, wasn't getting down to Stack 1—I just took the elevator on my next break. The problem was getting into the Special Collections once I was there.

Abigail was on Stack 1 with Francis. It was a long room like the other stacks, with the same buzzing fluorescent lights, but for some reason it felt different. It felt dangerous.

"Hi, Leo. Do you need something?" asked Abigail. She didn't sound like her usual friendly self.

"No, I was just getting familiar with the stacks. I've only really been on Stack 5 and Stack 6. What's down here?"

"These are the Special Collections."

"What's in them? Can I take a look?" I asked.

"They're locked," said Francis.

"They're restricted access," said Abigail.

"But what's in them? Is it, like, a big secret?" I asked.

Abigail and Francis looked at each other. "You have to ask Dr. Rust," said Abigail at last.

"Okay." I turned to go.

"Sorry! I didn't mean to be rude, Leo, it's just, we're not supposed to—it's one of those things where you need permission," she said.

"Talk to Dr. Rust," said Francis.

"It's okay, I understand."

But Dr. Rust wouldn't tell me either. "There's no point in getting ahead of yourself. Your exam was quite impressive, but let's give you a chance to settle in first before you go messing with the Special Collections."

I wasn't going to give up that easily. I headed upstairs to the Catalog Room. Mr. Reyes was sitting at his desk under his beam of sunlight.

"Mr. Reyes, does the repository have its own subject thesaurus?" I asked.

"We mostly use a modified version of the LCSH—the Library of Congress Subject Headings—over there at the end," he said, pointing.

That wasn't exactly an answer.

"So there aren't any specialized thesauruses here?" I asked.

"Not for any of the collections you'll be using." That sounded evasive too. Did it mean I was on to something?

The LCSH was a big book in several volumes. I looked under *Time*. No time machines. That was a disappointment, but not a surprise.

I put the volume back and scanned the nearby shelves. There were dictionaries of this and that—music, biography, medicine, slang—and some volumes in languages I couldn't read, but I didn't see anything that looked like a subject thesaurus.

Then the clouds shifted in the skylight and a beam of sun hit a shelf above my head. I saw bright motes of dust doing their Brownian-motion dance in the sunbeam. The light was illuminating one of the books I'd thought I couldn't read. Had the words on the spine changed? Before, they'd looked like some kind of snaky foreign alphabet, but now I saw they were written in ordinary English characters.

They said *Special Collections Thesaurus*.

My hands shook as I pulled the book down. It had little round cutouts along the edge of the pages, with alphabet tabs, like a dictionary. I flipped quickly to the *T*'s. *Taxi, telescope, timbal.*

There: *Time machine: use anachronizing apparatus.*

I stared at it. It was really there.

I blinked hard. It was still there.

Mr. Reyes was staring at me and the sunbeam. I shut the book and put it back on the shelf. The sunbeam faded.

I hurried over to the card catalog and pulled out the *A–Ap* drawer. *Afterburner, aglet, ambergris.*

And there it was: *Anachronizing apparatus.* I ★WB 530.11 Z8485.

With trembling fingers I copied the call number onto a call slip and hid it in my pocket.

On my next shift, Ms. Callender put me on Stack 5 again with Jaya.

"Hey, Jaya." I took out the time machine call slip, then hesitated.

"What?"

"I have to ask you something." I hesitated again. She would think I was crazy.

"What? Come on, Leo, spit it out."

I handed her the slip.

"What's this?" she asked. She read the call slip, frowning. She turned it over, then turned it back again, looking worried. "Well?" she said.

I took a breath. "Remember how I was thinking about do-ing my science project on time machines? So I thought—I know this sounds crazy, but I thought if time machines really did exist, maybe they'd have one here in the repository. So I did some research in the Catalog Room. And I found it."

"How did you know what search term to use?"

"I looked in the Special Collections thesaurus."

"Who gave you that?"

"Nobody. I found it myself."

"You *found* the Special Collections thesaurus? All by yourself, without any help?"

"Yes, it was right there in the Catalog Room. It was weird—I couldn't read it at first, until this strange sunbeam shone on it. So is it true? Is there really a time machine here?"

Jaya looked at me for a long time, like she was trying to make up her mind. At last she said, "Yes."

Yes. She'd said yes.

Not "I can't believe you fell for that ancient gag." Not "Get away from me, you dangerous lunatic." *Yes.*

"Have you seen it? Have you used it? Where did you go to—*when* did you go to? How does it work? Where is it? Can I borrow it?" I was gabbling. A time machine! My time machine! I wasn't crazy—I really *had* seen myself riding a time machine!

"Calm down, Leo. Unfortunately, it doesn't work."

"How do you know? You've tried it?"

She nodded. "We all have."

It couldn't not work! "Then we'll fix it," I said. "I'm good at fixing things. I know I can get it to work—I know for a fact."

"It's never worked," said Jaya. "It's been in the repository since the 1930s, and nobody's ever been able to get it going. What makes you think *you* can?"

"Because I saw myself," I said. "I saw myself riding it—my future self. And you were with me."

Jaya hit me—hard. It wasn't as much fun as it looked when she did it to Francis.

"What?" she yelled. "You saw me riding a time machine and you *didn't tell me*?! Where did you see us? How old were we? What were we *doing*?" She hit me again on the word *doing*.

"Hey!" I rubbed my shoulder. "I'm sorry. I didn't want you to think I was crazy. I wasn't completely sure I wasn't."

"I'm not completely sure either," said Jaya. "But not because you saw us riding a time machine. That's not crazy. If you saw it, clearly it's going to happen."

She believed me! I would never believe me myself if I hadn't seen it with my own eyes. She must know the time machine actually existed!

"Let's go, then," I said. "Let's get it. Let me see that slip. Where's I ★ WB 530.11 Z8485? Come on, let's find it!"

Jaya caught me by the sleeve. "Settle down, Leo. We can't. We're working, remember? We have to run call slips."

"But there's a time machine! A *time machine*!"

"A nonworking time machine. It'll still be there when we finish our shift. Still nonworking, too."

"How can you be so calm about this?"

"You newbies are so cute," said Jaya, smiling patronizingly. I wanted to hit her myself. "Now, tell me about this time machine you saw us riding. Where did you see it?"

"In my bedroom. I don't know what we were doing—we didn't tell me."

"We came back from the future on a time machine and we didn't tell you *anything*? Not even the winning lottery numbers? What was the matter with us?"

"The time machine only stayed for a few seconds. You wanted to say things, but I stopped you—Future Me stopped you. Future Me said it was dangerous to change the past. I'm sure he's right. I'm sure *I'm* right."

"When were we coming from?"

"Like I just said, I don't know—we didn't tell me anything."

"Well, how old were we?"

"We looked like the same age we are now. Which means we're obviously supposed to find it soon. Let's go!"

"All right. We'll talk to Dr. Rust after our shift's over."

"Okay, but at least tell me what other crazy stuff they have here in the repository. Do they have beam transporters? What about interstellar rockets? Force fields? Invisibility shields?"

"I can't talk about any of that."

"Come on! I could find out myself, easily, just by looking in the Catalog Room."

"Then look in the Catalog Room. After our shift is over. Meanwhile, run this slip." She handed me a pneum that had just thudded into the basket.

I don't know how I made it through the rest of the shift. When it was over at last, we went upstairs and Jaya knocked on Dr. Rust's open door. "Got a minute?"

"Sure, come in. What's up?"

Mr. Reyes was sitting with Dr. Rust.

"Leo has—well, I'll let him tell you himself." Jaya elbowed me.

I wasn't sure exactly what part she wanted me to tell. "I was looking in the card catalog and I found a time machine and I asked Jaya about it and she said I should ask you." I held up the call slip where I'd written the time machine call number.

"Is that what you were looking up in the Special Collections thesaurus?" asked Mr. Reyes.

"Rick was just telling me you'd found the thesaurus," said Dr. Rust.

"Yes, but that's not the important part," said Jaya. "Go on, Leo, explain about how you saw us," she told me.

"Oh, okay. That was why I was looking up time machines in the first place. Before I knew about the repository, when I was first working on my science project, a time machine showed up in my bedroom. We were riding on it—me and Jaya. So I thought, since time machines really exist, maybe you would have one here. Maybe that's where we got it. The one we were riding."

"How did you know it was a time machine?" Dr. Rust asked. "Did your future self tell you?"

"No, not exactly. There wasn't much time before it disappeared. But what else could it be? If it wasn't a time machine, why would there be two of me? And Future Me told Then Me to read *The Time Machine,* by H. G. Wells," I said.

Dr. Rust and Jaya exchanged significant looks.

"Well, there are plenty of possible explanations for multiple yous," said Dr. Rust. "You might be visiting from a parallel dimension, for example. Or it could be a shape-shifter."

Parallel dimensions! Shape-shifters! Did those really exist too? If I hadn't seen a time machine with my own eyes, I would have thought they were messing with me.

"But the Wells reference certainly is indicative," continued Dr. Rust. "What did this purported time machine look like?"

"Kind of like one of those electric wheelchair-scooter things, only really old-fashioned. It was made out of metal, with gears and knobs. We were riding on a leather saddle." I remembered how Future Me had been hugging Future Jaya and blushed slightly.

"Hm. That does sound like ours. Jaya, would you mind asking Ms. Minnian to join us? She's on Stack 6."

"Sure thing, Doc," said Jaya.

When she was gone, Dr. Rust said to me, "Well, what a . . . what a surprising young man you turn out to be."

"I'm sorry."

"No, no, don't apologize. We like surprising at the repository. It's one of our favorite qualities."

Jaya came back with Ms. Minnian, the unsmiling librarian.

"What is it, Lee? Jaya says you wanted to see me?"

"Yes, thank you, Lucy. It seems our newest page has had an experience you'll want to hear about. Leo, tell her about the time machine."

Ms. Minnian listened silently to my story. When I was done, she said to Dr. Rust, "How do we know this isn't a ploy to get into the Special Collections? Remember that trouble a few years ago with the Grimm Collection? A page was involved—several pages."

For some reason that made Jaya mad. "Yes, several pages *were* involved!" she said fiercely. "Several pages saved the Grimm Collection! And it almost got them turned into dolls forever—including Anjali! I almost lost my sister!"

"That's exactly why I'm urging caution," said Ms. Minnian.

That made Jaya even madder. I could see why Ms. Callender had called her a dragon. I could easily imagine her breathing fire.

"It's okay, Jaya—no one's questioning your heroism, or your sister's," said Dr. Rust. "Lucy, I see your point, but this doesn't seem like a very effective ploy. If Leo wanted to gain access to the Special Collections, all he would have to do is work and wait. This way he draws attention to himself. He puts us on our guard."

"Leo's our kind of page," said Mr. Reyes. "He found the Special Collections thesaurus by himself. When was the last time a page did that? The only other one I can think of was Anjali."

"He did an impressive job with the assembly test too," added Dr. Rust.

"I'm not trying to gain access to anything," I said. "Not with a ploy, anyway. I'm just trying to figure out what I'm going to do and how. I mean, if I used a time machine to come back from the future, that means I'm going to use a time machine to come back from the future pretty soon no matter what, so why not get started now?"

Dr. Rust laughed. "You're right. Shall we pay a visit to the Wells Bequest?"

CHAPTER NINE

The Wells Bequest

The five of us took the elevator to the basement. We walked past several doors with letters stenciled on them and stopped at one marked *WB.

"Lucy, do you have your key?" asked Dr. Rust.

Ms. Minnian opened her purse and took out what looked like an old remote control. She pointed it at the door and punched a bunch of buttons. I heard a soft click.

"Thanks," said Dr. Rust, pushing the door open.

The room looked like any other room in the repository stacks, with the same fluorescent lights and rows of shelving, but for some reason my heart started pounding. I took a deep breath. "Is this the Wells Bequest?" I asked.

"Yes," said Dr. Rust. "May I see your call slip, please, Leo?"

I handed it over.

"530.11 Z8485," Dr. Rust read. "That'll be with the oversizes."

Jaya started down the room through the rows of shelving. The librarians and I followed. We walked past cabinets with ancient-looking padlocks on the doors and open shelves with neatly tagged machines lined up on them. Some had exposed brass gears and steel rivets. Some had complicated antennas and coiled electrical cords.

The place gave me an excited, tingly feeling. It felt like the moment just before you solve a math problem or figure out how to fix a machine, the moment when you can feel the solution arriving, before you quite see what it is.

I paused to look at one of the machines close up, but Ms. Minnian said, "Don't touch anything, Leo. It's dangerous." She hurried me forward by the shoulder.

We caught up to Jaya, Mr. Reyes, and Dr. Rust at the end of the room. They were facing a blank wall.

"Lucy, will you do the honors?" asked Dr. Rust.

"Of course," said Ms. Minnian.

"Let me!" said Jaya. "Please? I've been practicing."

"Successfully?" asked Ms. Minnian in her discouraging voice.

"Well, no, I haven't actually gotten in yet. But I'm sure I will soon," Jaya admitted.

"On the way out, maybe," said Dr. Rust. "Going in is more complicated. Lucy?"

Ms. Minnian ran her hands over the wall as if looking for cracks. Apparently she found some invisible irregularity. She probed the spot with her fingertips. Her fingers actually *sank* into the wall—at least, that's how it looked.

Then she did something I couldn't quite understand. She sort of shook the wall and flipped it, as if she were turning a shirt inside out. It felt as if the whole room was turning inside out. It felt as if *I* was turning inside out.

I squeezed my eyes shut and swallowed hard, feeling queasy.

When I opened them again, the four of us were standing in a vast, dim room surrounded by shadowy shapes. The repository seemed to have disappeared.

"Where *are* we?" I asked. Something was wrong with my voice. It came out squeaky.

"I'm sorry, Leo. I should have warned you," said Dr. Rust.

"Warned me about what? What *happened*?" I was still squeaking.

"We're in the Wells Bequest Oversize Annex, that's all," said Dr. Rust.

All around us were rows of big machines. They ranged in size from a motorcycle all the way up to an ocean liner. There was a huge metal sphere on three spiderlike legs, as tall as a tree. There was a gigantic mechanical elephant—gigantic even for an elephant—harnessed to a house on wheels. There were streamlined machines and boxy machines and machines with knobs and tubes and propellers. And from where I stood, I could see at least five things that looked like rockets.

"But where did the repository *go*? How did we *get* here?" I couldn't quite catch my breath.

"I did a birational transformation," said Ms. Minnian.

"Nice, isn't it? I know, it takes a little getting used to," said Mr. Reyes.

"It was Lucy's idea. So elegant," said Dr. Rust. "It allows us to store large objects in minimal space."

"You mean we went into another dimension or something?" I asked.

"We're in the projectivized tangent space," said Ms. Minnian, as if that would mean something to me. I bet Sofia would know what they were talking about.

"But where's the repository?"

Ms. Minnian waved her hands around vaguely.

"We're still in it," said Dr. Rust. "We're just . . . more *deeply* in it, you could say."

"Don't worry about it, Leo. This is just sort of a storage area," said Jaya.

"A storage area for what? What *is* all this stuff?"

"These are the Wells Bequest Oversizes—objects that don't fit in the main ★WB room," said Mr. Reyes.

"Okay, but what's the Wells Bequest? Nobody's actually *told* me." It's not that I minded being birational transformationed into a projectivized tangent space—I mean, I wasn't *scared* or anything—but I wished somebody would explain.

"The core of the Wells Bequest is a collection of objects assembled by the great industrialist Alfred P. Steel," said Dr. Rust, not really answering my question. "His collection passed to us in 1931, according to the terms of his will. We've added to it over the years, of course."

Jaya interrupted. "Hey, why isn't it called the Steel Bequest, then? I've never understood that."

"Mr. Steel chose the name," said Dr. Rust. "He acquired a number of objects from H. G. Wells. He was a big Wells fan."

"H. G. Wells the writer?" I asked. "The author of *The Time Machine*?"

Dr. Rust nodded.

"What did Mr. Steel get from Wells?" I asked.

"Well, the time machine, for one thing," said Dr. Rust. "Though there's some question about its authenticity—there's no record of it ever having worked. We also have a small sample of cavorite, along with some Herakleophorbia IV, a heat ray, and a black smoke. And a flask of invisibility potion, but no antidote. There's a tripod too, over there." Dr. Rust waved at the three-legged spider-sphere.

"What's cavorite?" I asked.

"A gravity repellant. Wells describes it in *The First Men in the Moon.*"

"You mean like an anti-gravity machine?!"

"More or less—an anti-gravity substance. They used it to make anti-gravity devices in the novel."

Time machines! Anti-gravity devices! Invisibility potions! And they all sounded perfectly serious about it! But the objects were all around me—I could see them with my own eyes, rockets and mechanical elephants and so forth. And the whole birational transformation thing had really happened, hadn't it?

"What's Hera—Hera whatever you said?" I asked.

"That's from *The Food of the Gods.* If you eat it, it makes you grow bigger."

"But don't," said Jaya hastily. "You're plenty big enough already."

"I'm not all *that* big," I said. Even though Sophia said I was growing so fast.

"If you ate Herakleophorbia IV, you'd be four or five stories tall. Come on, the 530s are this way," said Jaya.

I fell in step beside her; the librarians followed us. We walked past robots and jet cars and big, scary guns the size of buses.

"Hang on," I said. "What are those robots?" I paused beside them. "Is one of them that Czech one I wasn't allowed to look at?"

"Rossum's Universal Robot? Yes, it's here somewhere," said Jaya. She checked a tag. "This is it."

It was life-size and looked just like a man. It was wearing crazy metallic clothes with pointy shoulders and elbows.

"Come on, Leo. You can borrow it later," said Jaya, taking me by the arm. I gaped around me as she pulled me along.

"That looks like a spaceship! Is it really?" I asked as we passed one.

"Mm-hm," said Jaya.

"That too?" I asked, pointing to another.

She nodded, then shook her head. "Technically, it's a starship."

"What about that one?"

She checked a tag. "No, it's an exodriller from the Cyprian system."

"What's an exodriller? What's the Cyprian system?"

"I'm not sure. I'm not all that into space operas."

"What's a space opera?" I wished I didn't have to ask all these questions. I sounded so ignorant.

"You know—like a soap opera in space. Those books where advanced alien civilizations battle each other with all their advanced technology until the prince of the Borlechians kidnaps the daughter of the Argoralite emperor, only instead of him killing her, they marry and make an alliance to bring peace to their feuding families. Or whatever."

"Oh," I said. I loved books like that, but Jaya clearly thought they were silly, so I didn't say anything.

We passed some very large telescopes and what looked like a helicopter covered with feathers.

"Why is that helicopter covered with feathers?" I asked.

Jaya shrugged. "Aerodynamics, probably. Or maybe because it's a bio-mechano hybrid." She patted the helicopter's side. It fluffed its feathers, shook itself, spun its rotors a couple of times, and smoothed itself down again, like a pigeon resettling on a branch.

"Jaya," said Ms. Minnian behind us, disapprovingly.

"Sorry, sorry." Jaya grinned, flashing her crooked canine at me.

"Is that thing—*alive*?" I gasped.

"Sure, depending on your definition of alive," said Jaya. "Half alive? Alive enough that we have to feed it, anyway. It likes sunflower seeds soaked in petroleum. This way," she said, turning left.

After a couple of modest-size submersibles, we came to a huge submarine that looked strangely familiar. It was almost as long as a football field, tapered at both ends. It had a propeller in the back, with four vicious-looking blades, and a wheelhouse in front. The whole thing was covered with overlapping metal scales. It looked like a gigantic, reptilian cigar.

"Hey, Jaya," I said, catching her by the arm. "Hang on a sec. That looks just like the *Nautilus,* in *20,000 Leagues Under the Sea*. By Jules Verne, your favorite." Mine too. I loved that book. I had read it three times so far.

"Of course it does," said Jaya. "It *is* the *Nautilus*."

I stopped dead in my tracks, still holding her arm. "*What?* That's the *Nautilus*—the actual *Nautilus*? But what's it *doing* here?"

The librarians caught up to us. "Ah," said Dr. Rust. "The French keep asking us the same question. My counterpart at Phénoménothèque Centrale Supérieure de la Ville de Paris calls it a *trésor du patrimoine*—a national treasure—and would very much like to get her hands on it. But the international tribunal ruled that our title to it is airtight. Airtight, get it? Like the

Nautilus herself?" Dr. Rust paused to chuckle. "Jules Verne loved American technological know-how—and American greenbacks. He was happy to sell the gems of his collection to Mr. Steel."

"He charged a lot, but Mr. Steel could afford it," said Ms. Minnian.

"We have a hydrogen balloon from Verne's first book," said Dr. Rust. "And his Columbiad space gun from *De la terre à la lune,* and the *Albatross*—the flying machine from *Robur-le-Conquérant.* What a racket that thing makes. And of course you saw *la maison à vapeur*—the steam house? I've always had a soft spot for the elephant."

"That's that steam-powered elephant we passed when we first got here," said Jaya helpfully. "The book it's from is appallingly racist, but you gotta love the steam house. A steam-powered elephant!"

I had been listening with my mouth open. Now I shut it, opened it again, and said, "But that's fiction! The Verne books and the Wells books and the space operas too! All those books are *fiction*—stuff the authors made up! How can the objects actually *exist*?"

"Ah, so you're interested in literary-material philosophy," said Ms. Minnian. She sounded almost as if she approved.

"That's a rather profound question," said Dr. Rust. "Scholars have been looking into it for some time. Lucy's our literary-material philosopher around here."

"The simplest solution is that those books *aren't* all fiction," said Ms. Minnian. "As evidenced by the existence of these objects." She waved her hand again. "Though I admit that's not an entirely satisfying solution."

"So the stories are true?"

"That's one way of looking at it."

"But if they *are* true, then the *Nautilus* shouldn't be here! It gets scuttled at the end of *The Mysterious Island,* after Captain Nemo dies. Then it gets buried by a volcano!"

"Well, that part clearly *is* fiction," said Ms. Minnian, "since the *Nautilus* is right here."

"No way! Then how do you know what's fiction and what isn't?"

"Come on," said Jaya impatiently. "We're not going to get to the bottom of all the philosophical stuff today. Let's just find the time machine, okay? It should be right around this corner."

We passed a few more looming hulks and suddenly there it was: the time machine.

I stopped short and stared.

"Well?" asked Jaya. "Is that the one you saw us riding?"

"I—I don't know. It looks a lot like it. But this one's so . . . big."

"Bigger than the one you saw before?"

I nodded.

"Well, how big was that one?"

I held out my hands a few inches apart.

Jaya made a skeptical face. "What? How could the two of us ride on a machine that small?"

"We were only this big ourselves," I said, showing her with my hands.

"You're kidding! Six inches tall? And you only just thought to mention that?"

"You didn't ask."

"How was I supposed to know I should ask something like that? 'Oh, by the way, we didn't happen to be six inches tall, did we?'" She imitated herself questioning me earnestly. "'And did we by any chance happen to be kangaroos? No? What about Popsicle sticks? Balls of pure energy?'" Her sarcasm prickled like tiny claws.

"Fine," I said. "I guess I didn't think it through. I guess I forgot you weren't there yet—I mean Present You wasn't there, so you wouldn't know the things Future You is going to know."

"Did Future Us happen to tell you how we happened to end up six inches tall?" asked Jaya.

"Well, you said something about a shrink ray."

"Of course," said Dr. Rust without a trace of Jaya's sarcasm. "That makes perfect sense. And did Future Either of You say anything about how you got the time machine to work?"

"No," I said. "But . . . there's something wrong." I went up to the time machine for a closer look. "Can I touch it?" I asked.

Ms. Minnian nodded, her lips pursed. "Carefully."

"It looks . . . different," I said, touching a gear.

"Different how?" asked Jaya.

I stared at it, imagining the machine that had appeared in my bedroom. As I concentrated, my memory sharpened into one of those visions I get.

I pointed to the big machine. "Well, this part looks like it's made of brass. Some of those gears were silver-colored when I saw it before. So was this rod. And this seat is much fancier. The other one looked more like a plain bicycle saddle. It was leather, at least the part I could see. Of course, we were sitting on it . . ."

"What else?" asked Dr. Rust.

"There's something missing. There was a clear rod on the little machine. It looked like glass, maybe."

"The 'crystalline substance,'" Dr. Rust said to Ms. Minnian. "Quartz, probably."

"And there was a bar that was kind of . . . sparkling. I think it was this one"—I touched it—"but here it just looks normal."

"The 'twinkling' bar," Ms. Minnian said to Dr. Rust.

"And these levers were white, like they were made out of plastic or china instead of wood," I went on. "Ivory, maybe, like piano keys. And the whole thing looked kind of—" I squinted at my vision. "I don't know how to describe it. Kind of geometrically *off*. Of course, it was tiny and this one is life-size, so I could be wrong, but I don't know. . . ." I trailed off. "It just seems *different*," I said.

Dr. Rust, Mr. Reyes, and Ms. Minnian looked at each other, then at the machine, then at each other again. "Well," said Dr. Rust at last, "there are two possibilities. Either somebody will make a great many very specific alterations to this machine before you use it or it's not the same machine."

"I'm going to try it anyway," said Jaya. She jumped up onto the seat.

"Jaya, don't!" said Ms. Minnian.

"Which lever is future?" she asked. Without waiting for an answer, she reached out and pressed one.

"Jaya! NO!" shouted all three librarians.

But nothing happened. She sat there on the fancy velvet saddle going nowhere. "Nope. Still broken," said Jaya cheerfully, hopping off.

Ms. Minnian's nostrils flared. Her lips stood out red against her pale skin. "Jaya! You know better than to do things like that," she hissed. "What if it had worked?"

"What if it had? Then I would have pressed the other lever and come right back—after looking around a little first, of course. Anyway, we all knew it wouldn't. We've tried it a zillion times."

"She's right," said Mr. Reyes.

Ms. Minnian was still pale. "Someday, young lady, you'll go too far," she said.

"Well, I think that's all we can do here today," said Dr. Rust. "Lucy, will you bring us back?"

"Oh!" Jaya practically squealed. "Let me! Let me!"

"Haven't you done enough, Jaya?" said Ms. Minnian.

"No, I haven't. I haven't done *anything*. Please, Doc? You promised!"

Dr. Rust shrugged.

Taking that as permission, Jaya stooped down and felt the floor the way Ms. Minnian had done with the wall. She dipped her fingers into it, grabbed something, and made that flipping motion.

This time I managed to keep my eyes open, but I still couldn't catch the transformation. It happened too quickly. Suddenly we were standing back in the original Wells Bequest space, the fluorescent lights buzzing, facing the blank back wall.

"Well done, Jaya." Dr. Rust was smiling.

Ms. Minnian led us back to the front of the room, took her remote out of her purse, and pointed it at the door. She ushered us upstairs into the suddenly ordinary light of the fading day.

CHAPTER TEN

Simon's Sabotage

Going back to plain old normal life after spending an hour in a projectivized tangent space full of starships and time machines was the hardest thing I'd ever done.

I wanted to run back to the basement and look at every single one of the objects. I wanted to sit down with the time machine and figure out how to fix it. But Ms. Minnian had said, "Go home now. That's quite enough for today." And I couldn't get into the Wells Bequest Oversize Annex on my own anyway.

So here I was, losing badly to Jake at Gravity Force III.

"What's wrong with you today?" he asked. I'd just crashed my ship three times before getting wiped by a space raider.

I threw down my game controller. "Sorry," I said. "I guess I'm preoccupied."

"Obviously. What are you thinking about?"

I shrugged. "My science project."

"Are you still doing robots?"

"I guess," I said.

"How's it going?"

I shrugged again. "Okay . . . Hey, Jake. What would you do if you found out . . ." I stopped. I shouldn't talk about this. They would kick me out of the repository.

"If I found out what? That my best friend suddenly sucked at Gravity Force III?"

It's okay, I told myself. He would just think I was speculating about silly stuff, the way I always do. "If you found out the things in science-fiction books really existed," I said.

It was his turn to shrug. "They do," he said.

My stomach clenched. Did he *know*? "What do you mean?"

"We have rockets. We sent men to the moon. We sent rovers to Mars. We have submarines and videophones and artificial eyes."

"Oh, *that*. That's not science fiction. It's just science," I said.

"Well, before it was science, it was science fiction."

"Yeah, but that's not what I'm talking about."

"What *are* you talking about, then? You mean things like aliens and artificial intelligence and pork chops that grow on trees?"

"Yeah, I guess," I said. "What if you found out they really existed?"

"They probably do. It's a big universe. A few zillion light-years past Pluto there are probably aliens planting pork-chop trees with their pet artificial intelligences, talking about whether *we* exist. And you know what? Every single one of them could beat you at Gravity Force III. Come on, pick up your controller. And this time, concentrate."

For my next shift at the repository, Ms. Callender put me on Stack 5 again. Abigail and Simon were there when I arrived.

The door opened and Jaya came in. Her hair looked a storm

cloud—dark and wild, with strands shooting out like lightning. My heart did its usual thumpy thing.

Simon jumped up. "Jaya," he said. "Have you heard from the Burton yet? Aren't you supposed to find out this week?"

"I haven't heard anything yet. Has it been busy down here today?"

"Totally dead," said Abigail. "We only got two slips for the whole shift. Do you know where I'm supposed to go next?"

"Ms. Callender wants both of you up in Preservation," said Jaya.

Simon put away his notebook. "Right," he said. "Do let me know if you hear from London."

"Of course," said Jaya.

"What's the Burton?" I asked after they left.

"The Burton Memorial Material Repository, in London," said Jaya. "I'm applying for their summer guest page program."

I remembered the conversation she'd had with Simon back when I first met her. "Would you be gone all summer? I would really miss you!"

"Thanks. I'd miss you too. I have mixed feelings about the whole thing. I mean, Simon really wanted me to apply, and it would be fun to work at another repository. I'd love staying with my aunt in London. But Francis is applying too and he really wants it."

I wanted to say I hoped she wouldn't get the job, but that seemed mean. Besides, it wasn't really true. I did want her to get it, if it would make her happy. But I'd much rather have her being happy on the same continent as me.

After a pause, I cleared my throat. "So," I said. "About last week. Did that . . . did all that really happen?"

"What, you mean the Wells Bequest?" said Jaya. "Yes. It did."

"There really are spaceships and time machines in a crazy room down in the basement?"

"Yes. There really are."

"Who else knows about it?"

"The librarians and most of the pages. And some of the patrons too."

"Simon? Abigail?"

"Yes, and Francis and Alan and Mariela. Most people don't find out as quickly as you did. You're pretty special."

I blushed. "When did *you* find out?"

"Oh, I've known for years and years. But that's different. I kind of grew up in the repository. There was some trouble with the Grimm Collection back when I was ten—my sister, Anjali, got turned into a doll, and I had to rescue her."

"What?!"

Jaya laughed. "Yeah, I know, crazy, right? I was a pretty resourceful ten-year-old. I'll tell you all about it someday."

"Tell me now!"

"I can't. It's way too long a story, and Dr. Rust doesn't like me talking about it."

"All right, but what's the Grimm Collection? At least tell me that."

"The ★GCs. It's another Special Collection down in the basement—objects from fairy tales."

"From *fairy tales*?" I couldn't believe it.

She nodded. "Magic mirrors, seven-league boots, flying carpets, things like that."

"No way! That's impossible!"

"Why? You saw the science-fiction objects in the Wells Bequest. How's the Grimm Collection any more impossible?"

"But science fiction is based on *science*! Science is *real*. Like my friend Jake says, a lot of those things ended up getting invented later on, and the ones that didn't, they might soon. But magic—that's just nonsense! There's no such thing. There can't be. By definition—otherwise it wouldn't be magic."

"Well, what can I say? There *is,*" said Jaya. "Right down there in the basement."

I hated the idea. Not as much Sofia and Dmitri would hate it, but a lot. "That's just wrong," I said. I guess I was a real Novikov after all.

"Not nearly as wrong as the Lovecraft Corpus," said Jaya. She was clearly enjoying watching me get so upset.

"What's the Lovecraft Corpus?"

"Stuff from gothic stories and horror," said Jaya.

"Like what? Ghosts? Vampires? Severed heads?" What a horrible thought!

"You don't want to know. I went in there once—it was really, really creepy. That's the one Special Collection I'd rather not explore."

I shuddered. "What else do they have here?"

"What other Special Collections, you mean?" She counted them off on her fingers. "There's the Grimm Collection, the Wells Bequest, the Lovecraft Corpus, and the Gibson Chrestomathy."

"The Gibson what?"

"The Chresto, for short. It's is a collection of cyber stuff—artificial intelligences, computer viruses, bionic body parts, that kind of thing."

"Oh, okay." That didn't sound so bad. More like the science-fiction collection—stuff that theoretically *could* exist. I thought of something else. "Are all the Special Collections all objects from fiction?" I asked.

"That's one of those philosophical questions Ms. Minnian was talking about," said Jaya. "What is fiction? If the objects exist, don't the stories have to be true, not fiction?"

"Unless somehow the fiction comes true and produces the objects," I said.

"That's one theory," said Jaya.

"It's easy enough to test," I said. I took a handful of scrap paper and a stumpy little pencil from the cabinet next to the card file and started scribbling. I covered four little squares of paper. "There," I said, handing them to Jaya.

She read out loud. "'Once upon a time there was an . . .' Wow, you have messy handwriting. What's this word?"

"'Awesome.'"

"' . . . awesome boy named Leo Novikov. One day he wrote a story on some pieces of paper about an awesome boy named Leo Novikov. The awesome boy in the story invented an awesome machine. When you pressed a button, the awesome machine would fix everything that was broken that you put on the platform.' What platform?" asked Jaya.

"The platform on the machine, of course."

"You didn't say there was a platform on the machine."

"Obviously there is, or where would you put whatever you wanted fixed?"

Jaya rolled her eyes and went on reading: "'It would also make your teeth straight and make you get A's in all your classes.

When the awesome boy Leo Novikov NOT in the story finished writing about the awesome boy Leo Novikov IN the story, he looked around and what did he see? He saw the machine that the awesome boy Leo Novikov in the story had invented! It was right there in front of him! And it worked perfectly! The end, by Leo Novikov.'" Jaya handed me back the slips of paper. "Well? What did that prove?"

"Well?" I said. "Where's the awesome machine? If writing a story makes science-fiction objects exist, it should be right here in front of me."

"Not necessarily," said Jaya. "Maybe it only works with *good* stories."

"Hey! You're talking to the next Jules Verne here," I said.

"Right," she said. "Or maybe it doesn't work until after seventeen years have passed."

"Why seventeen?"

"Why *not* seventeen? Or maybe the story needs to be published for it to work. Or maybe it needs to be popular. Who knows how it might work? All you've proved is that *you* writing *that particular* story didn't do anything. Except make me laugh my head off, deep down inside." She grinned. Her one crooked tooth looked like it was laughing at me too.

I crumpled up the pieces of paper and threw them at her. One of them stuck in her hair. "So if this is a circulating library, do all those objects in the Special Collections—you know—*circulate*? Can people borrow them?" I asked.

"Sure," said Jaya. "But you need to leave a serious deposit. And some objects are so dangerous they don't really let you take them out. Technically you can do it, but you would have to leave your life behind as a deposit, and there's not much you can do without your life." She picked up the pieces of paper, including the one in her hair. She uncrumpled them and handed them back to me. "Here's your masterpiece," she said.

"Thanks." I put it in the recycling basket. I thought about how cool it would be to borrow a spaceship or a very powerful telescope. I wondered if I could afford the deposit.

When our shift was over, Jaya and I clocked out and walked downstairs with Francis. The three of us paused on the steps outside the repository to say good-bye.

Simon burst through the doors. "Jaya? Jaya! There you are! This came for you," he said. He handed her a blue envelope with a foreign stamp.

"What is this? Where did you get it?"

"Ms. Callender had it on her desk. It's from the Burton—it must be," said Simon. "Open it!"

Jaya slid her finger under the flap and tore the envelope open.

"Well? What does it say?"

"Hang on. I can't tell you till I read it." She pulled a letter out of the envelope and unfolded it. Then she gasped. "I can't believe it! I got it! I got the guest page position!"

"Yes! I knew you would!" said Simon. He threw his arms around her. She looked a little uncomfortable, but not as uncomfortable as I wished she looked.

"Congratulations, Jaya. I'm very happy for you," said Francis. He smiled, but his voice sounded flat.

Jaya wiggled out of Simon's embrace. "I'm so sorry," she said, hugging Francis's arm.

He shrugged slightly. "They made an excellent choice. You deserve it—you'll be a great guest page," he said. "Well, I'd better go. I'll see you guys next week." He freed himself from Jaya and walked quickly down the stairs. Jaya frowned after him.

"Aren't you happy, Jaya?" said Simon. "This means we'll be together all summer. It's very good news."

"Sure, I guess," said Jaya. "But I feel bad for Francis. He really wanted the job. And it involves the music collection, so he's more qualified than me."

"Well, they must have liked your application," I said. "They chose you, didn't they?" I didn't want her to go away. But I couldn't imagine anyone not choosing her for anything, no matter who else applied.

"I guess so. And I love London. It's just—I hope they didn't think they had to take me because Auntie Shanti's on the board of directors! I would feel terrible about that."

"Oh, it wasn't your aunt. If you really want to know," said Simon confidentially, "there was a . . . an irregularity with Francis's application."

"What do you mean?"

"Well . . ." He leaned closer to her and spoke so softly that I almost couldn't hear him. "I happen to know that his letters of recommendation went to the Burton on the slow boat with the oversize inter-repository loans. The Burton wouldn't have had his complete file by the deadline. And Dr. Pemberley-Potts is very particular about that sort of thing."

"What? How do you know that?"

"Because I was the one who . . . Well, let's just say, I know it firsthand."

Jaya took a step back and stared at him in horror. "What are you saying? You mean you sabotaged Francis's application?"

"Well, no, I didn't say that. I just helped *yours* a little, that's all."

"By ruining Francis's chances? That's horrible! I can't believe you would do that!"

Now Simon looked angry. "I thought you would be pleased, Jaya," he said. "You wanted that position! You told me you were sad I was leaving New York! You said you would enjoy working with me again. I was just helping make that happen! I didn't do anything actually wrong. I made sure the recommendations got sent—just not by courier."

"You call that *helping* me—sabotaging my friend?" Jaya's eyes flashed. I hoped she would never aim those weapons at me. "Come on!" she said, grabbing Simon by the elbow and pulling him toward the repository door.

"Where are we going?"

"Upstairs to Dr. Rust's office. You're going to explain what you did and you're going to ask Dr. Rust to call Dr. Pemberley-Potts and fix things for Francis. And after that I never want to speak to you again!"

CHAPTER ELEVEN

My Brilliant Idea

That evening I texted Jaya to find out what had happened with Simon. Dr. Rust had fired him, she told me. When I got to the repository for my next shift, I found the pages clustered around Ms. Callender's empty desk gossiping about what had happened.

"He went back to London yesterday," said Abigail. "Good riddance! I never liked him. He was so self-involved."

"Did he get fired at the Burton too?" I asked.

"No, they're giving him a second chance," said Jaya. "His father is the president of their board of directors."

"I wish I didn't have to work with him when I get there," said Francis.

"So you got the summer page job after all?" I asked.

He nodded vigorously.

"Congratulations, Francis! That's awesome!"

"It's because of Jaya. I couldn't believe it! She told Dr. Pemberley-Potts she wouldn't take the job, and she got Doc to talk her into reconsidering my application. Jaya, you're an amazing friend!"

"Doc just had to get Pem-Po to ignore the missed dead-line—your application speaks for itself," said Jaya.

"Pem-Po?" asked Francis.

"That's what Auntie Shanti calls her. Not to her face. I would stick to 'Dr. Pemberley-Potts' if I were you."

"Does your aunt work for the Burton?" I asked. "I thought she invested in start-ups."

"She does, but she's also on the Burton's board of directors," said Jaya.

Alan Stein—a tall, redheaded page I didn't know very well—said, "What I don't get is, why did he do it? Simon, I mean."

"Because he was in love with Jaya, duh!" said Abigail. "Didn't you see how he was always staring at her? And how he was al-ways trying to get Ms. Callender to put them both on the same stack? He wanted her to go to London."

I blushed. I wondered whether I was always staring at Jaya and whether Abigail had noticed.

"But did you hear the funny part?" Abigail went on. "After Doc fired him, Simon tried to borrow the time machine!"

"Abigail! You know you're not supposed to talk about . . . you know," said Alan.

"It's okay, Alan," said Abigail. "Leo knows all about the Spe-cial Collections already. Doc took him downstairs."

"But what did Simon want with the time machine?" I asked.

"He said he wanted to go back in time and fix things," said Alan. "Stop himself from sabotaging Francis's application."

"Fix things, ha," said Abigail. "He probably wanted to *fix things* so he didn't get caught. Our librarians would have to be crazy to let a creep like that run around in the past, changing the future."

"Well, they didn't," said Jaya. "They revoked his borrowing privileges and took away his keys."

"But I don't understand—I thought the time machine didn't work?" I said.

"It doesn't. I guess he was desperate," said Abigail.

"The sad thing is, I kind of liked him before," said Jaya. "I mean, I wouldn't have gone out with him or anything, but I thought he was a decent person, just a little shy or something. When I ran out of the Wilkins tawny orange marmalade that my aunt sends me from London, he ran all over town looking for a shop that carried it. I know the rest of you think he's snobby and self-involved, but he was always nice to me."

"Of course he was nice to *you*," said Abigail. "He had a big, fat, juicy, creepy crush on you. He wanted to touch you all over with his squishy marshmallow fingers."

"Ick, Abigail! Stop it, that's disgusting!"

"Well, he did."

Jaya hit at Abigail with her scarf. Abigail ducked, giggling.

"Everybody here?" asked Ms. Callender, coming up behind us. "Jaya, why don't you take Leo up to Preservation and show him what to do? Abigail, you and Francis take Stack 5. Alan, I'm putting you on 3 with Mariela . . ." She went down her clipboard checking off pages and stacks until we were all distributed.

Jaya led me to a long, tall room on the top floor. Daylight poured in through high skylights in the slanted roof. There were cabinets all around the walls and a long table down the middle. I was glad to be alone with Jaya again.

"Welcome to Preservation," she said. "Ready to work?"

"Of course. What do we do?" I asked.

"We fix things." Jaya opened a cabinet and took out a toaster and a doll's chair. "Here, start with something easy," she said, handing me the chair. "The arm needs regluing."

"What's wrong with the toaster?"

"Not sure. Doesn't toast, probably. It should say on the tag."

"Could I fix that instead?" I asked. "I'm pretty good with toasters."

"Sure, if you want. Can you hand me the wood glue? It's right behind you."

I used my multi-utility tool to unscrew the toaster's bottom panel. A zillion crumbs fell out. "Why was someone borrowing a toaster?" I asked, pulling out something sticky. It looked like a burnt raisin.

She checked a tag. "They were using it as a theater prop. So tell me, little toaster—how did it feel to be a Broadway star?"

Almost to my surprise, the toaster didn't answer.

"What do the librarians do when people break things?" I asked. "Do they just have us fix them? What if someone loses something?" I had lost my share of library books when I was little.

Jaya uncapped her glue. "The patrons pay fines. Not that much for a broken toaster—that's easy to fix. Seriously high fines for something really valuable—or for stuff from the Special Collections."

"Like how high?"

"Well, one time this guy Aaron—he was a page when my sister worked here—once he lost a cooling cloak—"

"What's a cooling cloak?"

"Just what it sounds like," she said, a little impatiently. "A normal cloak keeps you warm. A cooling cloak keeps you cool. There are two of them in the Grimm Collection. They're very popular in August. Anyway, when Aaron lost the cloak, he had to give up his sense of humor."

"His *what*?"

"His sense of humor."

"But how? Is a sense of humor even . . . I don't know, detachable?"

"Sure. Sense of humor, sense of proportion, ear for music— all those things. Dr. Rust collects them as deposits and keeps them safe in a special box. When Aaron lost his sense of humor, his girlfriend broke up with him. She said he was pointless without a sense of humor. I knew they'd be miserable without each other, so I had to find it for him. I'm good at finding things."

"Where was it?" I asked.

"It had fallen behind the radiator."

"His sense of humor fell behind the radiator?"

"No! Weren't you listening? Doc was keeping his sense of humor in a special box. The *cooling cloak* fell behind the radiator. I thought that was hilarious, but Aaron didn't see what was so funny. Not even after he got his sense of humor back."

"You're kidding, right?" I asked. She didn't look like she was kidding, though.

"Perfectly serious. How's that toaster?"

I pulled at a wire. "There's a loose connection. Should I just tighten it or rewire the whole thing? Maybe add a digital color sensor to check for proper browning."

"No fancy stuff. Just fix it," said Jaya, wiggling the loose chair arm into place. "The point is to put everything back as close as possible to how it was before it broke."

"Too bad," I said. "I could make it so much better."

"I'm sure you could. But don't. The librarians wouldn't like it." She clamped the chair arm to hold it tight while the glue hardened.

"What happened to that chair?" I asked, twisting together two wire ends. "Did a really fat doll sit on it?"

She laughed. "Looks that way, doesn't it? Here's a broken stove—want to fix that next? It's a salesman's sample."

"A what?"

"A salesman's sample." She held it out. It looked like a little kid's toy stove. "It's hard to carry around a bunch of full-size stoves, so the salesmen from the furniture company would take miniature samples on their sales calls instead."

I examined the sample stove. It was like a stove out of an old black-and-white movie, only mint green and a fifth the size. Everything looked functional: all the burner knobs turned, the oven door opened, and the little oven racks slid in and out. But the oven door wouldn't stay shut. I checked the tag. *Broken oven door hinge,* it said.

"So this is a working stove?" I asked. "If I hooked it up to a gas line, could I bake a cake?"

"Once you fix it, yes. A cupcake, anyway."

I opened and shut the oven door. A spring was missing on one side. "Where would I find spare parts? I need a spring."

"Try the drawers in the cabinet over there," said Jaya.

I chose a handful of different-size springs and brought them back to the worktable, but they were all either too big or too small. "Oh, this one's so *almost*! If only it were a quark smaller," I said.

"If you really can't find one that fits, we can use the shrink ray to resize it," said Jaya.

I jumped up. "We can? Let's go now!"

Jaya stayed put. "Only if you can't find one that works. It's a pain in the neck to shrink parts down to exactly the right size, and we're not really supposed to do it unless we really need to."

"But I *really need* to see the shrink ray," I said. "Come on, Jaya! You can't tease me like that! Anyway, none of these work," I said, trying the last spring to make my point.

To my disappointment, it fit perfectly.

"Good. It's much better when it's the right size to begin with. But you'll go back to the Wells Bequest soon, I promise," said Jaya.

I fitted the spring in the hinge and tested the door. It snapped shut with a click. As it did, something clicked in my mind too. I could almost hear the ideas clicking into place.

"Hey!" I said.

"What's the matter? You look like you just swallowed a corn chip without chewing."

"I think I thought of something." I put the stove down and started digging through my backpack. "Here—look!" I pulled out the copy of H. G. Wells's *The Time Machine* that I'd been carrying around with me. "The time machine, *our* time machine! It's like the spring—it was the right size to begin with!"

"What are you talking about?"

I flipped to the scene in the beginning of the book where the mad scientist demonstrates his invention for his friends. "Look," I said. "The Time Traveller invents a time machine. But before he builds the full-size one, he makes a little demo version. Fully functioning, just like the salesman's samples."

"And you think—?"

"Yes," I said. "That must be why I told myself to read *The Time Machine*! Listen." I read from the book: "'The thing the Time Traveller held in his hand was a glittering metallic framework, scarcely larger than a small clock, and very delicately made. There was ivory in it, and some transparent crystalline substance.'" I flipped forward a bit. "'"This little affair," said the Time Traveller, resting his elbows upon the table and pressing his hands together above the apparatus, "is only a model. It is my plan for a machine to travel through time."'"

"Is that what you saw? Could that be our time machine? The little demo model?" asked Jaya.

"I think so," I said. "And I think I know where it goes."

"Where?"

"You'll see in a sec," I said. I read some more:

"'"Now I want you clearly to understand that this lever, being pressed over, sends the machine gliding into the future, and this other reverses the motion. This saddle represents the seat of a time traveller. Presently I am going to press the lever, and off the machine will go. It will vanish, pass into future Time, and disappear."'"

"Well, does it disappear? I don't remember this part of the book that well," said Jaya.

"Yes. Listen," I said. "'There was a breath of wind, and the lamp flame jumped. One of the candles on the mantel was blown out, and the little machine suddenly swung round, became indistinct, was seen as a ghost for a second perhaps, as an eddy of faintly glittering brass and ivory; and it was gone—vanished! Save for the lamp the table was bare.'" I shut the book triumphantly. "What do you think of that?"

"Where does it go?"

"Into the future, of course," I said. "But that was over a century ago. And you know what the future was over a century ago? It was *now*!"

"But *where*? Where *is* it?"

"Right where it was when it went into the future, of course," I said. "In someplace called Richmond, in England."

"Oh, Richmond! That's part of London now," said Jaya. "My auntie Shanti lives there."

"That's perfect!" I said. "Your aunt can help us find it."

"But I don't understand—why does the model time machine disappear if it's still there?"

"It's still right there on the table. He explains that in the book. The people in the story just can't see it because it's moving through time so much faster than they are. It's going so fast it's invisible, like a wheel spinning or a bullet flying. So we just have to find the Time Traveller's house and figure out how to stop time and then grab it."

Jaya jumped out of her chair and threw her arms around me. "Leo Novikov, you are a genius," she cried. "And so am I, for finding you!"

I didn't bother to argue that she hadn't found me—that *I* had found *her*. Instead, I lurched out of my chair and threw my own arms around her. We stood there in a crazy, awkward hug with the model stove getting tangled in her hair, and all I could think was how this had to be the happiest moment of my life.

Like all moments, happy or not, it had to end. So I decided to end it before the hug made Jaya uncomfortable. I opened my arms and backed away slightly.

"Ow," said Jaya. "You're pulling my hair."

"Sorry! The stove's caught. Stop wiggling, you're making it worse." I freed it and then carefully pulled a few of Jaya's long hairs out of the hinge.

"Come on," said Jaya, tugging me by the arm.

"Okay. Where are we going?"

"To Richmond."

"Richmond, England? Just like that? How are we getting there?"

"I don't know yet, but Doc will," said Jaya.

Ms. Minnian was sitting in the guest chair by Dr. Rust's desk. "Jaya! Leo! Aren't you supposed to be in Preservation?" she asked.

"Yes, but this is important. It's the time machine," said Jaya. "Leo figured out how to find it."

"You mean how to fix it?" asked Ms. Minnian.

"No, how to find it. Tell them, Leo."

I explained about the demo model.

Doc cocked an eyebrow. "That sounds distinctly plausible. What do you think, Lucy?"

"Very clever. We've thought about trying to capture the big time machine on one of its trips through time, when we know it was working. But nobody ever thought of looking for the demo model! Shall I alert our friends at the Burton and see if they can capture it?"

"No, don't," said Dr. Rust, just as Jaya was yelping, "No! Let us! We thought of it!"

Doc waited until she was done and said, "Dr. Pemberley-Potts has doubts about the legality of the Wells Bequest. If she got her hands on the demo model, she'd be sure to declare it a cultural treasure and claim it for the Burton. The lawyers would squabble over it for years, and there's no guarantee the council would side with us—after all, it technically wasn't in Steel's possession when he died."

"That's nonsense," said Ms. Minnian. "It's clearly covered in the 'artifacts to be found' clause."

"Yes, and most likely the ruling would come down in our favor eventually. But *eventually* can take a long time. I think we'd better go to London ourselves—as quietly as possible."

"All right," said Ms. Minnian. "I'll book us plane tickets."

"But that's not fair! It was Leo's idea! *We* should go," objected Jaya in a near wail.

Ms. Minnian glanced at her impatiently.

I said, "Won't it look weird if our head repositorian suddenly shows up in London for no reason? If you need it done quietly, you should send me and Jaya."

"Nobody'll notice a couple of kids," said Jaya. "We can go spend the weekend with my aunt. That wouldn't draw any attention."

"I don't know. It's an awfully important mission for a couple of pages," said Ms. Minnian.

"For the head page, you mean! Remember that Grimm Collection thief? The pages were the ones who caught him, not the librarians."

"You'll never let us forget it," said Doc.

"Besides, what's the worst that could happen?" Jaya went on. "We go to England, we try to find the time machine, we fail, and we have a nice weekend with Auntie Shanti."

Dr. Rust nodded. "True. Since we're talking about expropriating an artifact in a foreign jurisdiction without due process, it has to be done very, very quietly. That all argues for the pages doing it. This is a clandestine operation. No commercial plane flights."

Ms. Minnian frowned. "Well . . . if you think so, Lee."

"In fact," said Dr. Rust, "if you two do get hold of the model time machine, don't bring it here. Keep it somewhere safe at home. I don't want it in our possession until we've been over every inch of the legalities. I'll get in touch with our attorney."

"Does that mean you're letting me and Leo go? Great!" said Jaya. "How are we going? Jet packs? Flying carpet? Dirigible?"

Jet packs! Flying carpets! Would I ever get used to this place?

"Jet packs would be fun," I said, trying to sound calm. "Or could we take the *Nautilus*?"

"Too loud and too slow," said Dr. Rust. "You need something fast, silent, and unnoticeable. We don't want them shooting you down with fighter jets or blowing you up with depth charges."

"What about the dissolution transporter?" suggested Ms. Minnian. "Is it still checked out?"

"Let's see." Doc went over to a card file and flipped through it. "No, it's back downstairs in the Chresto. Excellent idea."

"What's a dissolution transporter?" I asked.

"Sort of like a fax machine for objects," said Dr. Rust.

"What's a fax machine, then?"

"Oh, you young people!" said Ms. Minnian.

"Never mind about the fax," said Doc. "A dissolution transporter deconstructs an object—in this case, you—taking note of its exact structure and composition. Then it transfers that information to another location, where the object is reassembled from material there."

"Kind of like the transporter on *Star Trek* except it only works one way," said Jaya.

That sounded alarming. "But if we're deconstructed here and reassembled someplace else, won't we turn into other people?"

"Technically, yes. But you'll be other people with the exact same memories. And exact duplicates of your bodies, down to the last quark," said Ms. Minnian.

"Yes, but I'll be dead! Just because someone else has my memories, that doesn't mean it's me!" I objected.

"It's okay, Leo," said Jaya. "I've used the diss tran a zillion times and I still feel like myself."

"Of course you do. You have all of the original Jaya's memories, so of course you *think* you're her. That doesn't mean you *are*."

"What makes you so sure you're the same Leo who went to bed last night?" said Ms. Minnian. "Dissolution transportation is no more discontinuous than falling asleep and waking up again. But you don't have to go if you're afraid."

"No, I'm not afraid! I want to go."

"Great," said Jaya. "Let's go get beamed."

CHAPTER TWELVE

Chocolate at the Time Traveller's House

We told our parents we were participating in an educational weekend project for the repository—which, if you thought about it, was true. Dr. Rust gave us forms for them to sign.

"Though I don't see why I need a permission slip to visit my own aunt for the weekend," said Jaya, once we had all reassembled in Doc's office.

"Because the rules apply to you too, young lady, much as you'd like to believe otherwise," said Ms. Minnian, putting our forms in a folder.

Jaya winked at me behind her back. "You talked to my aunt, right, Doc?"

"She knows you're coming. I caught her at the office, but we didn't have much time to talk. I told her you'd explain when you get there," said Dr. Rust, handing Ms. Minnian a fist-size metal globe. "Will you do the honors, Lucy? You're so precise."

"Of course," said Ms. Minnian. "Stand over here by the window, you two. No, closer together. You've both got your backpacks?" I swiveled slightly to show her mine. She lifted the globe to her eye as if she were looking at us through an old-fashioned camera's viewfinder. "Get closer together—I don't want to leave parts of you behind. Leo, put your arm around Jaya's shoulders. That's right."

Ms. Minnian lowered the globe. I stood there awkwardly with my arm around Jaya—her shoulders felt surprisingly sharp—while Ms. Minnian fiddled with some rings on the globe's surface.

"Jaya, what's Shanti's address?" she asked.

"Number 127 Sidney Terrace."

"Is that the north or south side of the street?"

"North."

"You sure?"

"Positive."

"Hang on—here's the Time Traveller's address," said Dr. Rust, scribbling something on a blank call slip and handing it to me. "Travel safely, kids. Warm regards to your aunt, Jaya."

Ms. Minnian lifted the globe to her eye again. "All right. Stand still now. I said *still,* Jaya! Don't fidget, you could lose a finger. Ready, you two?"

"Ready," said Jaya and I together.

Ms. Minnian pressed something on the globe and the world blinked black.

A second later—or maybe a lifetime—the world went bright again. I found myself standing on something unstable, looking down at a small living room from an odd angle. It was evening. Little lamps with colored shades spilled pools of cozy light around the room.

"Jaya, really—your shoes!" said a woman with an English accent. "Aren't you a little old to be bouncing on the furniture?"

I looked down, clutching Jaya's shoulder. We were standing on a velvet couch with carved wooden arms. I still felt like myself, only more unsteady.

Jaya shrugged out of my grasp, tumbling me off my feet like a load of laundry. She jumped off the couch and threw her arms around the woman. "Hi, Auntie Shanti!"

"Hi yourself, incorrigible," said her aunt, hugging her back.

Shanti Rao had her niece's snapping black eyes and long thin arms. She wore her black hair pulled back firmly, but I could almost see it scheming to get loose. "You must be Leo," she said, holding out her hand. With her accent, she sounded like the narrator on a Masterpiece Theater program.

"Thank you for having us," I said, taking her hand to shake it. She pulled me to my feet and looked me up and down.

"Too tall to sleep on the sofa," she said. "Pity. I've only the one guest bed."

"He can have it," said Jaya. "He's the guest."

"I don't mind the floor," I said. "Really, Ms. Rao."

"Well, we'll sort it out later. Please call me Auntie Shanti. Hungry?"

Jaya and I nodded.

"Good. Fish and chips? And then you can tell me what on earth the two of you are doing here."

Richmond, where Auntie Shanti lived, had bendy streets lined with houses made of red or yellow brick. Some were whitewashed, some trimmed with stone. Some had arched doors or bow windows, some had slate roofs and little gardens in front. It was very pretty and very old.

But it wasn't raining. Wasn't it supposed to rain all the time in England? The air felt cool and pleasant.

Jaya's aunt bought fish and chips "to take away" at a little shop on one of the wider streets. We ate sitting on a bench in a park where a few people were walking their dogs in the cool evening air.

I bit through the crisp crust. It was salty, vinegary, and greasy, in a good way. My teeth met in tender, steaming fish. "This is awesome," I said. "Why don't we have this stuff at home?"

"I know, right?" said Jaya. "There's that place in the Village where I used to go with Simon, but it's not really the same."

"You have better pizza in New York, though," said Auntie Shanti, crumpling up her empty fish paper. "Now, tell me what brings you here."

I ate my fish while Jaya explained.

"Clever boy," said Auntie Shanti when she finished.

"You won't tell Pem-Po, will you? I promised Dr. Rust you wouldn't," said Jaya quickly.

"No, of course not," said her aunt. "The Wells time machine belongs to the New York repository."

"Doesn't the Burton have its own time machine anyway?" asked Jaya.

"Well, yes. A few of them," said Shanti. "But that never stops any repository from wanting another. Besides, the ones at the Burton are weaker than the H. G. Wells machine."

"Of course—that makes sense," said Jaya.

"What are you guys talking about?" I asked.

"Each machine follows the principles of its underlying fiction," said Jaya.

"What does that mean?"

She licked a crumb off her upper lip. "Say you want to travel faster than light. You would need to find a spacecraft from a science-fiction story where faster-than-light travel is possible. If you tried to go faster than light in a rocket from a novel where faster-than-light travel isn't possible, it wouldn't work."

"But I thought Einstein had proved that *nothing* can ever go faster than light," I objected.

"Yes, he did, for all practical purposes. That's why the books are science *fiction*. It's what makes the Special Collections special. The objects in the Wells Bequest don't exist in the boring old ordinary world. Or they don't exist *yet*."

"The same's true of the objects in the other Special Collections—the ones in other repositories, like the Burton," said Auntie Shanti.

I thought about it. "So some of the things in the Special Collections violate the laws of nature?"

"Of course," said Jaya. "The whole Grimm Collection, for starters. You've got wishing rings and flying carpets and magic tables that make food appear."

"Okay, sure, but that's fairy tales. They're not supposed to make logical sense. Science fiction is different. It's supposed to be . . . I don't know. It's supposed to be *possible*."

"All the science-fiction objects *are* possible, in their own terms," said Jaya. "They do obey the rules of nature—just *different* rules of nature."

"But what if those rules contradict each other?" I objected.

"The stories all have different rules. They shouldn't all be able to coexist in our world. It's impossible."

Jaya shrugged. "Would you really want to live in a world where only the possible is possible?"

I laughed. "You're right, I wouldn't. You can be pretty impossible yourself, but I'm glad you're here."

"Thanks! You're pretty impossible too. Especially that curl."

I blushed and pushed it out of my eyes. "So how does all this work for the Burton's time machines?" I asked quickly.

"Same as any other science-fiction objects," said Jaya. "They follow the laws from their stories of origin."

"Which are what?"

"Well, one of the Burton's time machines, the Tuck machine, comes from a can't-change-the-past story," said Auntie Shanti. "Whenever the characters in the Tuck novel try to use their time machine to change the past, they fail. They try to shoot Hitler and the gun misfires or they try to launch a missile, but they trip before they can reach the on switch—that sort of thing. According to the rules in Tuck's book, you can't change the past. So the Tuck machine really is only good for tourism. You couldn't use it to correct a mistake or prevent 9/11 or anything like that. And you can't even use it to collect souvenirs—it won't let you take anything home with you."

"What about the others?" I asked.

"The other two are both weak also. The one from *Tomorrow's Tomorrows Today* only goes to the future. It doesn't have a past setting. Which means if you use it to go to the future, you're stuck there," said Auntie Shanti. "Some people would say it doesn't really count as a time machine."

"And the third one?"

"The Kerr machine? That one's a little more interesting. It's from an alternate-worlds story. You know about alternate worlds, right?"

I nodded.

"The Kerr time machine opens a portal to the past or the future. When the characters in the Kerr novel use it to change the past, they splinter off a new future," said Auntie Shanti. "The world is different for the versions of the characters who exist in the new future. But their actions don't affect the future that they themselves come from."

"You mean their original present?" I asked.

"Exactly."

I thought about it. I guess I looked confused because Jaya said, "Look at it this way. Suppose you used the Kerr machine to open a portal and travel back to 1930 and kill Hitler. Then in the world where you did that, World War II would never happen. But that wouldn't affect the world you left from. If you went home in the Kerr time machine, your own world would be the same as ever—World War II would still have happened in that world."

"I see," I said. "So you couldn't go back in time and change your *own* past even though you could change the past for other people in alternate universes. Including other versions of you."

"Right," said Auntie Shanti. "You would never experience the new past yourself."

"So how does the Wells machine work? What rules does it follow?" I asked.

"As far as anyone knows, it's unrestricted," said Auntie

Shanti. "H. G. Wells doesn't say anything about not being able to change the past or bring back information from the future, or alternate universes, or anything like that."

"Wells doesn't even mention the grandfather paradox," said Jaya. "I bet you could even use his machine to go back in time and kill your grandfather before he met your grandmother, and then you'd never be born. You would probably just disappear."

"That sounds unbelievably dangerous," I said. It was exactly what I'd been worrying about when the tiny time machine first appeared in my bedroom.

"All powerful objects are dangerous," said Jaya. "I like to think things work out all right anyway."

"Only if you're careful," I said.

"Don't be a worrywart, Leo," said Jaya.

"I'm not a worrywart. I'm sensibly cautious!" I finished my fish and chips and crumpled up the wrapper. "Here, want me to throw that away for you?"

"Thanks." Jaya and her aunt handed me their wrappers. I walked over to a trash basket a few yards behind our bench.

When I came back, someone was talking to Jaya and her aunt. He had his back to me, but I recognized his stiff posture and reddish-blond hair. It was Simon FitzHenry!

"You came to tell me you forgive me, didn't you?" he was saying.

"I'm just here visiting my aunt for the weekend," Jaya said.

"But you do forgive me, don't you? You're not still angry?"

"Not angry, just disappointed. I thought you were a different kind of person."

"I will be. I'll be whatever kind of person you want me to

be. You and me—we're not like everyone else. We've always un-derstood each other. Please, Jaya!" He sounded a little desperate. Jaya looked uncomfortable.

I went around the bench and stood next to her. Simon's face contorted when he saw me. "Leo? What are *you* doing here?"

"He's visiting my aunt with me," said Jaya.

Simon stared at me murderously. Then he turned to Jaya. "I thought you came here to see me, but clearly I'm wrong. I can see I'm not wanted." He turned on his heel and walked off.

"That was weird," I said. "How did he know we were here?"

"Well, he does live in London," said Jaya. "Maybe he was just walking in the park. Should I go after him? I feel bad for him. He really did sound sorry."

"*Do* you forgive him?" asked Auntie Shanti.

"Sure, I guess. Now that Francis has the job."

"Would you—you know—go out with Simon?" I asked. "Because that's what he'll think if you stop him."

"No, I guess you're right," said Jaya. "Poor Simon, though."

After Simon had disappeared over the crest of the hill, Auntie Shanti said, "Let's talk about tomorrow. I have some questions about your plan."

"Okay," said Jaya.

"First off," said Auntie Shanti, "why bother with the mini demo time machine? You could use that same technique to capture the full-size machine instead. After all, the full-size machine should be right there in the laboratory too, going forward into the future. It would be far more useful than the mini model."

"But we already have the big machine in the repository—not that it works," said Jaya. "How can it be in two places at once?"

"Of course it can be in two places at once," said Auntie Shanti. "It's a time machine. That's what time machines *do.*"

"Oh, right. Duh," said Jaya, hitting her head.

"I don't want to wrestle the Time Traveller for the full-size machine, do you?" I said. "The Time Traveller is riding the full-size machine. He's not going to just let us take it. The demo is empty. There's nobody at the controls. All we need to do is stop time and grab it."

"Good point," said Auntie Shanti. "That brings up my second question. How do you plan to stop time?"

I had been worrying about that myself. But not too much—after all, I *had* seen my future self on the time machine. "I was hoping we'd think of something when we get there," I said. It sounded pretty lame, but we were bound to come up with something that worked.

"Actually, I have a plan," said Jaya.

"Great! Tell me!" I said.

"When we get there, I need you to almost kill me."

"What?!!"

"Choke me or hold a knife to my throat or something. When people almost die, their life flashes in front of their eyes. That's because time slows down and compresses. It should slow down enough for me to grab the mini time machine."

"No way, Jaya! That's the stupidest plan I've ever heard," I said, horrified. "It won't work."

"Why not?" She sounded offended.

"Well, for one thing, there's no way I'm going to choke you or hold a knife to your throat."

"That's not my plan not working. That's you being too stubborn and wimpy to try it," said Jaya.

"Not wanting to hurt you is not *wimpy*! But it wouldn't work anyway. You know I would never hurt you! Your life only flashes in front of your eyes when you think you're really going to die, not when you know someone is pretending to try to kill you."

"All right, fine. I'll use plan B, then."

"What's plan B?" I asked.

"I can't tell you yet. Or else it might not work."

"Oh, come on! That's ridiculous. I've told you all *my* plans."

"No, really. I can't. It depends on the element of surprise," said Jaya.

Nothing I said would change her mind.

I did win the fight about who got the guest bed. What with the hard floor, jet lag, excitement, and worry, I didn't get much sleep.

The next day, the three of us headed out after breakfast to the Time Traveller's house. Well, breakfast for me and Jaya—it was lunch for Auntie Shanti. It's five hours later in London, so we'd had some trouble waking up.

Before we'd gone a block, it started to rain, little misty drops that stuck to Jaya's hair like glitter. I turned up my collar and stuck my hands in my pockets.

The Time Traveller's house was big and fancy, made of red brick with white trim. It had an octagonal turret and all sorts of peaks and dormers in the roof. The whole ground floor had been converted to shops: a chocolatier, a yarn shop, and a florist.

The Time Traveller must have made a good living, I thought. Maybe that would be a good career choice for me too: mad scientist in a work of fiction.

I stood on tiptoe and peered over the low garden wall. Behind the house were a glass greenhouse, a shed, and a little building that might have been a stable or carriage house.

"That was his lab, I bet," said Jaya.

"We want what used to be the parlor," said Jaya. "Which one do you think that is?"

"The chocolatier, I should think," said Auntie Shanti. "With the bow window."

"All right," said Jaya. "Here's the plan. I'll stop time. Leo, right away—the *instant* it stops—you grab the time machine and switch it off. Pull the lever upright. Perfectly straight up and down. Make sure you get the lever that's sending it into the future, not the one that would send it into the past!"

"I know," I said. "I read the book too. And I saw myself using it, remember?"

"All right, just making sure you know what to do. Meanwhile, Auntie Shanti, you distract the shopkeeper and whoever else is in there. Buy some chocolate or something. Make a fuss. Can you do that?"

"Oh yes, I think I can manage," said Auntie Shanti. "I'm rather good at buying chocolate."

"We need a bag or something to put the time machine in," I said. "It's going to be pretty distinctive looking—it glitters.

We don't want people wondering what it is and where it came from."

"Half a sec," said Auntie Shanti, rooting in her purse. She pulled out a folded plastic shopping bag that said *Fortnum & Mason*. "Will that do?"

"Perfect. Thanks."

"I'd better take that," said Jaya. "Okay, here goes." She opened the door. A bell tinkled as we stepped into a cool room smelling of chocolate.

There were plaster flowers on the ceiling. Shelves piled with fancy candy tins lined the walls. A long glass counter ran along one side with trays of chocolate laid out in rows, which made them look more like jewelry than something you'd eat. Aside from a saleswoman standing behind the counter, we were alone in the shop.

"May I help you?" asked the saleswoman.

"Yes, please," said Auntie Shanti. "I need—oh, shall we say five hundred grams of chocolates? They're for my sister. She's quite particular. Have you got anything from Madagascar?"

"Yes, let me show you our single-estate bars," said the saleswoman. "They're very popular."

"Oh, no, that won't do," said Auntie Shanti. "My sister loathes anything popular. What's your worst seller?"

"I think you must mean our most exclusive collection," said the saleswoman.

"Quite," said Auntie Shanti.

"Perhaps your sister would enjoy our florals?" suggested the saleswoman.

"Nasturtium and borage—with chocolate? Really? I can see why they're . . . exclusive," said Auntie Shanti.

"Indeed. Would you care for a taste?" offered the saleswoman. Auntie Shanti wrinkled her nose but nodded.

Meanwhile, Jaya had been looking around the room. "The demo time machine should be near the fireplace," she said.

I followed her across the room to a marble fireplace with long chocolate boxes stacked in it like logs. Jaya pointed to a spot by her feet. "In the book, Wells says the demo was sitting on a little octagonal table in front of the fire, 'with two legs on the hearth rug.' So that should be right here."

"There's no table there now, though. Do you think the demo would have fallen down? Or will it be standing in mid-air?" I asked.

"I'm not sure," said Jaya. "If it's not on the floor, get ready to catch it." She glanced around. Auntie Shanti and the saleswoman were deep in conversation, inspecting boxes of candy. "Remember, grab the lever the *absolute second* time stops," said Jaya. "Don't wait! We won't have long."

"Yes, yes, I know," I said. "Hurry up and do whatever you're going to do, before the saleswoman notices us."

"Okay. Here goes." Jaya took a deep breath.

Then she leaned forward and kissed me.

CHAPTER THIRTEEN

Jaya Stops Time

Time stopped.

For a split second—or maybe forever, I couldn't quite tell—the world vanished. My heart pounded. There was nothing but me and Jaya and the kiss. Despite a strange, sharp pain in my left shin, I felt like I might explode with joy.

The sharp pain in my left shin got sharper. It was Jaya kicking me.

The reason the world had vanished, I discovered, was that I had closed my eyes. I opened them. Right in front of me, at waist height, something shimmered, complex and brassy. The time machine!

Like a frog snapping a fly out of the air, I reached out, grabbed the lever, and pulled it upright.

My movement broke the spell. Jaya let go of me, the kiss ended, time started up again, and the tiny time machine thudded onto my toes.

"Leo!" hissed Jaya. "You were supposed to catch it! Is it broken?"

"I hope not!"

I handed it to Jaya. She bundled it into the Fortnum & Mason bag.

The saleswoman had heard the thump and turned around. "Did you drop something?" she asked.

"My gram's clock," said Jaya. "We're taking it to be repaired." She pulled down the plastic so that the top of the time machine peeked out. It did look like a clock. "Are you done yet, Auntie?"

"Almost. I think I *will* take those florals, please. Two hundred fifty grams," said Auntie Shanti.

The woman filled a box with brown lumps. "Will that be all?"

"Yes, I think so—or no, shall we get some rose creams for your mum, Jaya?"

"I think she'd like the ginger better," said Jaya. She muttered to me, "I know *I* would."

"Two hundred fifty grams of the chocolate ginger as well, then. And that's the lot," said Auntie Shanti.

I walked down the front steps to the pavement, twitching and zinging with excitement. Jaya had kissed me! I'd found the time machine!

Auntie Shanti paused at the bottom of the steps. "How did you manage it? Stopping time, I mean," she asked.

Jaya looked embarrassed. "I used the subjective startle effect," she said a little stiffly. "I induced a moment of emotional anomaly, altering Leo's experience of relative temporality."

"Emotional anomaly?" Auntie Shanti sounded puzzled. Then comprehension washed across her face. "You didn't! Little Jaya! Don't tell me you—"

She broke off and looked at me. I blushed.

"Well," said Auntie Shanti with a laugh, "whatever works!"

"Jaya!" called a voice on the street behind us.

I whipped around. There stood Simon FitzHenry in all his reddish-blond hatefulness.

"Simon!" I growled. "Are you following us?"

He ignored me. "What are you doing here, Jaya?" he asked.

"Visiting my aunt, like I told you. Buying chocolate. What are *you* doing here?"

"You're buying *chocolate*? At the Time Traveller's house?" His voice dripped with incredulity.

"Oh, is this the Time Traveller's house?" Jaya sounded almost innocent. "We came for chocolate."

"You know perfectly well it is. What are you up to?"

"Buying chocolate, like I just said. What are *you* doing here? Are you buying chocolate too, or is this just another really un-likely coincidence?"

"I've been tracking your movements with the Burton's peo-ple finder," said Simon.

I could see Jaya's pity turning into anger. "You disgusting sneak! You've been *spying* on me?"

"I'm not spying, just . . . watching. I couldn't bear things the way we left them. I couldn't bear not knowing where you were."

"You're *stalking* me!"

"When you showed up in London last night, I thought you'd come to see me. But I was wrong. And then today, when you went to the Time Traveller's house, I knew why you must be here! To try to recapture the time machine! But I *need* it. Where is it? Did you get it?"

"Don't be ridiculous. Do you see a time machine here?" said Jaya. "That thing's the size of an armchair."

"You could have hidden it in the house. Or made it invisible."

"Well, I didn't. And if I had it, there's no way I would ever give it to *you*," said Jaya.

Simon narrowed his flinty little eyes. "I wouldn't taunt the man who controls Tesla's death ray, Jaya."

"What death ray? Tesla never built one. And even if he had, why would *you* have it?"

"My grandmother's grandfather worked in Tesla's lab, remember? He sailed for England the night the lab burned down. He took three chests of plans and models with him."

"Oh, so your grandmother's grandfather was a cheat too? It figures."

"Please, Jaya," said Simon. "I don't want to hurt you. If you have the time machine, let me use it. I need to go back to last month and fix my mistake so you won't hate me and we can be together." His voice shook. I almost pitied him.

"Go away, Simon. Your little plan isn't going to work," Jaya told him.

"Please, Jaya! Don't make me use the death ray!"

I stepped in front of Simon and looked him straight in the eyes. The guy was really sounding crazy!

Simon stopped, surprised.

"Get . . . out . . . of . . . here . . . *now*," I said. My voice felt different—it had never before sounded that controlled and intimidating. "And stop threatening Jaya. *Do you understand me?*" My fingers tightened into fists.

Simon looked down at my hands. My eyes never left his face. He began to tense up.

Auntie Shanti put her hand on my right arm. I lowered it slowly.

"That's enough, Simon," she said. "You ought to be ashamed of yourself. Leave us alone, or I'll make sure Dr. Pemberley-Potts hears about this."

"You're making a mistake. You'll see." With a last glare at Jaya and me, Simon stalked away down the street.

It takes a moment to recover from that kind of anger. We all stood there silently. Then what Simon had said sank in.

"Does Simon really have a death ray?" I asked. "The histories all say Tesla never finished inventing it."

"But his lab burned down," said Jaya. "Lots of his inventions got lost. Maybe the death ray was one of them—maybe Simon's ancestor really did steal the plans for it before the fire."

"Highly unlikely," said Auntie Shanti. "I've known Simon's father for years—we're both on the Burton's board—and he's never mentioned it. He's not what you'd call modest. Though I suppose even he might hesitate to boast about owning weapons of mass destruction."

"Well, let's not stand here in the rain," said Jaya. "After that ordeal, I need a crumpet."

"I can carry the time machine, Jaya," I offered. She handed it to me.

"There's a good tea shop around the corner," said Auntie Shanti, leading the way.

• • •

The waitress pointed us to a tiny table by the window.

"That whole thing with Simon was really disturbing," said Jaya.

Auntie Shanti frowned. "Not here," she said, glancing around at the crowded tea shop.

"You're right," said Jaya. She changed the subject: "What do you hear from Meena and the boys?"

While Jaya and her aunt discussed family matters, I spaced out and thought about the confrontation with Simon, the time machine, and the kiss. What was Simon capable of? I wondered. How much danger was Jaya in? And what could I do to protect her? But mostly, I wondered about the kiss. What did it mean? Did Jaya . . . like me? I mean, she obviously liked me, but did she like me the way you like someone you kiss? Or did she just know *I* liked *her*?

She'd kissed me for a reason: to make time stop. Obviously time wouldn't stop for just any old kiss. Her kiss was amazing. Nothing remotely like what had happened when I kissed Rachel Mintz in sixth grade. Clearly it had to be with someone you felt strongly about.

Had time stopped for Jaya or just for me? I opened my mouth to ask, then shut it again. I couldn't possibly ask her a question like that.

If the kiss wasn't real for her, then there was something sad about being kissed by the most awesome girl in the known universe for a reason that had nothing to do with how she felt about me.

Well, at least we had gotten a time machine out of it. I felt for it with my toes to reassure myself it was still under my chair, which made me jostle Jaya with my knee.

She smiled and jostled me back. "Sorry, we're being rude," she said. "How's your scone?"

"It's great. Want a bite?"

I held out my scone and she bit it. I watched her lick clotted cream off the corner of her mouth and wished I could do it for her.

Back at Auntie Shanti's apartment we shook rain off our jackets.

"Let's have a look at it, shall we?" said Auntie Shanti.

I pulled the demo time machine out of the Fortnum's bag. The fall didn't seem to have hurt it. Nothing was bent or broken.

"It's very detailed for a model. I love these little lion-paw feet," said Auntie Shanti.

Jaya touched a bar with her fingertip. "Is this supposed to be twinkling like that? The big one doesn't twinkle."

"It's supposed to. At least, that's how H. G. Wells describes it in the book," I said.

"Now what?" asked Auntie Shanti. "Care for a spot of sightseeing, you two? Or would you rather take the model back to New York right away?"

"I've always wanted to see the Tower of London. And Kew Gardens. And I'm curious about the Burton Repository, of course," I said. "But what I really want to do is try out the time machine!"

"The Tower of London would be super-fun with a time machine," said Jaya. "But I don't want to risk Simon finding us again. We should get it home."

"Pity, but I expect you're right," said Auntie Shanti. "Better pack your things, then."

I didn't have much to pack. I shoved my dirty clothes in the bottom of my backpack for padding, then wrapped the model time machine in my last clean T-shirt and tucked it away too.

"So how are we getting home, Auntie?" asked Jaya, coming back with her bag. "The dissolution transporter we used to get here is back in New York. Do you have one here?"

"No, and even if we did, we shouldn't use it on the time machine. It's never a good idea to use objects of power on each other without testing them first. Who knows what damage we might do."

"How will we go, then? Are there jet packs?"

Auntie Shanti shook her head. "I thought we would take the *Épouvante.*"

"What's that?" I asked.

"From Jules Verne's *Master of the World,*" she explained. "In English, it's the *Terror.*"

"That sounds ominous."

"It's not ominous, it's awesome. It's a land-air-sea sub-ship," said Jaya. "But isn't it in the Phénoménothèque in Paris?"

"Usually, but it's here on inter-repository loan. Jane Random and I took it on holiday to Minorca two weeks ago. I might as well run you over before we return it—that way I can have a nice visit with your mum and dad."

"Great! Where is it? Can I drive?"

"It's in the river. Leo will get his wish to see Kew Gardens— we'll be passing beside them on our way to the Channel."

CHAPTER FOURTEEN

The Terror

We shouldered our backpacks and wound our way downhill along Richmond's curving streets, through a tidy green park to the Thames River.

"Just over here," said Auntie Shanti.

A sign read *Private Pier. Strictly No Mooring.*

Jaya hopped over a chain, ran down a metal stair to water level, and stepped out on the swaying wooden pier. "Where's the *Terror*?" she asked, scanning the water.

We followed her down. "Cloaked," answered Auntie Shanti.

"It has a cloaking device? I don't remember that from the book," Jaya objected.

"It didn't have one in the book," said her aunt. "But it got hit by lightning, remember? When the Phénoménothèque Centrale Supérieure de la Ville de Paris rebuilt it in the mid-twentieth century, they put in a number of improvements. People weren't as strict about authenticity back then."

"If it's from a Jules Verne novel, why isn't it in the New York repository?" I asked. "I thought Mr. Steel bought all Verne's objects."

"He did, most of them. But he thought the *Terror* was too badly damaged to rebuild, so he traded the pieces to the Paris Phénoménothèque," said Auntie Shanti.

"What did he get for them?" I asked.

"Something of General Lafayette's, I think. A sword, maybe."

While she was talking, Auntie Shanti stooped by the edge of the pier, running her fingers along it. She caught hold of something invisible and pulled. The water beside the pier churned and buckled, as if an invisible whale were surfacing. She strained at her invisible rope, splashing and sluicing water.

"Hold this, will you, Jaya?"

Jaya grabbed the air behind her aunt and helped tug. I felt a thump and the pier swayed. Then Auntie Shanti stepped over the railing and leapt into air.

She landed in the middle of the disturbance and stood, rocking but upright. She looked like she was walking on water. "Give me your hand, Leo," she said. "I'll help you over."

That water looked really unsteady. It was stupid to jump before I understood it. "If the boat's cloaked, doesn't that mean it's invisible? Shouldn't it look like a hole in the water?"

Auntie Shanti shook her head. "It's not invisible, it's camouflaged. It looks like its surroundings—in this case, water. Come along." She held out her hand impatiently. Between the two of them, Jaya and her aunt had about as much patience as the number 2 express train.

I stepped over the railing, shut my eyes, and jumped.

I landed on my left foot. My right shot sideways, but Auntie Shanti caught me by the backpack before I fell. "Steady now," she said. "Ready, Jaya?"

I held out my hand to Jaya. She took it, leapt, stumbled as she landed, and fell into my arms. She righted herself quickly. Too quickly—I wouldn't have minded if she'd stayed awhile.

Auntie Shanti bent and lifted something invisible. "Down the hatch," she said. Jaya scampered over and climbed down.

Auntie Shanti untied the invisible rope. As soon as she detached it from the cloaked vessel, it popped into visibility. She coiled it and tossed it onto the pier. It lay there like a snake, hot pink and glaring yellow.

I felt a tug at my heels. "This way, Leo," said Jaya from below. She fitted my feet onto the ladder rungs as I climbed down into nothingness.

The moment the top of my head cleared the hatch, the ship became visible. We were in a little room with hanging bunks. A round porthole let in water-green light. It smelled of metal and brine and old grease.

"Come on, I'll give you the grand tour," said Jaya. She led me through the narrow sleeping cabin to a kitchen and a tidy paneled dining room—"the mess," she called it—and the engine room, with its silent electric engines. The batteries were hidden under benches in the next compartment, the smoking room. I wanted to stop and figure out how it all worked, but Jaya hurried me through. "We need to get moving. There'll be plenty of time for that later, while we're crossing the Atlantic."

She opened the next airtight door. A long room tapered

dramatically toward the front end—the bow, said Jaya. Brass handrails ran along the sides. Instead of portholes, the entire front end of the vessel had a big, pointed windshield.

"Cool!" I said, running over to it. "It's like the ship on Gravity Force II: Planetbound!"

Below the windshield were the controls. Jaya plopped herself down in the captain's chair by the steering wheel.

"Out," said Auntie Shanti.

"But you said I could drive. You promised!"

"I did not."

"Come on! Please? Dad let me last summer."

"Maybe once we've cleared the Channel. There's far too much traffic on the river here. Up!"

Jaya made a face and flounced out of the chair. "You just want to drive in the exciting part!"

"Can you blame me?" With a Jaya-like grin, Shanti sat down, twisted a knob, and pulled a lever. The *Terror* kicked into life.

It lived up to its name. "Grab the handrail, Leo!" she warned as I barreled into Jaya. I braced my feet wide apart, hung on like crazy, and hoped I wouldn't fall flat on my face. It was like playing Gravity Force III with my whole body. We sped furiously through the water, skimming around barges and diving under ferries. Our wake sent the little vessels bobbing like toys. I hoped the cloaking would keep us hidden.

"Watch out! There's the Richmond Lock up ahead!" yelled Jaya. "It's closed!"

"I see it, Jaya," said her aunt calmly. "We'll go over. Hold on tight."

I was already holding the handrail, but I grabbed tighter and bent my knees. Auntie Shanti pressed a button. With a metallic shriek, a pair of wings sliced outward from the *Terror*'s sides. They gave three beats and we leapt into the air like a flying fish, just clearing the footbridge over the lock. We landed in the river and dove under, pulling a veil of bubbles around us.

"That was fun," said Jaya. "Why don't we fly the whole way?"

"Not till we clear the populous areas," said Auntie Shanti. "We might ghost."

"A ghost? Where?" I asked. Nothing could surprise me now. It made sense there would be ghosts in a place this old.

Auntie Shanti laughed. "Not *a* ghost—ghosting. That's when the cloaking leaves a glint in air. It's best to stay under when the water's deep enough. Oh, but I'll make a quick exception." She pulled the *Terror*'s sharp nose straight up out of the river. "Look to starboard, Leo."

A green vista flashed past on the right-hand side. "What was that?" I asked, craning my neck as it vanished behind us.

"Kew Gardens. See? I kept my promise."

"Uh, thanks."

As we went deeper into London, the river deepened too, but it got more crowded. We dodged and dove and zipped around vessels of all sizes. It looked like fun—I wished I were driving. Auntie Shanti pulled us out of the water from time to time to show me sights: the Houses of Parliament, the giant Ferris wheel, and the dome of St. Paul's Cathedral. The Tower Bridge winked past from a cockeyed airborne angle.

"How did you like London?" asked Auntie Shanti, plunging into the Channel.

"Charming city," I said.

"It is, actually," said Jaya. "You'll like it next time we come. Can I drive already, Auntie Shanti?"

Next time—Jaya expected to come back here with me!

"I said *after* the Channel."

"But we're past the exciting part, and I'm good at this. You know I am."

"Fine," said Auntie Shanti, climbing out of the chair. "If you crash, make sure I die. That way I won't have to explain it to your father."

Jaya climbed into the chair, then looked at me. "Leo, you're the guest. Want to take the wheel first?"

How generous! I could have hugged her. "No, you go first," I said. "You've been dying to." I hung over the captain's chair, watching her take us under ships and over shoals. She would be killer at Gravity Force III, I thought.

Dim green light sifted through the window. Plastic bags floated like jellyfish. Marine life loomed into view, then flicked away. We nosed through a school of fish. They parted around us like a shiny beaded curtain.

"Whiting," said Auntie Shanti. "They live in shipwrecks. You'd better pull our nose up. There must be a wreck nearby."

"Ooh!" Jaya slowed down abruptly. She spun us around, snapped on our headlights, and dove. Glinting bits of who knows what came at us in the twin cones of light. It was like driving through snow.

"Up! I said up, not down!" shouted Shanti.

"I just want to take a look."

"Oh, very well. I'll admit I'm curious myself."

The wreck swam into view: an ancient pirate-looking ship

lying on its side. Its masts had broken off and lay buried in the seafloor. A brown-gray layer of muck covered it like a velvet blanket. Little fish darted through the wreckage.

"Maybe it's a Spanish galleon full of gold!" Jaya said, hovering over it. "Let's get out and look."

"You know we can't. It would be a legal nightmare," said her aunt. "Jaya! *Now!*"

"Spoilsport," said Jaya. She reluctantly turned us back around and sped us forward. "Leo, want a turn?" she asked.

"Yes, please!"

She got up and offered me the captain's chair. "Okay, we're in the Atlantic now. Stick to the mid-depths and watch out for whales," she said. "Check the sonar and the GPS."

I followed the course she'd set. The engines whispered. We followed our headlight cones through the brown darkness.

Suddenly Jaya shouted, "Watch out! Shark!"

I whipped around to look. Something loomed on the sonar, and a moment later the headlights illuminated a huge, blunt snout dripping with teeth. I swerved just in time. With a flip of its tail, the shark vanished. "Will he follow us? Can he hurt the ship?" I asked.

"Of course not. Are you afraid he'll try to eat us? He's not a goat. We're basically a big tin can—pretty indigestible. I was worried about *him,* not us! We would hurt him if we rammed him."

"Or her," said Auntie Shanti. She glanced at the GPS. "We'll have cleared the coastal radar surveillance by now. It's time to fly," she said.

"Me, me, let me!" cried Jaya.

"All right. Take us up to eight thousand feet. Use the air button and the—"

"Yes, I know. The alt lever. May I, Leo?" asked Jaya.

"Buckle up, Leo," said Auntie Shanti.

I gave Jaya the captain's seat and buckled myself into an armchair. She took us upward through the lightening sea. Just as we burst into sunlight, she pressed the air button, snapped the wings out, and leapt us into air.

Up, up, up we went, the wings pumping like a heartbeat. The acceleration pressed me back into the armchair. We flew toward a fluffy cloud, which engulfed us, then let us go. We popped out into clear blue.

"Engage the autoflight and the traffic avoidance now," said Auntie Shanti.

"I *know*. Please stop backseat piloting," said Jaya.

"Aye, aye, Captain," said Auntie Shanti, grinning like her niece.

We flew west over the ocean on autopilot, stretching out the day into one long afternoon. Auntie Shanti made cauliflower curry for lunch, or maybe it was dinner. We ate in the mess, with sunlight slanting through the portholes. She and Jaya kept hopping up to check the sonar and make sure the avoidance system hadn't missed anything.

After lunch, Jaya found two copies of *The Master of the World* in the main cabin, one in French and one in English. "Have you ever read this?" she asked. "It's the Jules Verne novel the *Terror* comes from."

"Cool!"

"French or English?"

"English, please."

"I was hoping you'd say that. It's better in French," she said, curling up in an armchair and opening it.

Show-off, I thought. And the annoying thing was, she had so many impressive things to show off.

A few chapters in, I said, "This book is hilarious! First they were all trying to climb an unscalable volcano in west North Carolina, and now the *Terror* is diving in a giant lake high in the mountains of Kansas. The mountains of *Kansas*!"

"What's the matter? You've never been to the mountains of Kansas?"

"There aren't any."

"Maybe not in *this* universe."

"Really? Are there other universes where Kansas has mountains?"

"Sure! Jules Verne's fictional universe, for one."

"But that's fictional. By definition, it's not real."

"Depends on what you mean by real. The *Terror* is fictional, but it feels pretty darn real to me," said Jaya, thumping the floor with her feet.

I put my book upside down in my lap. "I still don't understand how science-fiction objects get out of their fictional universes and into the real world."

"You mean *this* world? What makes you so sure this is the real world?"

"Come on, Jaya. Be serious."

"I am being serious."

"All right. How do they get out of their fictional worlds and into *this* world, then?"

She shut her book on her finger to keep her place. "There isn't one single answer. Lots of the objects come through the authors—that's how Mr. Steel got most of the things in the Wells Bequest. Or sometimes we can capture them ourselves."

"Like we just did with the model time machine," I said.

"Exactly." She paused, smiling. Could she be thinking of the kiss? "But there are lots of objects that nobody's captured yet, and maybe they never will. Maybe those stories aren't good enough to have real objects in them. Or maybe I'm wrong, and there is no fictional universe with Kansan mountains in it. Maybe when Verne wrote the story, he put in some true stuff—like the *Terror*—and some stuff he just made up, like the mountains in Kansas."

"That answer stinks," I said. "It's totally unsatisfying."

"Then maybe you should do some literary-philosophy experiments and try to find a better one," said Jaya. "Ms. Minnian would like that."

"I wish the judges would let me do that for my science fair project!"

Auntie Shanti put her head in the doorway. "Are you done solving the mysteries of the universe yet?" she asked. "You'd better finish fast—it's time to take the vessel down."

CHAPTER FIFTEEN

The Death Ray

Auntie Shanti folded our wings and dove into the Atlantic. We surfaced so we wouldn't scrape the bottom, engaged the cloaking, and docked at the yacht club marina by Battery Park.

I followed Jaya and Shanti up the swaying pier toward the tall buildings of the Wall Street district. The sailboats poked their masts at the setting sun.

"Here, I'll take the time machine," said Jaya.

"No, you'd better let Leo keep it for now, until Doc speaks with the attorneys," said Auntie Shanti. "Your apartment might count as an official repository location. After all, your father's the board president."

"Oh, good point. Do you have someplace safe to put it, Leo?"

I nodded. "My closet, under my laundry. My whole family's terrified of my dirty socks."

"Schist! Socks!" said Jaya. "Come meet us at the repository after you've dropped it off—Doc's going to want to hear all about it."

It felt odd carrying a time machine on the subway. The three blond tourists chattering away in German, the African American man in a suit reading a neatly folded newspaper, the tired Chinese woman carrying four red shopping bags full of vegetables, the two little boys elbowing each other for a better view out the window—what would they say if they knew?

I met Jaya and her aunt again in the repository. We headed upstairs with Ms. Minnian.

"Guess what?" cried Jaya, bursting through the doors into Dr. Rust's office. "My plan worked, and Leo—"

"Stop, Jaya. We're not alone," said Dr. Rust, pointing at the wall.

"What?" said Jaya. We both spun around to look.

A large tinted sepia photograph in a fancy frame was hanging on the wall. Wires attached the picture to a complicated brass device that looked like an old-fashioned telephone. The photo showed Simon standing in front of a big machine that looked a little like a World War I anti-aircraft gun. It was almost twice as tall as he was. It had five mean-looking barrels, five big, brassy boxes, and a cube with scary-looking swirly things sticking out of it. Somehow those swirly things were the focus of the photo. They seemed to glow.

But it couldn't be a photo. Simon was moving. He was talking, too.

"There you are, Jaya," he said.

"That's not the shifting picture from the Grimm Collection, is it?" Jaya asked Dr. Rust. "The frame looks different."

"No, it's the telelectroscope from the Wells Bequest."

"The what?" said Jaya.

"What's a telelectroscope?" I asked.

"It's a sort of networked videophone—an early version of the Internet. From an 1898 short story by Mark Twain."

"Mark Twain, the guy who wrote *Huckleberry Finn*? I didn't know he even wrote science fiction."

"Oh, he wrote pretty much everything," said Dr. Rust. "He had a wide-ranging imagination."

The image of Simon cleared his throat sarcastically. "If you're quite done with the literary critique, I have a small matter to discuss," he said.

We all turned back to Simon.

"As you know, I made a mistake. I would like a chance to rectify that. To do that, I need the time machine. Please send it today by pneumo-courier." His voice came out hollow and crackly.

"Simon," said Dr. Rust, "you know perfectly well that the time machine in the Wells Bequest doesn't work. And you also know perfectly well that you've lost all borrowing privileges at the New-York Circulating Material Repository."

"I also know perfectly well that Jaya and Leo were just in Richmond trying to recapture the time machine from the Time Traveller's house, and I just heard Jaya admit that her plan worked."

"Don't be an idiot, Simon. You saw us. Did we look like we were carrying the time machine? It's huge."

"You might have taken it home already when I saw you. Or shrunk it, or made it invisible. I know you have it. Doc, you would be well advised to restore my borrowing privileges and send it to me by the next pneumo-courier."

"Why would we do that—even if we did have it?" asked Ms. Minnian.

Simon waved his hand at the machine behind him. "Because I have Nikola Tesla's death ray, and I won't hesitate to use it if you don't. I'll destroy New York."

For a moment nobody could speak. Then Jaya said, "This is supposed to convince me that you're not evil, Simon? Fail!"

Simon said, "I know you think that now. But you'll see. It will all work out. Once I've used the time machine to correct my mistake, you'll never know about any of this because it will never have happened."

"And what if we don't have the working time machine—which we don't? Or if we choose not to negotiate with a terrorist?"

"I would be very sad to have to use the death ray, but believe me, I will if I have to," said Simon. "Don't look at me like that. I'm not a monster. Be sensible! Once I have the time machine, I can change the past and undestroy New York."

"Not if it's in New York and you destroy it!" said Jaya.

"That's why you'll give it to me," said Simon.

"But we don't have it!" I said.

"That's crazy, Simon! You're not thinking clearly," said Jaya.

"All right. I'll destroy San Francisco first. You have cousins there, don't you?"

"Why should we believe that the machine behind you is Tesla's death ray, Simon?" asked Ms. Minnian in a reasonable voice. "There's no record that he ever actually built one. The models and plans are thought to have been destroyed in the

South Fifth Avenue lab fire of 1895. The Burton certainly doesn't own such a thing."

"It's not the Burton's. It's mine," said Simon.

"What are you doing with Tesla's death ray?"

"My grandmother's grandfather worked in Tesla's lab. He sailed to England the night the lab burned down. He took a lot of models and plans with him. He met my great-great-grandmother on the ship crossing the Atlantic, and they built the death ray together from the plans."

"Oh, come on. *That* thing?" said Jaya. But she sounded worried.

I was worried too. Even in the sepia motion photo, that big gun looked way too real.

"You have twenty-four hours to hand over the time machine," said Simon. "Then I'll do a little demonstration to show you what the death ray is capable of. Dallas, shall we say? Or Paris?"

"I don't believe you. You wouldn't do that," said Jaya. "You're not really that evil."

"Twenty-four hours," said Simon, and reached behind him. The photo image went uniformly brown.

Dr. Rust unplugged the telelectroscope, took it down from the wall, put it outside the office, and shut the door. "We can talk freely—he can't hear us now. What do we do?"

"I know one ought never to negotiate with terrorists," said Auntie Shanti. "But mightn't it be safer simply to give him the time machine?"

"That's crazy! Why would we do that?" I said.

Auntie Shanti said, "The death ray—if that's what it really

is—could destroy a city. And all Simon wants with the time machine is to undo a mistake he made. That seems harmless."

"No," said Dr. Rust. "The Wells machine has no restrictions. Simon could use it to alter the past and the future any way he liked. We can't put an object so powerful in the hands of someone so unstable and untrustworthy. And anyway, we don't even know for sure whether that thing *is* the death ray. I'm inclined to think he's bluffing."

"But what if he isn't?" asked Jaya.

"It looked pretty convincing to me," I said.

"How could he possibly aim a beam at New York from London unless he was in orbit? Which he's not," said Dr. Rust.

"Well, we don't have an answer to that," said Ms. Minnian. "There are no records of what the Tesla death ray was or how it worked."

I'd just read a whole book about Tesla and his inventions. "Wasn't he trying to use tiny particles of mercury, accelerated in a vacuum?" I said.

"Yes, that was one idea he was playing with. But we don't know for sure what his final concept was, if he ever finished it. The ray could arc along the lines of force of Earth's magnetic field, for all we know. Or it could obey parabolic or ballistic laws, like a missile. We have no idea what that thing behind Simon is."

"It looks like a really pretentious boson's idea of what a death ray would look like," I said. "Boy, is that guy full of himself! He's got to use a telelectroscope—he can't even use a cell phone like a normal person."

"That's not just pretentiousness," said Ms. Minnian. "He's threatening to use a weapon of mass destruction. The telelectroscope can't be detected with the methods used by national security agencies like the NSA or MI5. Cell phones can. If they heard him and took him seriously, he would be the subject of one of the most massive manhunts in history. And they would find him."

"Shouldn't we call in the FBI or the NSA or something?" I asked.

"No," said Dr. Rust. "They would declare us a national threat and confiscate half our collection. We're on our own."

"Well, couldn't we threaten him back? Are there any deadly weapons in the Wells Bequest?" I asked. As soon as I said it, I realized what a bad idea that was.

"I *have* always wanted to try out Washington Irving's moonstones and concentrated sunbeams," said Jaya. "But I don't think Simon would react well to threats."

"Let's not go there," said Ms. Minnian.

"To be safe, we have to assume the death ray is real," said Dr. Rust. "I'll reach out to Dr. Pemberley-Potts, and we'll pull together a team to send to London."

"Can I go?" asked Jaya eagerly. "It's my fault this whole thing started. At least, he said he's doing it for me. I should be the one stopping him."

"No," said Dr. Rust. "It's too dangerous."

Jaya got a stubborn look on her face, but she just said, "All right. I guess you don't need me here, then," and ran out of the room.

"You'd better go calm her down," Auntie Shanti told me.

"I'll try. I hope you catch Simon fast."

CHAPTER SIXTEEN

The Shrink Ray

I found Jaya in the Catalog Room. I hurried over to her. "Don't worry, Jaya. It'll be okay. That death ray thing's probably just a big cardboard fake," I said, with way more confidence than I felt.

Jaya looked up. "Oh, there you are, Leo." She didn't sound nearly as upset as I expected. "Help me find a good map of the city. Or, no—maybe you should get the money while I find the maps. Get plenty of nickels."

"What are you talking about? What do you need nickels for?" I checked my pockets. I had a five-dollar bill and sixty-two cents in change, none of it in nickels.

"For the buses and trams and things. Put that away—modern money won't work in 1895, silly!"

"1895? Schist, Jaya! What are you planning?"

"Not so loud. We can't let the librarians know or they'll try to stop us."

"Try to stop us from doing *what*?"

"From using the time machine, of course. We're going back

in time to 1895, before Tesla's lab burned down, and we're stopping Simon's great-great-grandfather from taking the death ray with him when he left for England. Leaves for England? Left for England? Which is it?"

"Jaya! We can't do that!"

"Or we're stopping him from taking the plans for the death ray—Simon's ancestor, I mean. Or maybe we're stopping Tesla from inventing it in the first place. I'm not sure. But we're stopping the death ray at the source so Simon can't get his hands on it."

"No way!" I said. "That's crazy! The Wells time machine is far too powerful. You know how I worry about changing the past in some horrible way. . . ."

"We won't. We're just going back for a few hours and making one little stop. That won't change much, if anything."

"Yes, it will! We'll be messing with the lab of one of the most important scientists who ever lived! We could change *everything!*"

"Don't be such a worrywart," said Jaya. "We'll be careful. This isn't the first time I've operated dangerous equipment, you know."

"That's the opposite of reassuring," I said.

"Look," said Jaya. "I don't actually need you to come with me. I could take the time machine and go back to 1895 by myself. But it'll be much, much better if you help. And I know you're going to agree because you *did*. I mean, you *will*. I mean, you saw your future self already doing it. So can we please just skip this argument and get on with it?"

She was right—I was going to time travel with her, no matter what I said. And Simon hadn't left us a lot of options. "Fine," I said. "I'll go with you. Not to help, though. To stop you from doing anything too rash."

"Whatever you say, boss," said Jaya. She didn't sound like she meant it.

I suppressed the urge to strangle her. "So what are we going to need?" I asked. "Money from 1895 and an old subway map—did they even have subways back then?—and old-fashioned clothes." So that's why Future Me and Future Jaya were dressed funny! "And the time machine, obviously. What else?"

"The shrink ray from the Wells Bequest. We'll never fit on the model time machine at this size."

I remembered her mentioning a shrink ray. "Wait—do you have to plug it in? Was this place wired for electricity back in 1895?"

"Oh, we're not leaving from *here*! We can't bring the time machine to the repository, remember? And you saw us in your bedroom. We're leaving from your place."

"We are? Oh. You're right, we must be."

"Your building was built already back then, right? It must have been, or we wouldn't have gone there," said Jaya.

"Yeah, the cornerstone says 1894," I said. "We'd better bring batteries just in case there wasn't electricity there yet."

"All right. You take care of the electric stuff and the maps, okay? I'll get the shrink ray and the clothes and the money. What's your shoe size?"

"Nine and a half," I said.

"Really? Your feet look bigger than that."

"Thanks," I said.

"I have to stop at home first to pick something up," said Jaya. "Meet me at your place. What's your address? Here, write it down."

Mom and Dad had gone upstate for the weekend and Sofia was staying with Sara, her best friend, so the apartment was empty when I got home. If Simon really acted on his threat, I wouldn't even get a chance to say good-bye to my family.

He wouldn't really do it, would he? He couldn't be *that* evil—could he? But when I remembered the look on his face when Francis teased him about his family, I wasn't so sure.

I got to work at my computer hunting up maps and reading about how people used to get around New York before the subways opened in 1904. I packed up batteries and an adapter. What could I put them in? My backpack would look really out of place in 1895, and they wouldn't invent plastic bags for another few decades.

Maybe my laundry bag?

Emptying it made me realize what a gigantic mess my room was. Dad says a messy desk is a sign of a fertile mind, and Mom doesn't care what I do to my room as long as she doesn't have to look at it.

I kicked things under the bed, shoveled things into the closet, bundled the trash out of the room, threw a sweater over the more delicate projects on my workbench, and straightened the blankets on the bed.

I was engineering a tower of books when the buzzer rang.

"Come on up. It's the sixth floor," I told Jaya through the intercom.

I stood in the hallway waiting for her elevator and trying to look calm. No big deal, right? Just a coworker I was goopy about, coming over to travel back in time a century or so and stop a supervillain from destroying the city. Not a supervillain, exactly. A dweebervillain. Just the most amazing girl in the city, coming to my own apartment to bend the laws of physics with me and defeat a boy without a conscience. Just the girl—

"Hi, Leo!" called Jaya, stepping off the elevator. She was carrying an old-fashioned leather traveling bag. I led the way to my room.

"I plotted our route downtown," I said. "Let me show you. We'd better take the Sixth Avenue elevated train, which actually runs on the same track as the Eighth Avenue line up here, and we can catch it at—"

Jaya cut me off. "That's fine. Do you think we could move those books? I need at least five square feet of floor space to work in and a wall outlet." She took a little gadget out of her traveling bag. It looked like a cross between a pencil sharpener and a vacuum cleaner.

"What's that?" I asked.

"The shrink ray from the Wells Bequest."

"That's a shrink ray? But it's so . . . small," I said.

"That's because I shrank it. It's way too big to carry. Come on, help me move these books."

We pushed the books under my desk. Jaya plugged in the gadget.

"I need to turn it on, but now the switch is too small for my finger. You don't have a needle or a pin, do you?" asked Jaya.

"I have a microprobe. Will that do?"

"What's a microprobe?"

I rifled through the mess on my workbench, found the probe, and handed it to her.

"This is just a needle stuck through a cork," Jaya pointed out.

"Yeah," I admitted. "A needle makes a pretty good microprobe, and the cork makes a good handle."

"Whatever," said Jaya. She set the shrink ray down in the middle of the cleared space, kneeled beside it, and poked at it with the microprobe.

I peered down at it.

"Get out of the way, Leo! Move back from the shrink ray," said Jaya impatiently.

"I'm nowhere near it," I said.

"You will be soon. Get back!"

I retreated to the wall. The little machine suddenly began to swell, pushing a stray book along the floor beside it. It blew up so fast I was afraid it would burst. I leapt out of the way as the machine's side zoomed toward me.

Just when I was sure it was going to hit the wall and bring it crashing down, Jaya threw herself on it and hit a switch.

The thing stopped growing. It was about the size of a motorcycle. It took up all the spare space in my room.

"Wow," I said. "I wasn't sure you'd stop it before it knocked over the building."

"Yeah, sorry about that," said Jaya. "I guess I went a little too fast. I had to leave my patience as a deposit when I borrowed the shrink ray."

"Your *patience*?"

"Yes, remember? Dr. Rust collects functional deposits when

we borrow objects from the Special Collections. I generally leave my patience—I don't have all that much of it anyway, so I don't really miss it. Now, what did you do with that time machine?"

"What a thing to leave! Couldn't you leave—I don't know, your *im*patience?" I went to open the closet door. "Close your eyes—it's a mess in here."

"I'm not afraid of a few dirty socks!"

I dug the Fortnum's bag out from under my laundry, then took out the time machine and handed it to her. "We should use the shrink ray to expand it," I said. That would be way more practical than shrinking *us*. But I knew I was going to lose this argument—after all, I'd seen us riding the tiny machine.

Jaya shook her head and put the time machine on my desk. "Too risky," she said. "We don't really understand how the time machine works. The time-travel engineering might depend on fixed distances or surface-volume proportions. Remember what Auntie Shanti said about not using Special Collection objects on each other without testing them thoroughly first? You can seriously disturb their functionality."

"But you just used the shrink ray to expand itself," I said. "Why doesn't that 'seriously disturb its functionality'?"

"That's different. I used the autoexpand setting—it's designed to do this. I've done it a zillion times. It's perfectly safe as long as you manage to hit 'off' in time."

"And what if you *don't* manage to hit 'off' in time?"

"Oh, the shrink ray could go on growing out of control until you couldn't reach the off switch, and then the increased mass could throw the earth out of its orbit and plummet us into the sun. Or if you were autoshrinking instead of autoexpanding, the off switch could get too small for your fingers, and then the shrink ray would shrink out of existence. But none of that's ever happened. I'm always careful."

I thought about how close she'd come to knocking down my bedroom walls. "I don't think leaving your patience as a deposit is such a great idea," I said. "It makes you take even more risks than usual."

"The problem with you, Leo, is you worry too much."

"You sound just like my sister."

"Whatever. We can argue after we stop Simon," said Jaya. "Let's get going now. Stand over here, and I'll shrink you."

"Wait a sec," I said. "Can we talk about this some more first? Like, for one thing, are you sure we can control the time machine precisely enough? We're on the sixth floor. The cornerstone was laid in 1894, and Tesla's lab burned down on March 13, 1895. What if they weren't done building this place by then? If you send us back in time to before this building was finished, we'll go crashing through the floor because the floor won't be there yet. We'll die," I said.

While I was talking, Jaya was pushing me into position opposite the shrink ray's pointy nozzle. "It'll be fine," she said. She fiddled with some knobs on the shrink ray.

"You can't know that. It's too dangerous! We have to at least look up exactly when the building was finished," I said.

"Nah, that would take too long. If we see the walls coming unbuilt, we'll stop and reverse the time machine. Are you doing okay there?"

She asked that because I was screaming. I had started

screaming because she turned the shrink ray on me. A green light shot out of its nozzle, and everything suddenly went really weird. The walls scampered away sideways, the ceiling shot upward, and Jaya expanded like a shapely, bright-eyed balloon. Everything I'd kicked under the bed loomed up at me like a reproachful army. My whole body itched and tickled, inside and out. It felt like someone was crumpling aluminum foil inside my bones.

"Jaya! Jaya, stop!" I screamed.

"What's wrong?" She hit the off switch. The green light went out and my bones stopped squeaking. "Are you feeling okay? That's probably enough anyway. You look around the right size."

"Jaya!" I sputtered. "You didn't warn me! I wasn't ready!"

She bent down, bringing her gigantic face close to me, and giggled. She actually *giggled*. "I'm sorry," she said. "But you sound so funny! And the look on your face! It's so—so cute."

"I am not *cute*," I spat.

"There's no point saying you're not cute when you're six inches tall and you look like a kitten who wants to scratch me but doesn't quite know how," said Jaya.

I actually gnashed my teeth. I'd read about tooth gnashing, but I had no idea people really did it. I wished I *were* a kitten—then at least I would have claws to scratch her with. "Can you please stop shrinking the whole world for ten seconds and tell me what the quark you think you're doing before you do it?" I said.

"Well, first I'm going to see if you're the right size to ride the model time machine," said Jaya. She reached down toward me with her vast, brown, bony fingers.

CHAPTER SEVENTEEN

Time Passes—Backward

I tensed every muscle in my body, prepared for a bruising squeeze. But she held me gently. She lifted me up to the desk and put me down next to the time machine.

I was amazed at its workmanship. I was used to looking at things through magnifying glasses and microscopes. Usually the objects looked crude up close, with splinters and loose ends. But not the demo time machine—every edge was clean and polished. The Time Traveller who made it must have been an amazing craftsman. I wished I could make things that well.

"Climb on the seat for a second, will you? That looks like a good fit," said Jaya. "Don't touch the controls! Wait for me. Okay, now I'm going to shrink the stuff I brought," she continued. "Do you have anything you need shrunk?"

"The maps and stuff. They're in that laundry bag. Wait, don't shrink the battery pack and the adapter."

Jaya must really have been impatient because she didn't stop to ask why. She took out the items and put my bag next to hers.

I climbed down from the time machine and ran over to the edge of the desk, dodging around pencils, to watch them shrink.

"Then—let's see—I'm going to shrink myself," said Jaya, plopping the leather bag down on the desk beside me with her fingertips. She had chipped coral-pink polish on her gigantic fingernails. "Okay, here I go."

"Wait!" I said. "My desk won't be there back in 1895. You better put the time machine on the floor."

"Oh, you're right." With her gigantic fingers, she moved the time machine, the bag, and finally me down to the floor.

I looked up at enormous Jaya and the enormous shrink ray. "How are you going to reach the switch?" I asked. "You can't touch it and stand in front of the nozzle at the same time. I would do it for you, but I'm too small."

"Watch," she said. She took an unsharpened pencil off my desk and expanded it to the size of a spear. Then she placed the end with the lead in it against the shrink ray's on switch, twisted a knob, and stood in front of the nozzle, where I had been standing when she shrank me. She leaned against the eraser, turning the machine on.

"Jaya! No!" I yelled. She was writhing and shrinking. How would she be able to keep hold of the pencil and turn off the machine before she shrank out of existence?

But somehow she managed it. When she was eye level with the desk, she writhed hard against the pencil and threw the switch. The green light went off and she stopped convulsing. She still looked enormous, but a lot less enormous.

"Relax, Leo," she said. "I'm good at this. Now I'm going to

put the shrink ray on autoshrink and make it smaller. I need to keep it more or less the same scale as me."

"This would be a lot easier with a third person," I said. "You should have asked Francis to help us."

"You're right. I didn't think of that. Well, too late now." She reached up, switched the shrink ray to autoshrink, and pressed the on switch.

I was impressed to see that while the machine shrank, its electric plug stayed the same size. It made sense—otherwise you couldn't plug it in.

Using the pencil as a switch-poker, she took turns shrinking herself and the shrink ray, back and forth, until she was just my height and the shrink ray was small enough to fit in her traveling bag.

"Here," she said, pulling a pair of black leather shoes and some clothes out of her bag. "Put these on."

I looked around for somewhere to change. There wasn't really anywhere good. "Turn around," I said, ducking behind my desk leg.

"Like I was planning to peek," said Jaya.

I changed into the old-fashioned clothes. The shoes were too small, and I didn't know what to do with the tie. "How do you . . . ," I asked, coming out from behind the time machine.

"Hang on, I'm not ready," said Jaya. "Stupid buttons! Why couldn't they have invented the zipper a few years earlier? Okay, you can come out now. Can you button me, please?"

Jaya was wearing the long, dark gray dress I'd seen her in when she appeared in my room and started the whole adventure. It had puffy sleeves, a tight waist, and a flared skirt that ended just below her ankles. She turned her back and I fumbled down a long row of tiny buttons. What with her undershirt thingie and petticoat, she was covered from head to foot. But somehow I still found it embarrassing to fasten her dress.

Embarrassing and exciting.

"Tickles," she said.

"Just two more . . . okay, done."

She turned around. "Well? Put on your tie. A gentleman always wears a necktie."

"I don't really know how," I confessed.

"What? You're kidding!" She stared at me like I was some kind of alien. "I'll do it for you." She reached around my neck with her cool fingers, twitched my collar up, and pulled the tie around my neck.

"Ow. Not so tight!"

"That's how it's supposed to be. Haven't you ever worn a tie? Put on your shoes now."

"They don't fit. You need to expand them with the shrink ray."

"I'll do it when we get there."

"No! I know you're impatient, Jaya, but I'm not going back a zillion years into the past wearing shoes that pinch. What if we have to run away from someone—or something? Do it before we go."

Jaya sighed. "Fine. But if Simon destroys the world while I'm fussing with your shoes, you're the one who's explaining it to Dr. Rust."

Jaya stowed her traveling bag under the time machine's saddle. She put the battery pack and adapter in my laundry bag—they took up half the bag—and stowed it next to her traveling bag, then scrambled on board, leaning forward in the seat. "Get up behind me, Leo," she said. "Time to go!"

"No," I said firmly. "I'm driving. Come on, move over."

She didn't budge. "I told you, I'm good with machinery."

"It isn't safe. You're way too impatient."

She shook her head impatiently.

"Also," I added, "it isn't fair. I'm the one who found the time machine."

That was a more effective argument. I could see from the way Jaya's forehead wrinkled that her sense of justice was fighting it out with her passion for control.

Justice won. "Go ahead, then," she said, scooting as far back as she could without falling off the saddle.

I climbed on. She put her arms around my waist, turning me into the tiny guy I had been jealous of way back when I first saw us, the one sharing a saddle with the beautiful girl. I savored the moment.

No savoring for Jaya. "Well? What are you waiting for? Let's go!"

I took a deep breath, leaned forward, and pushed the lever marked *PAST.*

Traveling through time is the weirdest feeling. When you go very fast through space—by car or speedboat, say, or if you've ever ridden a motorcycle—it feels urgent. Everything moves. The world whips past you, trees and houses or buoys and boats, the wind in your hair, *here* vanishing away, *there* looming up to meet you, then rushing by.

When you travel through time, you get the same headlong urgency but minus the *here* and *there*. The result is a horrible, unsettling feeling of motion in stillness. You hurtle without moving. Every second you feel you're about to crash into the unknown.

It's even worse when you're going backward, into the past instead of the future. Not only are you hurtling blindly at unnatural speed (if *speed* is even the word for it), but your body somehow knows that you're going in the wrong direction. Time closes over your head. It's like drowning.

For me, the feeling took the form of overwhelming dread. For Jaya, apparently, it came out as amplified impatience. She hugged me so tight it pinched. "Hurry up, Leo! Can't we go any faster?" she urged in my ear.

"Not without losing count." The sun was whipping across my south-facing window from west to east, over and over and over, ticking back the days. They flicked dark–light–dark–light. "We need to end up in March 1895. If we go back too far, we'll die!"

"That's decades away! We'll never get there like this! Can't we count the years instead?"

"It's not as safe."

"Come *on!*"

"All right, I'll try. Watch the sun. When it disappears under the building across the street, that means it's December." I pushed the lever farther toward *PAST.*

My sense of dread intensified as the flickering days smudged together into twilight. It was a brilliant dark blue. The sun blurred into a streak, an arc that rose and fell like a vicious yellow snake. Whenever it vanished behind the downtown buildings, we counted off another December.

"1927, 1926, 1925 . . . ," chanted Jaya in my ear.

I pulled the lever back.

"No, don't slow down yet! We have thirty more years to go!"

"We're getting close. I'm afraid we'll miss it. 1911, 1910, 1909 . . ."

Jaya dug her fingernails into my ribs. "Come *on,* Leo!"

But she didn't have long to wait. When we hit the winter solstice of 1895, I pulled the lever back almost all the way. Out the window, way over in the park, trees went from leafless to autumn yellow, then deepened from yellow to tired green. They brightened backward through June and May, shrank through April, turned into a yellow spring haze, and then vanished. I counted the days.

"This is it, I think," I said, pulling the lever almost to the stop position. "March 13."

"Go back one more day," said Jaya. "The lab fire starts at 3 a.m. We need to get there before that."

"Oh, you're right." I pushed the lever up gently and pulled us one more day into the past. The room was empty now, without even any furniture. The early spring sunshine backward darted across the floorboards and faded into a rainy night. Clouds hid the moon. The sun rose sunset orange in the west.

"Here we are, I think," I said. "March 12." I slowed us down in the morning, judging by the light. But there was someone in the room, a gigantic, ghostly-looking workman. He flitted jerkily around the room, sawing something with blurry movements like a video on fast-forward.

"Don't stop! Someone's there! Go forward again!" urged Jaya.

"I see him." I pulled the *PAST* lever upright and gently pressed the other lever, the one marked *FUTURE*. We slipped forward in time past the workman. When the room was empty, I pulled us to a stop.

Jaya let go of my waist and stepped off the time machine. The place smelled of sawdust and paint. There was an electric light miles away up in the ceiling, but it didn't have any bulbs.

I stepped off the time machine too. It was a huge relief not to be going backward anymore, but I also felt strangely empty.

The floor stretched out like a tan soccer field with the grass worn off. It was brand new—it hadn't even been varnished yet.

"So this is it," I said. "1895."

"Come on," said Jaya. "Let's get big, and let's get going."

CHAPTER EIGHTEEN

A Steam Train in Manhattan

"**I** hope the power's on," said Jaya, taking the tiny shrink ray out of her bag. It looked ridiculous with its gigantic, normal-size plug. "Where's the wall outlet?"

We couldn't find one. I guess they hadn't been invented yet. Good thing I'd brought the batteries! Twenty minutes and endless fiddling later, we were back to life size, with the shrink ray and the demo time machine tucked away in the traveling bag.

I wanted to stow the time machine in the apartment while we went downtown to Tesla's lab. I thought it would be safer than dragging it around town through who-knows-what terrible neighborhoods full of thugs and pickpockets. They had gangs called things like the Dead Rabbits and the Roach Guards, who would pour boiling water on people's heads before shooting them.

"That was back in the 1850s," said Jaya. "Schist! Don't you know *anything*?"

I laughed. "Okay, so maybe the Dead Rabbits are gone. But I'm sure there are new gangs."

"What's stopping the thieves from coming in here and taking the machines while we're out? Or the guy we just saw?"

She had a point. I shouldered the bag.

Having workmen around meant the doors would be open, so we could get back in when we needed to. We went out the back way, past what would be the janitor's door when the building was finished. Nobody saw us.

I looked back at my building. It seemed much more impressive in the 1890s. For one thing, it was the tallest one on the block. They hadn't yet built the skyscrapers that New York was going to be known for. My building was seven stories tall, with a fancy entrance and lions carved over the windows. It towered over the low brown houses.

"We can take the El downtown," I said. "It's over on Columbus Avenue."

We buttoned up our coats, tied our scarves, and walked down my street. It was weird how similar everything was, and how totally different.

The first different thing was the smell. You know how Central Park South reeks from the carriage horses? It was like that everywhere. Some of the sidewalks were paved with slate, and some of the streets had cobblestones. But there were also unpaved streets and streets so covered with mud and muck and horse droppings that I couldn't really tell whether they were paved or not.

The next thing I noticed was the quality of the noise. New York is a loud city, with horns honking, sirens screeping, jackhammers hacking up streets, and people shouting into their cell phones.

Back in 1895 it was just as noisy, but the sounds were different. There was a lot more clattering—all those horses' hooves and carriage wheels bumping over the cobbles. In the side streets, servants banged metal trash cans and ladies practiced pianos in their parlors. On the avenues, knife grinders and nut roasters and hot corn sellers spun their wheels and shouted for customers. Chickens crowed in empty lots—the neighborhood had been farmland just a few years ago. And the horse-drawn fire trucks announced themselves with deafening bells.

Traffic lights hadn't been invented yet, which made crossing the avenues exciting. With cars you only have one person to worry about: the driver. But with carriages, the horse also gets to have an opinion about whether you'll survive the crossing. And horses are a lot bigger than we are.

"Don't be so scared," said Jaya as we crossed Amsterdam Avenue. "It's just a horse. It's not going to eat you."

"Who's scared? It's just . . . big," I said.

As I spoke, the horse in question let loose a loud, yellow stream of pee. It foamed as it hit the cobbles. Jaya jumped back, pulling her skirt away. "All right, all right. I admit cars have some advantages," she said.

We heard the elevated railroad before we saw it. Smelled it, too. The air got even smokier and a tooth-shaking clatter came from overhead. Three stories up, on top of a looming iron track, a train roared and lurched past.

At the front was an engine like something out of an old children's picture book. Thick coal smoke poured out of its smokestack. I coughed.

"Wow, that thing is *cute*!" exclaimed Jaya. "It's like a whole old-fashioned steam train! On *stilts*! Did you see its little engine? Run, we're missing it!"

I caught her arm. "That's not ours. It's going the wrong way," I said. The train had been heading north, and we needed to go south.

We walked in the shadow of the track until we reached the staircase that led to the next station. The railings were decorated with curled ironwork.

"Did you bring the 1895 money?" I asked. "The fare should be a nickel."

"Here you go," said Jaya, handing me one. It had a lady's head on one side and a *V* on the other.

We climbed the stairs to the station. A guard was standing next to a tall wooden boxy thing. We tried to give him our nickels.

"You need a ticket, sister," he grunted.

"Oh, okay. Where do we get them?" said Jaya.

He jerked his thumb at another guard at a little window.

That guard was even surlier. He grabbed our nickels and pushed our tickets at us without a word.

The first guard took them, stuck them in the boxy thing, and pulled a lever. The machine gave a snap. He handed us back our tickets, now with holes in them.

The station was stuffy, with grimed-up windows and a little potbellied stove slamming out heat. Overhead, fancy sockets held dim, bare electric bulbs. The place smelled of damp woolen coats and the people wearing them. "Let's wait outside," suggested Jaya.

We pushed through the double doors to the platform. The wind was sharp, but we didn't have long to wait. Soon a roar shook the station and one of Jaya's cute little engines came tearing into view, pulling a tail of cars. The brakes screamed, the doors opened, and we stepped on.

The train was crowded. People glanced at us, but nobody stared. Either Jaya had found us convincing 1895 clothes or New Yorkers back then considered it part of basic politeness to mind their own business, just like they do today.

The train rattled past third-floor windows. We saw a man brushing his hair with two handle-less brushes, one in each hand.

"His hair must be really messy if he needs two brushes," said Jaya.

"*You* might need three," I said.

"Oh, thanks! My hair isn't *that* messy, is it?" She poked a curl back into her bun. "Yeah, I guess you're right."

"It looks good messy," I said.

We passed empty lots, some with brownstones going up, some with old barns falling down. "Look, is that a *goat*?" said Jaya. We passed a woman in an apron standing on a chair, polishing the window with a piece of crumpled newspaper, a cat with its nose to the glass and its ears turned forward, another cat with its ears flattened back against its head, a whole family sitting around a table eating soup, and a man at a desk writing in a big ledger.

It was funny only getting to see the beginnings of things. We saw a man start to walk across a room, a woman start to talk to someone out of sight, three men start to lift a piano—but we were always gone before they'd finished.

Jaya waved at a little girl in a window. We were gone before she could wave back.

"I'd hate to live next to this train, but it's fun seeing into all the houses," I said.

"My sister's boyfriend lives next to the El up in Harlem," said Jaya. "She complains about the noise, but Marc says he doesn't even hear it anymore."

"The trains are quieter in our time, though," I said.

"The lab is in SoHo," said Jaya. "Do we have to change to a crosstown train somewhere?"

"No," I said, "this is the right train. We get off at Bleecker Street. It should head east pretty soon."

It did, with a stomach-turning lurch and a screech that stabbed me through both ears and smashed together in the middle of my brain. After a block or two, it lurched, screeched, and turned again. From there it was a straight shot downtown.

"Isn't this our stop?" Jaya grabbed my sleeve as our train pulled into the Bleecker Street station. The doors banged shut behind us and the train roared away, shaking the platform. Jaya pushed through the station doors and ran down the stairs to the street, holding up her skirt so she wouldn't trip.

"43 South Fifth Avenue," she said, reading the number on the building on the corner. "The lab's at number 35—that's downtown from here. Wow, none of this looks the tiniest bit familiar."

I hurried after her. The elevated tracks threw gloomy shadows over the low, rundown buildings. "It's all NYU buildings in our time," I said.

Jaya stopped. "Look, I think this is it."

We had come to a large, dirty, plain-looking factory building on a block of similar buildings. It said *33–35* over the door.

"Do we just, like, knock?" I asked.

Jaya shook her head. "It's Tesla's lab. He's the greatest living
inventor. Want to bet it's going to have an electric bell, at least?"

It did. In fact, it had several. The chipped enameled plaque
next to the bottom button read *Gillis & Geoghegan, Steamfitters'
Supplies.* The one above it had a simple card that read *N. Tesla.*
Jaya reached out a gloved finger and pressed it.

Nothing happened for a long time.

Jaya pressed the bell again.

"Give him a minute, Jaya. I don't think they had intercoms
back then," I said.

"I don't see why not. They had telephones," she argued. She
was reaching out to press the bell again when the door opened.

According to the books I'd read, Tesla was a tall man, skel-
etally thin, with black hair and eyes like blue lightning. This
man was shorter than Jaya and stocky, with reddish hair and
freckles. He looked like an intelligent calf. He wasn't wearing
a jacket, just a shirt with the sleeves rolled up and held in place
with black straps. He had a smudge across his forehead, as if he
had pushed his hair back with sooty hands.

"Yes?" he asked.

"We're here to see Mr. Tesla," I said.

He frowned. "Do you have an appointment?"

"No, but we need to speak to him. It's urgent," I said.

"Well, he isn't here."

"That's all right—we can wait for him in his office," said Jaya.

Tesla's employee stared at her for a moment, halfway between puzzled and hostile. "I'm not authorized to admit strangers," he said.

"Can we talk to Mr. FitzHenry, then?" I asked.

"Never heard of him."

Jaya and I glanced at each other. Simon's ancestor must have some other name. That made sense, if you thought about it. The ancestor who was supposed to be Tesla's assistant wasn't on his father's side—it was his grandmother's grandfather.

"When will Mr. Tesla be back?"

"Not before tomorrow. If you'll give me your names, I'll let him know you called."

"But tomorrow's too late! We need to see him *now*," persisted Jaya.

The man frowned at her suspiciously. "Who are you? Did the Wizard send you?"

"What wizard? Mr. Tesla is a scientist," I said.

"You know exactly who I mean. The Wizard of Menlo Park—Thomas Edison. Tell him to stop sending his spies. It's useless. He won't get anything out of any of us."

"We have nothing to do with Edison! We've never even met him," said Jaya. She sounded convincingly outraged. "We need to talk to Mr. Tesla right away about a matter of extreme importance. Believe me, he will want to talk to us. Let us in at once, please."

"I'm sorry, but I can't do that."

"Then tell us where to find him. He'll be very angry when he finds out you kept us away."

The man's smudged forehead wrinkled. I could see he was picturing his boss angry. "All right. He's giving a lecture at the Electric Club," he said.

"The Electric Club? Where's that?"

"17 East 22nd Street, near Fifth Avenue," said the man. "He won't be back in the lab until tomorrow. If you'll leave a card, I'll tell him you called."

"We'll go see him at the Electric Club, thanks," said Jaya.

"Suit yourselves," said the man, and shut the door in our faces.

CHAPTER NINETEEN

Her Royal Highness, the Rani of Chomalur

We walked back to the El station. Just before we got there, a train rattled by over our heads. "Quark! That was our train," said Jaya. "Let's walk." She turned away from the station and started uptown, her legs kicking her skirt.

"It'll be quicker to take the next El," I said.

"I can't wait that long. It's only a mile or so," said Jaya impatiently.

"You realize you're so impatient you're actually wasting time?" I said.

She glared at me without slowing down.

"Fine," I said. A few minutes wouldn't make that much difference. We hurried north under the train tracks, passing rundown buildings that no longer exist.

Things started looking familiar again when we got to Washington Square Park. The fountain was still there—I mean already there. So was the white marble arch. It must have been brand new since it wasn't dingy with coal smoke yet like most of the buildings nearby. The air was about the same temperature as back home, but it felt different—softer. It was spring here instead of fall. The leaves were still bare, but there were a few crocuses in the flower beds.

"Listen, Jaya," I said. "When we find Tesla, you can't tell him about time travel and the lab fire and everything. That would risk seriously changing the future. We might never—"

"—Might never be born, we might trigger the apocalypse, blah blah blah. Don't worry, I'm not an idiot," said Jaya. "But we have to tell him *something*. We need him to let us into his lab so we can stop Simon's great-great-grandfather."

She had put her finger on the problem, but I didn't see the solution. "Right, but telling him about time travel would make it worse."

"I know. Don't worry. I have a plan."

"What's your plan?"

"Tesla was—Tesla *is*—famous for giving his friends and investors midnight tours of his lab."

"So what? We're not his friends or investors."

"We're potential investors. I'll tell him I'm the Rani of Chomalur."

"The *what* of *what*?"

"The Rani of Chomalur. Where my family's from. It's a small kingdom in India. The rani is the queen."

"You don't look like a queen," I pointed out. "You look like a tomboy stuck in the wrong clothes."

She made her fire-flashing dragon face. "How would *you* know what the Rani of Chomalur looks like? As a matter of fact, I look *exactly* like the Rani of Chomalur, because I *am* the Rani of Chomalur!"

"Oh, come on! You are not."

"Yes, I am . . . almost. I mean, Chomalur doesn't exist anymore, in our time. And even if it did, my grandmother would be rani, not me. The current, 1895 rani is . . . let's see . . . my great-great-great-grandmother. Or great-great-great-great? Something like that."

"Okay, so you're a princess." Big surprise—no wonder she was so bossy. "But you still don't look like one. You're not dressed like a rani, and you talk like a modern New York girl. You have to convince Tesla, remember?"

"I *will* be dressed like a rani when we get to Tesla's club. You'll see. And I have no trouble sounding like a lady who's been educated by the best English governesses," she added in a perfect imitation of her aunt's upper-class English accent.

"What about me, though? I *definitely* don't look like royalty."

"I'll tell him you're my servant."

"Oh, thanks." But it wasn't like I had a better plan.

By then we'd crossed the park and reached Fifth Avenue. It was less sketchy here than in Tesla's neighborhood. The big, square brick houses had neatly painted shutters and cast-iron lampposts. Men strode by in black coats and top hats, some swinging canes. A woman pushed a baby carriage past us toward the park. Every so often a horse carriage rattled over the cobblestones.

Jaya grabbed my arm. "Look, Leo! Isn't that the cutest thing *ever*? Even cuter than the steam engine! I didn't know they still had them this late!" She was practically squealing.

Turning to look at where she was pointing, I saw a carriage the size of a minivan coming up the street, pulled by three white horses. The driver—a man in a conductor's cap—sat on a little platform at the front. He held a long whip in one hand and the reins in the other. The carriage had a rounded roof with another, bigger platform on top and benches where people were sitting. On the side, in fancy gold letters, it said *Fifth Avenue*.

"What's so cute about it?" I asked. The back wheels were much bigger than the front ones, which was sort of amusing, I guess, in an old-fashioned-tricycle kind of way—but it sure wasn't anything to squeal about.

"It's a bus! A horse-drawn *bus*! Come on, we've got to take it!"

"Really?" I said. "We only have a few more blocks, and that thing looks kind of—shaky."

But there was no stopping Jaya. She practically ran in front of it, waving and calling to the driver. He pulled on the reins and the horses clomped to a stop, shaking their heads and bracing their shoulders against the carriage's momentum.

Jaya handed the driver a nickel.

"That's ten cents, miss."

"Oh, sorry," said Jaya. She took back the nickel and found a pair of dimes in her purse. "For both of us," she said. The driver put the coins in his belt and waved us aboard.

I held out my hand to help Jaya up the steps, but she didn't wait. She scrambled up to the top bench. I climbed after her.

The seats had hard, slippery leather cushions. The whole thing felt very precarious. What was wrong with me? Okay, I admit I'm naturally cautious. But I shouldn't be this nervous on some stupid *bus*. It was as if the trip backward in the time machine had left me with a gigantic load of extra dread.

The bus felt even more precarious when the driver flicked his whip at the horses and the three big animals lurched forward over the uneven cobblestones. The carriage bumped, rocked, and swayed.

"Isn't this fun? I wish he'd go faster!" said Jaya. Strands of hair were squiggling out from under her hat.

Since there were no traffic lights, pedestrians went dodging in and out of traffic and carriages crossed in front of each other without waiting. "I liked the *Terror* better," I said.

She laughed. "You're just scared of horses." Then she looked at me seriously. "You really are worried, aren't you?"

I nodded, wishing like crazy the dread would go away. "Not about the horses. About the death ray. About a maniac running around loose in our time trying to destroy our city. And my mom and dad and sister and the Empire State Building. I mean, I know it's kind of corny and touristy, but I really love the Empire State Building. What if I never see it again? It hasn't even been built yet here. And my sister can be totally irritating the way she always tells me what she thinks is wrong with me, but she's my *sister*."

"I know! Believe me, I know all about not wanting evil maniacs to destroy irritating sisters. Is your sister irritatingly perfect? Because mine is."

"Disgustingly perfect."

"Well, don't worry. I mean, I know you have to—you wouldn't be Leo if you didn't—but try not to, okay? I have *lots* of experience rescuing sisters from evil maniacs. Just ask my sister someday. Anyway, Simon's never going to win. We have way more going for us than he does."

"He has the death ray," I pointed out.

"Not necessarily. He says he has it, but he might not. Whereas *we*—" She counted on her fingers. "We have the time machine. We have the shrink ray. We have the librarians on our side. We have *justice* on our side. We managed to make it back to 1895, and we're on our way to meet Tesla. And we have the smartest, most kick-ass Wells Bequest page the repository has ever known."

"Don't be so modest!"

She gave me a hard nudge with her shoulder that almost knocked me off the omnibus and said, "Modest yourself! I'm talking about *you*, silly!"

The compliment shut me up. I was too pleased and embarrassed to say anything. I held onto the seat as the bus clattered up Fifth Avenue and we intersected with another wide street.

"Hey!" I said. "Wasn't that Broadway? We missed our stop!"

"It can't be—where's the Flatiron Building?" said Jaya.

"It must not be built yet. Come on!"

We yelled to the driver, scrambled down from the bus, and walked back toward the wedge-shaped block at 23rd Street, where the Flatiron Building should have been. The Flatiron is one of my favorite buildings. It was one of the earliest skyscrapers in the city. It's a tall, wedge-shaped tower that looks like an ocean liner sailing into the sky. In our time it stands by itself, taking up its whole pie-slice-shaped block. I always thought of it as really old. It's way older than the Empire State Building, anyway.

Somehow, the Flatiron Building's absence made the city feel more alien to me than anything else had so far, even horse-drawn buses and men in top hats. New York just didn't feel like New York without the skyscrapers.

In its place, three or four low buildings filled the pointy end of the triangle and a taller building stretched across the wide end. Awnings and banners covered with writing flapped from the haphazard collection of buildings. It looked like a cross between Times Square and a sailboat.

"Check out the wall spam," said Jaya, pointing at the tallest building.

It was covered with ads. On the uptown side, block capital letters testified that BENSON'S CAPCINE PLASTER *contains Medical Ingredients not found in Allcock's Porous Plasters, hence they are Superior to those of Allcock's.* Other signs, awnings, and canvas billboards advertised Swift's Specifics, the Turkish Bath at the Windsor Hotel, the Erie Railway, and Seabury and Johnson's Mustard Plasters.

"What's a mustard plaster, anyway?"

"It's like a wet cloth thing they put on your chest. It stings," said Jaya. "Your parents never gave you one for a cold?"

"No, did yours?"

"Not after the first time." She headed the wrong way down 22nd Street.

"Where are you going?" I hurried after her. "The Electric Club's on the east side."

"I know. I need to fix my clothes first." She opened her bag, fished around, and drew out a small box and a gray scarf made of thin silk. It had a pattern of flowers woven into it with silver thread.

"Wow! Where did that come from?" I asked.

"Chomalur." She wrapped it around her shoulders. Suddenly she looked a lot more like a princess.

She opened the box and took out a gold pin set with a big red stone.

I stared. The red stone glowed in the sunlight like transparent lava. It looked alive. "Is that from Chomalur too?"

Jaya fastened the scarf at her shoulder with the gold pin. "Yeah. I borrowed it from my mom. It's the famous Chomalur Ruby."

"Won't she kill you? What if you lose it?"

"I'm not going to lose it." Jaya handed me her bag. "Here, you'd better carry this. Ranis don't carry their own bags in 1895. And remember, you're my servant, so act deferential."

"Yes, ma'am," I said.

"You mean, 'yes, Your Highness.'"

We walked the block to the Electric Club. From the outside it looked like the other brownstones, with a high stoop. "Go ring the doorbell," said Jaya.

"Yes, Your Highness." I walked up the stoop and looked around for a bell.

To my surprise, the door swung open all by itself before I'd reached the top stair.

A doorman sat in a little office to the left. He stood up when I got to the door. "Yes?" he said. He was wearing white gloves and a yellow jacket, with lightning bolts embroidered on the sleeves.

"Her Highness, the Rani of Chomalur, is here to attend Mr. Tesla's lecture," I told him as pompously as I could. I hoped I sounded like a princess's servant.

Jaya ruined the effect by running up behind me through the

open door. He frowned and said, "I'm sorry, but ladies are not permitted in the clubhouse." He had an Irish accent.

"They are today, Jim," said a gentleman standing near the door. "Ladies are always allowed at Mr. Tesla's lectures. He supports the rights of women."

"Yes, Mr. Latimer." The doorman said to Jaya, "I beg your pardon, miss. Come back in half an hour."

"Really, Jim! You're not going to turn an Indian princess out into the cold! Surely she can wait in the library?" said Mr. Latimer. He was a middle-aged African American man with little round wire-framed glasses, a cleft chin, and skin about the same tone as Jaya's.

"That must be Louis Latimer!" Jaya whispered to me excitedly. "He was a big deal in Edison's company. Is, I mean."

I nodded. We'd done a unit about Latimer in science class last year. I thought he was really cool. His parents escaped from slavery, and he joined the navy at sixteen to fight for the Union in the Civil War. After the war was over, he taught himself mechanical drawing and worked his way up from office boy to draftsman in a patent law firm. He went on teaching himself—science, engineering, languages. He patented a bunch of inventions, including a better carbon filament lightbulb and an improved toilet for trains. He spent years working for Edison as a draftsman and electrical engineer. And he played the flute and wrote poetry.

"If you say so, sir," said the doorman. He stepped aside disapprovingly. Apparently he didn't like the idea of ladies in the lounge, not even princesses.

Jaya and I walked past him and the automatic door swung

shut behind us. Mr. Latimer gave it a satisfied look, as if he expected us to be impressed. Evidently automatic doors were still new and exciting here.

The place was super-fancy. On the right was a long double room with gold-and-white wallpaper and furniture upholstered in yellow. On the ceiling, painted angels were waving lightning bolts around their heads. The lightning forked and zigzagged, and the angels' hair stood out in sparky halos. You could almost hear it crackling with static electricity.

"Are you an electric angel?" I whispered to Jaya. "They have your hair."

"Shh!" she hissed. "Servants don't make personal remarks."

Mr. Latimer came over to us. "May I introduce myself? I'm Louis Latimer," he said.

"Jaya Rao, Rani of Chomalur," said Jaya in her best Auntie Shanti accent, holding out her hand. "And this is my . . . servant, Leo."

Mr. Latimer raised an eyebrow and shook her hand. "An Indian princess, are you? We don't get many of those here at the Electric Club."

Uh-oh, I thought. He doesn't believe her. And as Edison's patent guy, won't he be on Edison's side of the great current rivalry—against Tesla?

"Even in faraway Chomalur we have heard of this country's great electrical scientists and their inventions," said Jaya. "Our palace is lit with American technology. I wanted to learn about it for myself. Am I right that you are the author of *Incandescent Lighting*?"

"Oh, you know my book?" Mr. Latimer looked pleased.

Good one, Jaya, I thought. "*Incandescent Electric Lighting: A Practical Description,*" he said. "I hope you don't mind my saying—you remind me a little of my elder daughter."

That was promising. Latimer had to face plenty of prejudice himself and so did his daughters, probably. Even if he didn't believe Jaya about being an Indian princess, it sounded like he sympathized.

"And you remind me a bit of my royal father," said Jaya.

He looked amused. "Do I?" he said. "Well, well. Perhaps we're related somehow."

"Oh, we're all related somehow, if you believe in the theories of Mr. Darwin—or in Adam and Eve, for that matter," said Jaya, way too pertly. "Tell me, Mr. Latimer," she continued. "You're in charge of Mr. Edison's library, aren't you?"

"That's right," he said, surprised.

Uh-oh, I thought again. Where was she going with this? Latimer was a key figure in nineteenth-century technology. Without him, Alexander Graham Bell would never have filed his patent for the telephone in time to beat Elisha Gray. Latimer had worked on a lot of Edison's most important patents too. What if Jaya said something to him that changed the course of history?

"Your Highness," I hissed.

Mr. Latimer glanced at me.

"Later, Leo," she said dismissively. "And are you involved with the New-York Circulating Material Repository?" she asked Mr. Latimer.

"I think I've heard of it," he said.

"Jaya!" I hissed as quietly as I could, "what are you *doing*?"

She ignored me. "I imagine you would find it very interesting. I believe you could make an important contribution to the scientific collections," she said. "The repository provides study materials for workmen who are trying to better their condition. Physical objects—laboratory materials and so on."

Jaya was going way too far. How could I stop her? I couldn't kick her. Servants don't kick their bosses, and besides, even if I did, it wouldn't shut her up. Dragging her out by the hair wouldn't work either. Jaya would just march back in. If she didn't, we would lose our chance to talk to Tesla.

"Oh, that does sound interesting," said Mr. Latimer. "I've been teaching immigrants at the Henry Street Settlement. They could use some hands-on experience. I'll look into it—thank you."

"Wouldn't you like to start an important collection of electrical technology?" said Jaya. "I'm sure the librarians at the repository will be open to it."

Maybe if I started to choke or something, Jaya would have to stop talking and help me?

Then Jaya shut up all by herself. The automatic door had opened and a very tall, very thin man walked in.

It was Nikola Tesla.

CHAPTER TWENTY

Two Geniuses and
One Very Long Lecture

I recognized Tesla right away from pictures in history books, but no still photo could capture the man's intensity. With his flashing blue eyes, gaunt build, and spiky limbs, he looked like a walking lightning bolt. The room changed when he came in. The corners seemed to crackle.

Mr. Latimer strode over to greet him. "Good evening, Tesla. I've been looking forward to hearing you talk," he said.

"Latimer! I'm glad you could make it," said Tesla, shaking his hand. He spoke quickly, with a Serbian accent—he sounded like my uncle Dragomir. I was relieved that he didn't seem to hold Mr. Latimer's association with Edison against him.

Jaya hurried over too. "Mr. Tesla! There you are," she began.

Tesla trained his electric eyes on her, taking in her silk scarf, her ruby, and her Jaya-ness. "Madam," he said.

"Nikola Tesla—the Rani of Chomalur," said Mr. Latimer.

Tesla bowed over her hand and kissed it. "Enchanted, Your Excellency," he murmured.

"Mr. Tesla, I need to talk to you about . . . about a very important matter relating to your research," said Jaya.

"Nothing would give me more pleasure, Your Highness. Now I must prepare for my lecture, but you will do me great honor if you will be my guest for dinner afterward."

Jaya mastered her impatience. It looked like it almost killed her. "Thank you," she said.

"Can I help you set up, Tesla?" asked Mr. Latimer.

"You are very kind. If you'll excuse us, Your Excellency." Tesla bowed at Jaya, Latimer winked at her, and the two geniuses walked upstairs, leaving us alone in the room.

"Jaya," I growled, trying to keep my voice down, "what did you think you were *doing,* telling Latimer about the repository? You could change history! What if he interferes with the collections?"

"But that's *exactly* what he's going to do. It's what he was *always* going to do! Who do you think started the repository electro-technical collections in the first place? It was Latimer! He was a big friend and patron of the repository. Mr. Steel was so impressed with those collections that he left us the Wells Bequest. We wouldn't be here—you and me—if it weren't for Latimer! Ask Dr. Rust if you don't believe me."

"But maybe he was supposed to find out from somebody else, and now he'll never start the collections, and Steel will leave his stuff to the library in Pittsburgh or someplace, and none of this will happen, and you and me—maybe we'll never even meet!"

"Calm down, Leo. We did meet, didn't we? You're standing right here. It's the other way around. Maybe if I hadn't said anything to Latimer, he would never have started the electro-technical collections and *then* we wouldn't meet."

The automatic doors swung open. "Shh—someone's coming," I said.

A man walked in, swinging a cane. He had shaggy hair and a big, bushy mustache. His eyebrows bristled in opposite directions, like a pair of push brooms trying to get away from each other. He paused to take off his coat and joke around with the doorman.

I had definitely seen his picture somewhere. Where?

After a second I came up with it: on the back of a book.

"Oh, quark! *Top* quark! Is that who I think it is?" whispered Jaya.

"You mean Mark Twain?" I whispered back. "*Huckleberry Finn* Mark Twain? *Huckleberry Finn* and the telelectroscope?"

She nodded. "Samuel Clemens—Mark Twain is his pen name. But what's he doing here?"

"He's best buds with Tesla," I whispered. There was a picture of Mark Twain in my Tesla book, I remembered, taken in Tesla's lab, with Twain holding a glowing orb and looking a little like Einstein.

Jaya said, "Cool! I always wanted to meet Mark Twain."

"Don't you dare talk to him about his books!" I said.

"You goofball—writers love it when you talk about their books. Look at Latimer."

"I know, but it's too dangerous. You could mess up and talk about the ones he hasn't written yet."

"Oh, he wrote all the important ones years ago," said Jaya airily.

Mark Twain and the doorman burst out laughing at something Twain had said. He slapped the other man on the shoulder and came into the parlor. He was a large man, tall and loose limbed, like some big-headed western animal—a bison or something. He walked with a sort of energetic shamble.

When he caught sight of Jaya, he stopped dead. "Bless me!" he drawled. "Either I'm dreaming or you're real!"

"I could say the same thing about you," said Jaya. "Why shouldn't I be real?" She was talking in her normal voice, not her Rani-of-Chomalur Cambridge accent.

"I thought you were a dream, all those years ago!"

"Really? We've met before? Well, *that* makes things easier! Hey, why aren't you wearing a white suit?"

"Should I be wearing a white suit?"

"You always do in the movies."

"What are 'the movies'? And why don't you look older?"

"Moving pictures—cinema. Hasn't it been invented yet? If not, it will be soon. There's a really cool early movie where they build a rocket and fly to the moon—the rocket's in the Phénoménothèque Centrale Supérieure de la Ville de Paris. Quit it, Leo!"

I was kicking her hopelessly. "Jaya! *You* quit it!" I hissed.

Mark Twain looked at me. "Jaya! That's it! I've been trying to remember that name all these years. It *is* Jaya, isn't it?"

"Yes." She held out her hand. "Jaya Rao, Rani of Chomalur." This time she remembered to use the accent.

"Oh, so you're a princess now?" He folded Jaya's hand in his big paw and shook it vigorously. "What about you, young man? Are you a prince?"

"No, he's my servant, Leo," said Jaya.

"Your servant, eh?" Twain guffawed. "Well, how do you like *that*, young man?"

"I . . ." I didn't know how to answer. "But how do you know Jaya?"

"I met this young lady ten years ago. She crushed my favorite hat. And she told me all about *you*." He shook his shaggy head at Jaya. "Funny thing, you don't look a day older than you did then. Which makes sense, if what you told me was true. Well, well, well! I'm glad you're real after all. Bless your heart, you gave me a splendid idea for a novel—but I guess you already know that. I always wanted to thank you, and it's no use trying to thank a dream."

"What novel?" asked Jaya, forgetting the accent again.

"Why, *A Connecticut Yankee in King Arthur's Court*. It's the story of a modern man who visits the past. Don't they read it anymore in your time? No, don't tell me. The news of my book's death might finish me off, and I'm nowhere near ready for my own funeral."

"Oh, don't worry! *A Connecticut Yankee* is a classic. So I inspired it? Cool!"

"Jaya," I said, "is that true? Did you really go visit Mark Twain in the 1880s?"

"Well, no, not yet. But I'm obviously going to."

"When you do, will you do me a favor?" said Mark Twain. "Warn me not to invest a single penny in that diabolical typesetting machine."

"Sure," said Jaya.

At the same time, I said, "She can't!"

"Why not? I would take it as a great kindness."

"Well, she didn't, or you wouldn't have to ask her to now," I explained. "So that means she won't, so she can't. And if she did, it might change history, which could have terrible consequences."

"Oh, you and your terrible consequences!" Jaya snapped. "What makes you think all my consequences will be so terrible, anyway? I inspired *A Connecticut Yankee*—that wasn't such a *terrible consequence,* was it? And yes, I can *so.* The Wells machine is unrestricted, so the fact that I didn't warn him yet doesn't mean I won't. I can do whatever I like. But don't worry, Mr. Clemens—your financial situation isn't a problem in the long run. You'll sort it out soon."

"Thank you—that's a great relief," said Mark Twain.

"Jaya! You can't go around prophesying like that!"

"I don't see why not. He *does* sort out his finances, so what's wrong with telling him? But Mr. Clemens, I need you to do me a favor. Can you help me get a private word with Tesla?"

"Leave it to me."

To my relief, the electric door opened and the room filled with lecture guests, so Jaya stopped talking to Mark Twain about time travel. After a few minutes Mr. Latimer came down to usher us upstairs into the lecture room.

"Ladies and gentlemen, Your Excellency," said Tesla, bowing slightly toward Jaya, "I propose today to address you on a subject of universal concern. I will speak of nothing less"—he paused dramatically, glaring around the room at everyone—"than the future of mankind!"

The audience of thirty or forty men and three women—counting Jaya—sat up straight in their chairs to listen.

"The progress in a measured time is nowadays more rapid and greater than it ever was before," said Tesla in his quick, light, accented voice. "This is quite in accordance with the fundamental law of motion, which commands acceleration and increase of momentum or accumulation of energy under the action of a continuously acting force and tendency and is the more true as every advance weakens the elements tending to produce friction and retardation."

He paused. The audience had slumped a little. One man surreptitiously pulled out his watch, frowned at it, and tucked it back in his vest pocket. Another man sitting near us nudged the guy next to him and whispered, "Look! Isn't that Lillie Langtry—the actress?" He pointed his chin at a curvy woman in an enormous hat.

"For," continued Tesla, "after all, what *is* progress, or—more correctly—development, or evolution, if not a movement, infinitely complex and often unscrutinizable, it is true, but nevertheless exactly determined in quantity as well as in quality of motion by the physical conditions and laws governing it?"

Jaya squirmed. For the zillionth time, I wished she had chosen something else to leave as a deposit at the repository. Her bossiness or her perfect skin—anything but her patience. "Princesses don't squirm," I whispered.

"How do you know? How many princesses have you met?" she whispered back.

Mark Twain, who was sitting on her other side, whispered, "Princesses don't whisper, either."

"Neither do famous authors," whispered Jaya back.

A man behind us cleared his throat. We all shut up, trying fairly successfully not to laugh.

Tesla was saying, "What has been so far done by electricity is nothing as compared with what the future has in store. The safeguarding of forests against fires, the destruction of microbes, insects, and rodents will, in due course, be accomplished by electricity."

The audience perked up. I guess they didn't like insects and rodents.

"The safety of vessels at sea will be particularly affected," Tesla went on. "We shall have electrical instruments which will prevent collisions, and we shall even be able to disperse fogs by electric force and powerful and penetrative rays."

That sounded like a good idea, actually. Maybe I could adapt it to solve Jaya's problem of the hands-free umbrella. I got distracted trying to think of how you would do it, exactly—what kind of rays?

When I tuned in to Tesla's lecture again, he was saying, "Great improvements are also possible in telegraphy and telephony. The use of a new receiving device will enable us to telephone through aerial lines or cables of any length by reducing current to an infinitesimal value. This invention will enormously extend wireless transmission."

Scattered applause from the audience. "Wow, he really is a genius! He's describing the cell phone—decades before it was invented!" Jaya whispered.

Tesla continued, "The time is bound to come when high-frequency currents will be on tap in every private residence. We may be able to do away with the customary bath. The cleaning of the body can be instantaneously effected simply by connecting it to a source of electric energy of very high potential, which will result in the throwing off of dust or any small particles adhering to the skin."

Mark Twain muttered, "The very thought makes my hair stand on end."

Tesla paused dramatically again. "But let us turn now to a far graver question: that of warfare—and, far more important, of peace."

I nudged Jaya. "Pay attention! I think he's about to talk about the death ray."

I tried to listen, but his language was so dense and abstract that my mind kept wandering. From what I could tell, he thought that future wars would be fought by high-tech robots deep in the oceans or high in the atmosphere, leaving people on Earth in perfect safety and peace.

He described a new, astonishingly destructive weapon he was developing, which would draw power from the earth's electric field. Was that the death ray at last? It was hard to tell from his description. He claimed it would end war because nobody would dare risk using it or provoking their enemies to use it. But what if a terrorist got his hands on Tesla's death ray? Like, for example, Simon?

I dragged my attention back to the podium. "And now," Tesla was saying, "I require a volunteer from the audience. Today we have the honor to have among us Her Excellency, the Rani of Choba—of Chupu—that is, Her Highness, the rani of one of India's finest kingdoms. Madam, if you would have the kindness to assist with a demonstration of what I may with all modesty claim is a unique advance in electrical science!"

He held out his hand to Jaya. I shook my head vigorously. "He's going to electrocute you!" I hissed. She ignored me.

"The honor is mine," she said in her rani voice, walking up to the front of the room. Lillie Langtry looked annoyed. I guess she was usually the one singled out.

Tesla held up a lightbulb on a small wire ring. "I shall place this globe in Her Majesty's hands. Observe that the device is completely disconnected from any battery or electric source." He waved the ring around in the air to show us that it wasn't attached to anything. "If you will be good enough to grasp it, Your Highness, just here and here." He closed Jaya's hands around the wire on either side of the lightbulb. Nearby stood a big, mean-looking machine. "Please observe, ladies and gentlemen, that Her Excellency is standing beside a resonating coil through which, when I throw this switch, will pass currents of a voltage one or two hundred times as high as that employed in electrocution!"

Oh, no! The electricity was going to jump through the air from the machine to Jaya!

I guess I must have gasped because Mark Twain put his hand on my shoulder and said softly, "Don't worry, Leo, she'll be fine. I've done it myself. It doesn't even tingle."

"The currents will traverse Her Highness's body and, as they pass between her hands, will bring the lamp to bright incandescence. Yet the extremely high tension of the currents will prevent Her Excellency from experiencing the slightest harm or inconvenience. Gentlemen, if you would assist me in closing those curtains."

A pair of attendants in the club's yellow-lightning uniform drew heavy curtains across the windows, darkening the room.

"And now, Your Highness, if you are ready?"

"I am," said Jaya.

Tesla threw the switch.

The lightbulb lit up.

Jaya didn't die.

The audience went wild with applause.

Three or four more demonstrations followed: another bulb-on-a-wire trick, some "phosphorescent lamps," and what looked like a neon diner sign—it said *Light* and made everyone gasp.

Tesla wound up his presentation with a speech about the glories of the future. Apparently by 1995 we were all going to be living in peace and harmony and riding around in little two-seater electric planes.

As the audience made for the doors, Twain grabbed Tesla's elbow. "Can you spare a few minutes to speak with Her Highness?" he asked.

"Gladly. I had hoped to induce her to join us at Delmonico's for supper, with Madame Langtry."

"There's no time for that!" said Jaya. "We need to talk to you alone. Right now. It's important."

"Of course, Your Highness. The club has rooms for private interviews," said Tesla.

Jaya, Mark Twain, and I followed him up the staircase to a

little room with a portrait of Thomas Edison on the wall. Tesla scowled at it. "How may I be of service to Your Majesty?" he asked, turning to Jaya.

"It's really about how *I* can be of service to *you*," said Jaya. "At this very minute, one of your employees is stealing your death ray. You have to stop him!"

Tesla's nostrils flared. "Forgive me, but may I inquire as to the source of your information?"

"Listen to her, Nik," said Mark Twain. "Jaya and Leo here are from the future. I know it sounds unlikely, but it's true. They're the ones who visited me from the twenty-first century and inspired *A Connecticut Yankee*."

That was when Tesla showed the full force of his genius. Most people, if told by the greatest living satirist that a pair of weird-looking kids were visitors from the future, would snort and roll their eyes. Not Tesla. He accepted it without question. "If you come from the future, you must know which of my predictions are correct," he said. "Tell me!"

"Well, you're going to win the War of the Currents, but you probably already know that. You're right about the wireless telephones and remote-controlled missiles. But you're wrong about war and mmmphff!"

I had managed to get my hand over her mouth. "Jaya! Stop it! You can't tell him all that stuff! You'll change the future!"

Tesla swung his crazy lightning gaze at me. "But why *not* change the future? Why not speed humanity's progress to perfection?"

"Because we're not heading toward perfection! Humanity sucks!"

"The boy's right," said Twain. "Given half a chance, the average specimen of mankind is as crooked as a congressman."

"We don't have time for this," said Jaya. "Simon's ancestor could be stealing the death ray *right now*!"

Jaya and I explained about Simon, his great-great-grandfather, the repository, the death ray, the time machines, and the possible destruction of New York—with lots of pauses for me to put my hand over Jaya's mouth to stop her from blabbing too much about the future and for her to kick my shins.

"Which of my employees is trying to steal my inventions?" asked Tesla.

"That's the thing—we don't know," said Jaya. "It's Simon's great-great-grandfather, but we don't know his name. That's why we have to catch him in the act."

"It can't be Ted or Robert," said Tesla. "I would trust them both with my life. Maybe one of the new men?"

"We're wasting time. Let's go find out—and stop him," said Mark Twain, with something of Jaya's impatience.

CHAPTER TWENTY-ONE

A Firefight
on South Fifth Avenue

The sun had set while we'd been watching Tesla shoot electricity around the lecture room, and the gas streetlights didn't do all that much to illuminate the street. There were stars everywhere, just like in the country. I could even make out the Milky Way. I had never seen stars like that in New York.

Tesla hailed a horse cab. The four of us piled in and clattered down Broadway, dodging around carriages and cable cars. Jaya unpinned the ruby and tucked it into her bag with her scarf. She sat leaning forward, as if she could somehow make the horses go faster by gritting her teeth.

We drew up at Tesla's lab. Tesla unfolded himself through the carriage door, and Mark Twain sprang out after him.

The windows were dark, except for a faint glimmer on the fourth floor. "Someone's up there," said Tesla.

"That's your lab, isn't it?" said Twain. "It's probably him. Come on!"

• • •

The four of us ran clomping up the wooden stairs. We sounded like a horse in a hurry.

The lab door opened on a cavernous room full of shadows and looming dark shapes. A lone desk lamp shone on a table in one corner. The stocky assistant—the one who looked like a redheaded calf—was packing papers into a crate. The light glinted on his hair.

He straightened up when he saw us, looking less like a calf and more like a startled rabbit.

"Good—ah—good evening, Mr. Tesla," he said.

"Mr. Smith! What are you doing with my notebooks?"

"I was working late. . . . I was just . . . straightening up."

Tesla pushed a button in the wall. Electric light flooded the room. We could see that an entire cabinet had been stripped bare, its contents packed in crates.

"Why are you packing my notebooks, Smith? What are you doing with my models? Put them down at once!" Tesla's voice crackled with rage. His Serbian accent suddenly got much stronger. "Is Edison paying you?"

Mr. Smith was holding something that looked like a big, awkward pistol. There were several more of them in the crate in front of him. The pistol had a long barrel with two metallic rings around it and a sort of octagonal cap at the end. It had a brass boxy part above the handle and a scary-looking swirly bit. It looked very familiar.

Then I recognized it. It was a small version of the death ray that Simon had been standing in front of when we saw him on the telelectroscope, back in the repository.

"That's the death ray, isn't it?" gasped Jaya.

Mr. Smith looked at the model death ray in his hand. Then he looked at Tesla. Then he pointed the death ray at Tesla and said, "I'm sorry, sir. I have a boat to catch. If you leave now, I won't hurt you."

I snatched up the nearest object—a complicated copper rod—and pointed it at Mr. Smith. "Put the gun down!" I yelled.

He laughed and swung the death ray around to point at me. "Or what? You'll induce a magnetic field?"

Suddenly the room went dark. Mark Twain had turned off the lights. Only Mr. Smith was left illuminated. "Duck, Leo!" Twain yelled.

Mr. Smith switched his table lamp off, leaving the whole room in velvety darkness.

I ducked low and crept sideways. Maybe if I could get to Mr. Smith's crate, I could grab one of those model death rays myself. I had to stop him—if Tesla got hurt, the future would get scrambled up like shaken dice.

I was halfway there when Jaya yelled, "Turn on the lights, Mr. Clemens!" When they came on again, Jaya was standing by Mr. Smith's table, pointing another model death ray at his head. She must have grabbed it out of a crate when the lights were out. Hers was bigger than his—she needed two hands to hold it. "Drop it or I'll shoot!" she said.

"You? You're not going to shoot," he said.

Instead of answering, she pointed the death ray over his shoulder and pulled the trigger. With a horrible hiss, a stream of hot, blinding silver shot out of the muzzle and racketed into the wall behind him. The impact shook the lab.

Jaya pointed the model death ray back at Mr. Smith. "I said, put it down." Her voice was shaking a little.

He put his ray gun down.

"Come here, Smith," said Tesla. "Right now!"

Mr. Smith took a step toward the door.

Suddenly there was another earsplitting sound like a zillion fingernails tearing a chalkboard apart. The air next to Mr. Smith split open, and Simon stepped through.

We all stared at him with our mouths open. The gap in the air was still open. The edges pulsed with ribbons of blue and purple light. I could see through it, but I couldn't really make sense of what I was seeing. It was like looking through a kaleidoscope, but not just the flat kind—like a kaleidoscope with five or six dimensions. I saw tiny bits of trees and chairs and people and galaxies and daylight and night sky, all oozing and swirling. For a second I saw something sickeningly pink, like the inside of somebody's intestines. For a second I saw what looked like fire.

While we were all staring into the horrifying portal, Simon picked up the model death ray that Mr. Smith had been holding.

Simon pointed it at Jaya. That snapped us out of it.

"Put the gun down, Jaya, and take me to the Wells time machine," he said.

"Seriously?" Jaya said. "Seriously, Simon? You're going to shoot me?"

"If I have to."

"But you kept saying you loved me."

Mark Twain had recovered his voice. "Who is *that*?" he said. "How did he get here?"

"It's Simon! Mr. Smith's great-great-grandson, the one Jaya told you about! We have to stop him!"

Simon was saying, "I do love you, Jaya. I don't want to hurt you. So put the gun down."

"No, you put *your* gun down. Or I'll shoot your ancestor, and you'll never be born!" said Jaya.

Mr. Smith stared at Simon. "Who are you? Where did you come from?" he gasped.

"I'm on your side. I'm your great-great-grandson, from the future," said Simon.

Mr. Smith looked shocked. "My great-great—but where—but how—?"

"How did you even know we were here, Simon?" asked Jaya, still pointing her weapon at Mr. Smith.

"I used the people finder at the Burton. It has a time setting," said Simon. "It showed you in 1895, so I knew you'd used the Wells time machine. I knew you were trying to stop my ancestor. I came back to stop you and get the time machine. Where is it?"

I still had the copper rod in my hand. I was edging around toward Simon. I wasn't sure what I was planning to do, but I had to do *something*. Maybe I could knock the death ray out of his hand.

"Stop right there, Leo! Nobody moves or I'll shoot," said Simon.

Tesla had picked up a big metal object and was bearing down on Simon. "Get out of my lab! All you, get out!" he roared. He moved like a giant skinny gorilla.

Simon yelled, "Everybody stand still! Or I'll shoot her, I swear I will!"

Another tremendous noise—this time a deep boom that

made my bones itch—and another copy of Simon materialized in the lab. He was riding on what must have been the Burton's other time machine. It had rounded lines—it looked like something out of a 1950s space comic. He had the beginning of a black eye, his shirt was ripped, and his nose was bleeding.

He leapt at the first copy of himself, screaming, "Stop! Stop! You'll hurt Jaya!"

Then everything got very confusing.

The new Simon knocked the death-ray pistol out of the first Simon's hand. Then the two Simons were fighting like demons, punching and kicking and yelling. They were perfectly matched. Simon One was fresher and unhurt, but Simon Two knew every move he was going to make seconds before he made it.

Meanwhile, Mr. Smith dove for Simon's model death ray, and I dove to stop him. I grabbed what I could reach—his back and shoulder—and hung on tight. His jacket was pulling loose from him, and I was losing my grip. And he was strong! We went down together. I tried to get on top of him and pin him to the floor, but he wiggled his arms free, grabbing the model death ray.

"Get out of the way, Leo! I can't shoot him—I'll hit you!" yelled Jaya.

Mr. Smith lurched beneath me and I heard that horrible hiss as he fired his death ray. I pushed myself up with all my strength and threw my weight on him. He rolled over, throwing me off and hitting my head hard on the floor.

For a moment I couldn't move. I saw a flash through my closed eyelids and I heard the death ray hiss again. Something else crackled. Suddenly the air filled with crackling and hissing.

It was deafening and blinding, as if everyone in the lab were shooting death rays at once. And then, to my terror, I smelled smoke.

When I got my eyes open, some machine—a Tesla coil?—was shooting lightning all around the room and something in the far corner had caught fire.

I looked for Tesla and Mark Twain. They were wrestling the ray gun away from Mr. Smith. One of the Simons was yelling, "Drop it, Jaya! Drop it!"

Where was Jaya? I couldn't see her.

A voice was yelling, "Jaya, watch out! Help her, Leo!" The voice sounded really familiar—almost like mine. I looked around. Where was Jaya? Who was talking?

"She's over by the window. Quick, Leo! Go help her!" The voice *was* mine! How? Where was it coming from?

No time to find out. I hauled myself to my feet and ran to the window.

Then one of the Simons—they were both so bloody and messed up now that I couldn't tell them apart—got away from the other one and jumped at Jaya. He pushed her over and she fell, hitting her head on the table leg with a loud crack. The ray gun went flying from her hand, and I saw it hit a metal tank. From the corner of my eye I saw what looked like lightning. Jaya was moaning and holding her head, and Simon was on top of her.

I threw myself on Simon and tore him off her with a strength I didn't know I had.

"Get out *now*, Simon!" yelled the other Simon. "The dark energy is destabilizing the portal! Run!"

The Simon I was fighting wrenched himself away and ran for the portal that Simon One had come out of. The whole thing was getting smaller.

Screaming, Simon leapt in.

The portal snapped shut behind him with a zipping wail, like a subway car crushing a zillion kittens.

The other Simon yelled, "Run, Mr. Smith! You have to make your ship!"

But Mr. Smith wasn't going anywhere. Tesla and Twain had him firmly by the arms.

The fire was spreading. Mr. Smith's crates and papers were blazing brighter than the electric lights, and the lightning was brighter than everything.

Tesla yelled something in Serbo-Croatian. It sounded like a curse. "The hydrogen!" he yelled.

"Everybody get out!" shouted Mark Twain. "It's going to explode!"

Swearing, the remaining Simon—it must have been Simon Two—jumped onto the space-age time machine. It disappeared with another tooth-jarring boom.

Jaya still looked stunned. I pulled her to her feet. "Come on! We've got to get out of here!" I yelled. We started for the door.

Then I remembered. "Wait! The time machine!"

"There's no time! Come on!" screamed Jaya, pulling my arm.

"You go! I'll get it!"

I wrenched free and ran across the room to where we'd left the traveling bag. I grabbed the bag just as flames were licking at the handle.

CHAPTER TWENTY-TWO

I Meet Myself
Coming and Going

Jaya and I stood together in the street, watching the lab burn, standing back from the wall of heat. The explosion still echoed in our ears. Mark Twain had Mr. Smith in a hammerlock, his arm behind his back. My legs felt weak, and Jaya looked grim and shaken.

"Leo, you saved my life in there. Thank you." She looked into my eyes.

I looked back into hers. I didn't know what to say.

Tesla stared at his lab. The lightning seemed to have gone out of his eyes. "It's all gone, Sam," he said. "The work of half my lifetime, very nearly." I saw tears on his cheeks, red with reflected firelight.

"It's a damn shame, Nik," said Twain gently. "A damn shame."

Tesla turned on Mr. Smith. "How could you do this? I trusted you!"

Mr. Smith shrugged, or tried to—he couldn't move his shoulders much. "It's your own fault. You should have let me take the things and go. Then you wouldn't have lost everything."

Tesla roared. I thought he was going to tear his assistant apart. Twain spun Mr. Smith around, putting himself between the two men.

"It's not true, Mr. Tesla," Jaya said quickly. "It's not your fault. Your lab would have burned down tonight anyway. In the future where we come from, the fire starts in the basement. I think Mr. Smith was always going to start it."

"You knew that? Then why didn't you warn me?" This time I thought Tesla was going to tear *Jaya* apart.

"Well, Leo wouldn't—I mean, we didn't want to risk—" She stopped. "I'm sorry, Mr. Tesla, I really am. But don't worry, you'll build a new lab right away. I promise."

We heard fire engine bells. The sound seemed to remind Jaya of her impatience. "Come on, Leo. We have to go," she said.

"I'm really sorry about your lab, Mr. Tesla," I said.

Jaya said, "I'll see you very soon, Mr. Clemens. But—" She hesitated.

"But I won't see you, is that it?" said Mark Twain.

Jaya nodded. "You've already seen me back then."

The clanging was getting louder and closer. "Come on, Leo," Jaya said.

Mr. Smith said something unrepeatable. Twain wrenched his arm. We walked away quickly to the train, not looking back.

When we got uptown to my building, it was quiet and empty in the starlight. We slipped in through the back door and climbed the stairs to the top floor. Once we were all packed and shrunk, Jaya hopped on the saddle. "My turn to drive," she said. "Get on behind me."

I started to argue, but then I remembered that I had been sitting behind her when the time machine had appeared in my bedroom. "All right," I said, "but we have to make a stop on the way home."

"When you saw us in your bedroom, you mean? Okay," said Jaya.

I braced myself for that horrible feeling of wrongness, and Jaya pushed the lever marked *FUTURE*.

We poured through time again with the same headlong, motionless hurtling, but this time it was different—maybe because we were going in the right direction. I felt like I was winning a game, acing a test. An upside-down waterfall of hope cascaded through me, starting in the soles of my feet and babbling out through my head.

"We did it!" I cried, leaning against Jaya and hugging her tight. "We stopped Simon! His ancestor didn't get the death ray! The city's safe!"

She laughed and leaned back against me, her hands on the controls.

The years flew by. I lost count, but I didn't care. Out the window, buildings rose and fell. Trees sprouted and writhed their branches taller and taller.

Suddenly a building leapt jerkily into existence on the corner lot near my building. I recognized it: the new annex of the Brindley School. They'd just finished building it the year before. "Slow down, Jaya! We're almost there."

She pulled back on the lever. The days flicked past one by one. Vast shadowy shapes filled the room; I saw my own furniture. My chair jerked around from desk to window and back. My bed flung its sheets into wild heaps, occasionally making itself neatly for a few moments. My *self* flickered around too, transparent and ghostly, shimmering on the chair or making the bed lumpy.

What day was it now? I looked around for the pencil line I'd drawn on the wall back when I was seven and first getting excited about astronomy. That's where the sunlight falls at noon every summer solstice, the third week in June.

There! The sun hit the line, and I started counting days. "Get ready to stop," I told Jaya.

One more night. One more sunrise.

"Now!"

She pulled the lever to the stop position. We stopped with a bang, knocking over my lamp.

I don't love looking in the mirror. I mean, I'm a reasonably okay-looking guy, I guess, but it always feels so strange to see myself from the outside. Photos are even worse—I'm used to Mirror Me, so Photo Me looks backwards, distorted, with my ears all crooked and that bosonic curl on the wrong side of my forehead. But the worst of all was real-life 3-D Me. He was backwards and distorted and a zillion feet tall, with his mouth hanging open in surprise.

He closed his mouth, swallowed, and blurted something. I wished Jaya didn't have to see him—me—like this.

"Hi, um, me," I answered. "It's me, Leo. I'm you. Wow, you're big." Smooth! But wait—didn't I have to tell him something—something about the repository? No, not the repository, the time machine. *The Time Machine.* I had to tell him to read it. That's how he would figure out about going to England and capturing the mini time machine. "Listen, this is important," I said. "Read H. G. Wells—"

He interrupted me with questions. Then Jaya started talking, trying to warn him about Simon.

I couldn't let her do that. Suppose she told me what Simon was going to do—suppose I listened to her? Suppose she got me to stop Simon before he sabotaged Francis's Burton page application and made Jaya hate him? Then Jaya might actually make the mistake of dating that boson! And then Simon wouldn't try to hold the city hostage, so we would never visit Tesla to stop him from getting the death ray, and I would never show up in my own bedroom on a time machine, and I would never tell myself to read Wells, and I might never ask Ms. Kang for advice about my project, and I might never meet Jaya. I couldn't let that happen!

I put my hand over Jaya's mouth. I saw Past Me's enormous eyes get even more enormous, and I remembered how surprised I'd been when I saw myself treating her like that.

She bit me, of course, and started arguing, just like she had before.

I heard my sister's footsteps. I reached around Jaya and rammed the lever down. My vast, past face faded, and we poured into the future again, buoyed on hope.

We landed safely in my empty bedroom. Jaya wanted to dash out to the repository as soon as we were the right size, but I made her wash the soot off her face first and change back into her regular clothes.

"The first thing we have to do is get Simon on the telelectroscope and tell him we know he's bluffing," she said, tugging on her ridiculous hat, the one with the pom-pom on the end.

"No, that's the second thing. The first thing we have to do is get your patience back," I told her.

She was way too impatient for the bus. She hustled me into a cab and then kept glaring at the driver for stopping at red lights. "It was better in 1895, before they invented traffic lights," she said.

At the repository, she was too impatient to wait for the elevator. She thumped up the stairs two at a time and burst into Doc's office.

"It's safe!" she cried. "You can call off the team! Simon's bluffing—he doesn't have the death ray!"

"Shut the door and sit down, Jaya," said Dr. Rust. "What team? Who's Simon?"

CHAPTER TWENTY-THREE

A World Without Simon

Apparently Simon had never existed.

Jaya turned to me in dismay. "What happened? Simon's great-great-grandfather didn't die in the fire! Clemens had him—he was perfectly safe! So why wasn't Simon born? What went wrong?"

"Nothing went wrong," I said. "This is *good*! No Simon to destroy New York."

"Yes, but why doesn't he *exist*?"

I thought about it. "Didn't Simon say his great-great-grandfather met his great-great-grandmother crossing the Atlantic? He must have missed his boat and never met her."

Dr. Rust, who had been listening patiently, asked, "Who is this Simon who doesn't exist?"

"There's no time to explain! I have to go back to Tesla's lab and stop us from killing Simon!"

"We didn't kill him," I said. "We just made things so that he never existed. Big difference."

"He did so exist!"

"Not in *this* world."

"Oh! Don't be such a boson! Give me that time machine!" She was so impatient she actually stamped her foot.

"Hold your horses, Jaya." I pulled the shrink ray out of the satchel and put it on Dr. Rust's desk. "Before we do anything else, you'd better give Jaya back her patience," I said.

"Clearly." With a look of amused patience, Dr. Rust opened a dark metal box on the desk and rummaged around, pulling out something swirly and insubstantial. "Is this it?"

Jaya curled her lip at the thing. "Ugh, of course not!"

Doc squinted at it. "No, you're right. That was just a good intention. Is this—? No . . . Ah, here it is!"

Doc pulled out a small, thin object and offered it to her.

Jaya frowned. "I thought there was more of it."

"*Your* patience? Don't be silly."

Jaya rolled her eyes, but she took the thing, which melted into her arm. She gave a huge sigh. The difference was invisible but dramatic. I felt the air around her relax.

"And now," said Doc, "go find Lucy Minnian and Rick Reyes and tell us all about this Simon who doesn't exist."

"Hang on," said Ms. Minnian when Jaya had finished talking. "How did this Simon get back to 1895?"

That's what continues to amaze me about the repository librarians. Unlike every other adult ever born—well, except Mark Twain and Tesla—a kid can tell them an unbelievable story and they'll believe it.

"Two copies of Simon appeared in Tesla's lab using two different time machines," said Jaya. "One was a portal and one was a space-age-looking machine. They must have been the Kerr and the Tuck, from the Burton."

"But why did he use them at all if the Kerr creates alternate timelines and the Tuck can't change the past?" asked Ms. Minnian. "Neither one would do him any good."

"Here's what I think happened," I said. I'd been puzzling it out all the way home. "Simon was tracking us with the Burton's people finder. When he saw that we were in 1895, he knew we had a working time machine. He figured we must be trying to stop his ancestor from stealing the death ray. So he went back to stop us. Or maybe he was trying to get a death ray for himself or get the Wells time machine from us. He did tell Jaya to give him the Wells machine."

"But he didn't have any effective time machines!" Jaya said.

"True. But if he used the Kerr to get the Wells time machine, he would be *in* that new universe—the one in which he had the Wells time machine. And so would we since we were there with him when he took it."

That made Jaya scrunch up her face and think hard. "Oh. I guess you're right." She thought some more. "But why did he use the can't-change-anything time machine after that? Didn't he know that thing was useless?"

"I guess he was desperate," I said. "Remember? He was shouting at himself, 'Stop! You'll hurt Jaya!' He must have hurt you, gone home, realized he had to stop himself from hurting you, and used the other machine to try to stop himself even though he knew it wouldn't work. I guess he really does care about you."

"But why not use the alternate-universes machine again since the can't-change-the-past one is useless?" asked Mr. Reyes.

Doc said, "He couldn't. The alternate-universe machine only opens a portal once per user. If I remember the originating story correctly, once the machine has encoded your quantum imprint, you can't pass the wormhole threshold again in the same temporal direction."

Jaya thought about that. "Okay, but then why aren't I hurt? If Simon hurt me and came back again to change that and if he used the can't-change-the-past time machine to do it, then how did he succeed in stopping himself from hurting me?"

"I thought you said Leo saved you, not Simon," said Dr. Rust.

"He did, but clearly he wasn't going to until Simon showed up on the Tuck machine. I mean, Simon was sure he had hurt me—he came back on the Tuck machine to stop himself. And I'm fine now, except for a bump on my head."

"Maybe Simon was wrong—maybe he just thought he'd hurt you, but he really hadn't?" suggested Ms. Minnian. "You do have a bump on your head. Maybe he thought it was worse than it is."

"I guess that could be it," I said. "Things were pretty confusing with the whole fight going on." It wasn't a very satisfying answer, but I couldn't think of a better one for now.

"All right," said Jaya. "Now, how do we bring him back?"

"We don't," I said. "He was a total boson and he tried to kill you. The world is better without him."

"He also tried to save me, and he was my *friend*," said Jaya. "And you shouldn't make people not exist just because you don't like them."

"But he brought it on himself!" I said. "If he hadn't threatened us with the death ray, we would never have gone back to 1895 and stopped his great-great-grandparents from meeting."

This was crazy. Now *Jaya* was the one insisting it had been a bad idea to change the past and *I* was the one defending it.

"What's the rush?" asked Dr. Rust. "There's no need to decide right now. Simon doesn't exist, so he's not going anywhere. Let's all sleep on it for a few days."

We agreed to leave it at that.

Something else was bothering me. It nagged at the back of my brain while I walked home through Central Park and unlocked my apartment door.

Sofia was in the kitchen making a banana smoothie and blasting Mozart to drown out the blender. A wave of relief and happiness hit me. "You exist!" I yelled. I threw my arms around her, astonishing both of us.

"Leo, get off! What's the matter with you?" she said, licking smoothie off her thumb.

"I don't know—isn't it *your* job to tell *me* that?"

When Jake came over that evening, I managed not to hug him, but I lost five games of Gravity Force III.

"I can't believe you let me pulverize your sub with my death ray," said Jake. "That's like the easiest shot to dodge! What's wrong with you?"

I couldn't believe it either. Shouldn't riding around in real submarines and fighting with real death rays make it easier to handle the fake ones in a video game?

I had a lot on my mind. For one thing, I felt bad about Simon too. I mean, I didn't think causing someone to never have existed was really the same thing as killing him, and there could be lots of theoretical universes where he still existed, and

I certainly didn't want to ever see him again as long as I lived. But still, he *had* existed, and now he didn't, and to some extent it was my fault.

I also felt bad about not telling Jake—my best friend—about all my amazing adventures. And the thought of Jaya was distracting me too, of course. Did that kiss mean anything?

That night I dreamed I was riding the Fifth Avenue Stage with Jaya, too nervous to put my arm around her, while Simon whipped the horses and laughed at me and a voice in the background—my own voice—shouted, "Kiss her, Leo! Kiss her!"

CHAPTER TWENTY-FOUR

Jaya's Brilliant Idea

When I got to the repository on Tuesday, Ms. Callender sent me and Jaya down to Stack 5. It was a quiet day. I wished I had lots of call slips to run. I didn't know what to say to Jaya. Why did I feel so awkward? Shouldn't capturing a time machine and traveling back to 1895 with a girl make you feel more comfortable with her, not less?

A call slip arrived. I took as long as I could to run it. As I was wrapping up a jigsaw to send to the Main Exam Room, the stack door opened and a boy ran in. He looked about seven or eight years old.

"Sister Jaya!" he yelled.

"Brother Dre!" Jaya yelled back. "What are you doing here? Did you come with Marc?"

"Yeah, he's upstairs with Doc. Read me a story?" He handed her a book.

"I thought you had a sister, not a brother," I said, puzzled. The kid looked African American, not Indian.

"I don't have a brother yet, but I will. This is Andre, Anjali's boyfriend's baby brother."

"Baby yourself!" said Andre indignantly. To me, he said, "Hi. Who are you?"

"That's Leo," said Jaya. "He's a new page."

Andre grinned at me. "Hi, Leo. Can you get Jaya to read to me?"

"Can't you read to yourself? Or is the book too hard?" asked Jaya.

"Of course I can!" He sounded outraged. "But it's way more fun when *you* read it. You make all the stories more exciting."

I knew what the kid meant.

Jaya looked at the book. "What is this, Poe again? Boy, Andre, you love the scary stuff, don't you!"

He nodded gleefully. "Read 'The Tell-Tale Heart.'"

"I'm sick of that one," said Jaya. "How about 'The Purloined Letter'?"

A pneum thumped into the basket. I pulled out a sheaf of call slips. "A snarling iron, a cow's tongue, a beak iron, a riffler, a bastard file, and a burnisher," I read. "What the quark is all this stuff?"

Jaya laughed. "Those are all silversmiths' tools. They should all be close together."

I went off down the stack to look for them. When I got back, Jaya jumped up, calling out, "I'm brilliant! I'm a genius!" She handed me the book. "Here, Leo, finish reading Andre the story. I have to go check something."

The story was about a detective looking for a missing letter. The villain had hidden it in plain sight—in a rack of other letters. Andre wasn't impressed. "That wasn't scary at *all*. I like

'The Pit and the Pendulum' way better. Read that one next," he told me.

"The Pit and the Pendulum" was much more exciting. I'd just gotten to the part where the red-hot walls of the torture chamber were threatening to crush the hero and throw him into the pit when Jaya burst back into the room holding a transparent rod. It looked very familiar.

"Look, Leo! I think this is *it*!"

"*It* what?"

"The missing quartz rod! From the full-size Wells time machine!"

"But where did you find it?"

"In the geology collection, with all the other mineral samples. Call number X S&M 549.68 U556," she said, reading from a call slip.

"That *is* brilliant! How do you think it got there?"

"Someone must have hidden it in plain sight, like the letter in the Poe story."

"But who?"

"I don't know—maybe you or me, in the past or the future. Or both. I'm going to run downstairs and see if it fits."

"Wait! I'll come with you!"

"No, somebody has to stay here in case we get call slips," she said, and ran off. So much for her newly restored patience.

I hadn't even gotten to the end of the Poe story when she came back. Her hair was a mess and there were circles under her eyes.

"Jaya! What happened to you?" I gasped.

"Nothing—I just went back to the 1880s and had a little chat with Mark Twain about time travel."

"Without me? How could you do that!"

"I'm sorry. But I was always going to go alone—he never mentioned having met *you* before. Did you know the ladies wore bustles back then?"

"What are bustles?" asked Andre.

"They're these cage things ladies wore under their dresses, strapped to the back of their underwear, like fake rear ends. Very uncomfortable."

Andre laughed. "I bet you look awesome with a fake rear end stuck on your underwear, Jaya!"

"Jaya!" I said. "You can't go time traveling without me! It's not safe! And who's going to save you if Simon tries to shoot you with a death ray?"

"Simon doesn't exist anymore, remember?" said Jaya. "We need to talk about that. I've been feeling terrible about what happened to Simon. I really think we need to fix it."

But I was only half listening because suddenly I understood what had been nagging at the back of my brain all this time. *I* was the one who had changed the past and saved Jaya from Simon One. Not Simon Two—he *was* unable to change the past! It was me. And I knew how I'd done it—or rather, how I was going to do it!

"Your turn to keep an eye on the stack," I said. "There's something I need to do."

CHAPTER TWENTY-FIVE

I Save the Life of the Most Awesome Girl in the Universe

I ran upstairs to Doc's office to save Jaya's life back in Tesla's lab. I had to stop in the stacks on my way to pick up a few items I needed for the job: a GPS, a microphone, and a clock.

Balancing them in my arms, I knocked on the head repositorian's door.

"What is it, Leo? Come in, come in." Dr. Rust cleared an armful of priceless objects off the spare chair and gestured for me to sit down. The other chair was occupied by a grownup version of Andre. He looked a little older than my brother, Dmitri.

"Oh, sorry—you're busy. I can come back later," I said. After all, 1895 would still be there in half an hour.

"No, you stay. I've got to go anyway," said Andre's brother.

"Take care, Marc. Love to Anjali," said Doc. Marc shut the door behind him.

Doc turned to me. "Now, Leo, what can I do for you?"

"Do you still have that thing you gave me to use when I

took the test with the clock and the radio—the conceptual coupler? Can I borrow it for a sec?"

"Sure." Doc opened a drawer and took it out. "Do you want to check it out on your card? If so, I'll need a deposit."

"You mean like how Jaya gave you her patience?"

"Yes, your patience would do. Patience, sense of direction, ability to dance—something like that."

"I only need the coupler for a few minutes. What if I just use it here—would that be okay?"

"Help yourself." Dr. Rust handed me the conceptual coupler.

With my multi-utility tool, I attached the coupler to the clock, the GPS, and the mic. Doc watched me with interest.

I tightened the connections, plugged everything in, wound the clock, switched on the power, and located Tesla's lab in space. Then I spun time backward to the evening when Jaya and I had fought with Simon and Tesla's lab burned down. I switched the mic to *amplify,* turning it into a speaker.

The room filled with the sounds of the fight. I heard death rays hiss, lightning fizz and snap, and men curse. I heard my own grunt of pain when Mr. Smith knocked me out.

The bangs and hisses and static seemed to go on and on. How long had I been out cold?

"Drop it, Jaya! Drop it!" Simon's voice came thin and crackly through the device. There! That was what he'd said just before he jumped on her.

I pushed the button that switched the mic to *speak* and shouted, "Jaya, watch out!"

Silence.

What had happened? Had I lost the connection? Oh, right—the mic was still on *speak*.

I let the talk button go. More crashes.

I pressed the talk button and shouted, "Help her, Leo! She's over by the window! Quick, Leo! Go help her!"

I switched back to *amplify* and we listened. More shouts and crashes. That must be the sound of me tearing Simon off Jaya. Through all the noise, I heard Jaya's voice—she was still alive. *It worked!* I thought. *I just saved Jaya!*

"Fascinating," said Dr. Rust. "I wonder why you were able to access that scene? In this timeline, Simon never existed. Why should he exist in the past?"

"He shouldn't," I said, "but he does. That's the beauty of the Wells time machine. Paradoxes don't bother it."

"Everybody get out! It's going to explode!" yelled Mark Twain thinly through the microphone.

"That can't be Tesla yelling. Is it Mark Twain?" asked Dr. Rust.

I nodded.

"I always wondered what his voice sounded like," said Doc. "You can tell he's from Missouri."

More curses from the loudspeaker as Past Me grabbed the time machine and everyone scrambled for the door. I switched off the mic hastily. "Well, that's it. If we're still listening when the hydrogen explodes, we'll probably blow out our eardrums. Thanks for the coupler." I disassembled my machine and handed it back.

Out in the corridor I heard Present Jaya calling, "Where are you, Leo? The shift's over!"

"My pleasure," said Doc. "I take it your mission succeeded?"

"Seems that way. Jaya survived." I got up to go to her.

"Hang on a second, Leo. I think you've earned this." Dr. Rust opened a drawer and took out a folding multi-utility tool. "Keep it safe and use it carefully."

"Thanks! What does it do?"

It had a zillion tools folded into its case, which was made of some silvery metal I didn't recognize. I unfolded one. It looked like a screwdriver with a fractal end. I unfolded a teeny-tiny telescope, then a sort of curving scissors. Then a little hand the size of my thumbnail, complete with a thumbnail of its own. When I levered the hand away from the handle, it flexed and shook itself as if being folded up had given it a cramp.

"Careful. That one's willful," said Doc.

The tiny hand snapped its fingers at us.

"This is a fantastic tool! What is it?"

Doc smiled. "Oh, sorry, didn't I say? It's a key to the Wells Bequest."

"There you are! I was looking for you. What were you doing in there?" asked Jaya as I emerged from Dr. Rust's office.

"Oh, just saving your life and earning my Wells Bequest key." I felt jubilant. I wanted to celebrate. I'd saved Jaya! I'd almost lost her, but I'd saved her instead! I wanted to fold her in my arms and hug her forever.

But I still didn't know if she liked me that way.

"You're kidding! Congratulations!" She punched me hard on the shoulder.

"Thanks, and yet ouch."

She was standing so close. What was wrong with me? I'd

driven the *Terror* through sea and air. I'd ridden a time machine across more than a century, battled a villain with death rays, run the wrong way in a burning lab with hydrogen tanks about to explode—but I couldn't seem to kiss the girl I loved.

Even though she'd already kissed me first.

"Are you done for the day?" I asked.

"I just have to put the time machine back in the Wells Bequest oversizes," said Jaya. "I left it in the main room."

"Good. I'll go down with you," I said. "I want to see it."

One of the devices on the silvery multi-utility tool was a little skeleton key that fit into a keyhole in the Wells Bequest door. "I didn't notice this keyhole before," I said. "Was it always here?"

"Not sure. I don't think I've seen it before either," said Jaya.

"Hey, didn't Ms. Minnian use a remote control to open the Wells Bequest? Why is my key different?"

"All the Special Collection keys are different. They fit the users," said Jaya. "I like yours."

The time machine stood in the middle of the room. It was missing its crystal rod.

"Here," said Jaya, taking the rod out of her backpack and handing it to me. "Want to take her for a spin before I put her away? I got to visit Mark Twain—you should get a solo trip too."

"Sure! Thanks." I fitted the rod into its slot, using the hand tool on my Wells Bequest key to tighten the gaskets. It grasped them with its tiny fingers and twisted. "We should probably put the rod back in the geology section when we're done," I said. "It's been safe there for decades."

"That's the plan," said Jaya. "I guess we should tell Doc too."

Now that the quartz rod was in place, a metal bar on the machine started twinkling. I folded up my tool and climbed into the saddle. "Well, here goes," I said.

"Have a good trip! Come back soon!"

I braced myself and pushed the lever to the past.

The saddle was more comfortable than the one on the mini demo model, and the action was much smoother. Best of all, the full-size machine had a sort of dashboard with time and speed indicators, which made it easier to figure out where I was—I mean when.

That was good because the basement repository room gave almost no clues. The lights blurred on and off, and ghostly figures hopped around occasionally, retrieving objects or reshelving them with a flick of light. But mostly, nothing happened. I felt the familiar wrongness of traveling backward in time. The room and everything in it stayed still, waiting. Everything was motionless except me.

After a few minutes of darkness, the lights snicked on and a few figures danced backward around a familiar object—the shrink ray—before vanishing.

I glanced at the controls. I had gone back a few years. That was probably far enough. I pulled the PAST lever to stop and pressed the other lever, starting us back to the present.

The time machine hung motionless for a moment, then slowly started accelerating into the future. As it did, I glimpsed the guy I'd just met—Marc, Andre's brother, only younger—with another guy and a girl. The three of them looked around my age. The other guy was using the shrink ray on Marc and the girl. They writhed, shrinking down to the size of soda cans.

I reached out to stop the machine, curious to see what would happen next, but my momentum swept me on too fast. Before I could catch it, the moment was gone. *Oh well,* I thought. The now-familiar sensation of hurtling hope waterfalled me forward, back to the present. Back to Jaya!

Back to Jaya—and what? Just friends?

I eyed the controls. Almost there . . . just another few ticks . . .

As I pulled the lever back to stop the machine, I saw I had gone a little too far—a minute or two forward into the future. I saw myself standing a few feet away. Future Me had his arms around Jaya.

He was kissing her.

He was kissing her!

That meant I was about to kiss her!

And far more important—*she was kissing him back!*

As if he'd read my mind, Future Me opened his eyes. Without breaking the kiss, he looked straight at me and flapped his hand at me, waving me off.

I just barely nudged the *PAST* lever and waited for my shadowy future self to disappear. The instant he did, I halted the machine. I was back in the present, in the Wells Bequest the moment after I'd left.

I sprang off, ran over to Jaya, threw my arms around her, and kissed her.

And to my endless, delighted disbelief—even though I knew she was going to—she kissed me back.

CHAPTER TWENTY-SIX

The Green Mouse Machine

What does it feel like to kiss the smartest, bravest, most awesome girl in the world? Not just because you're trying to stop time and capture a time machine, but because the two of you both finally figured out you were made for each other?

A little like driving a flying submarine over a storm. No, a little like riding a time machine fast into the future . . . No, not really like either of those. I can't describe it.

"What took you so long?" asked Jaya when we stopped for breath.

"You mean you didn't like it? The kiss went on too long?" I asked, panicky.

"No, silly! I mean, why did you wait so long to kiss me?"

"I don't know. I guess was afraid you didn't . . ." I shrugged.

"You boson!" She hit me on the shoulder.

"Well, *you* could have kissed *me,* you know."

"I *did,* you complete quark-head!" She hit me again.

The hit turned into a hug and another kiss, and the air filled with a dizzy whirring.

Then I opened my eyes. That whirring wasn't just my blood in my ears—it was the time machine—me, from a minute ago! It was starting to materialize, right at the wrong moment.

I flapped my hand at Past Me, waving him off. The buzzing faded, and the time machine vanished like a rainbow. I closed my eyes.

Soon we were interrupted again. The door banged.

"Ooh," said a voice—Abigail's. "Looks like *somebody's* been using the green mouse machine!"

Jaya stopped kissing me. "We did not!" she said indignantly. "This is the real thing!"

"The green mouse machine always finds the real thing," said Abigail. "That's the whole point. I *knew* you guys were meant for each other—I knew it the day I met you, Leo!"

I straightened myself up awkwardly. "What's the green mouse machine?" I asked.

"It's a machine for finding true love," said Jaya. "It's around here somewhere—I can show you." She let go of my arm and ran away down the room.

I stared after her. "A machine? How can a machine find true love?"

Abigail said, "Something about 'wireless psychical currents' encircling the earth. Currents of fate, I think."

"But what do green mice have to do with true love?"

"That's the name of the book it's from—*The Green Mouse*. I don't know why it's called that, though. I never read it."

"I did," said Jaya, coming back from the other end of the room with a little box in her hand. "It's really old-fashioned in a not-so-great way. The green mouse machine only matches people up with people from the exact same background as them. It would never approve of the two of us. Other than that I liked the book okay. It has a lot of funny moments."

"But why's it called *The Green Mouse*?"

"I don't remember. Some silly reason. It's a very silly book. Look, here's the machine."

She opened the box. Inside was a little object that looked like the innards of a windup watch. I peered at it, wondering how it worked.

"Anyway," said Abigail, "I'm sorry to interrupt, but Ms. Minnian sent me down here to get Leo. She wants to talk to you."

"Go ahead, Leo," said Jaya. "I have something I need to finish up down here." She snapped the green mouse box shut and nodded significantly at the time machine. "I'll see you tomorrow."

I started to leave, then stopped. "You're not going to use the green mouse machine, are you?"

"Of course not, silly! I don't need to. I have you!"

Ms. Minnian was waiting for me in Dr. Rust's office. She wanted to congratulate me on earning my Wells Bequest key and lecture me about using it carefully.

"Relax, Lucy," said Doc. "Leo's a cautious boy."

"No such thing," said Ms. Minnian. But she smiled.

I told them about Jaya's discovery of the quartz rod.

"Brilliant!" said Doc. "Why didn't I think of that? I take it you tested it?"

"Yeah, I just took a very quick trip," I said. I found myself blushing furiously. Doc and Ms. Minnian raised their eyebrows at each other. I could tell the lecture about using the Wells Bequest items responsibly was about to flare up again. To distract them, I said, "Jaya and I think it would be safer to keep the rod in the geology section."

"Hm. You may be right," said Dr. Rust. "But I'd better talk to Rick Reyes about recategorizing it. He'll probably want to record its new category in the thesaurus."

"You know, Lee," said Ms. Minnian, "since we now have a working time machine, do you think we should offer the demo model to the Burton? We could trade it for the Poe gold bug. I'm pretty sure Pem-Po would go for it." She glanced at me. "I mean Dr. Pemberley-Potts."

"That's brilliant! It always kills me that we don't have the gold bug in the Corpus," said Doc.

"Then, if the Burton agreed, we'd just need to get the casque of Amontillado back from the Italians and that would give us all the Poe essentials," said Ms. Minnian, looking greedy. Were her teeth always so sharp?

Doc turned to me. "What do you think, Leo? As the person responsible for finding the mini model, I'd like to hear your opinion."

"Me?" I was flattered. "I think it's a great idea. Ms. Minnian's right—we don't really need it anymore."

"Well, we'll bring the matter up with the board."

I got to the repository a little early for my next shift, my heart beating fast at the idea of seeing Jaya again. Abigail was hanging up her coat.

"Is Jaya here yet?" I asked.

"She's upstairs in the Main Exam Room, talking to Simon."

"Talking to *who*?"

"Simon FitzHenry."

"What?! What the quark is *he* doing here? How do you even know about him?"

Abigail stared at me. "What are you talking about? He worked here for, like, months! He came over with Dr. Pemberley-Potts. She's meeting with Doc. She brought him over to apologize properly after that business with Francis."

"But—" Jaya must have used the time machine again today and brought Simon back to life. She must have gone back to the moment after we left Tesla's burning lab and gotten Mark Twain to let Simon's great-great-grandfather go, so he could catch his ship and meet Simon's great-great-grandmother.

My heart sank. Did Jaya really like Simon that much?

Then an even worse thought hit me. The time machine! Dr. Rust was about to give Pem-Po the working model! That meant if Simon could get the librarians at the Burton to let him use it, he would be able to go back in time and stop himself from cheating, and then Jaya and I would never—

I ran for the Main Exam Room. I didn't even to wait for the elevator. I charged up the stairs two at a time.

Simon and Jaya were near the door, standing by a table covered with teapots. "Please, Jaya," Simon was saying. "I would never have hurt anyone, not really. I just wanted to fix things!"

"Jaya," I said urgently, "I need to talk to you."

She glanced at me. "It's okay, Leo," she said. "Don't worry. I've got this."

"No—I need to talk to you *right now!*"

I guess she heard how exasperated I was. "Just a minute," she said to Simon. "Stay right there." She took me by the arm and marched me out into the hall. "Now, what's so urgent?" she asked me.

"Jaya, what did you do? Doc's giving Pem-Po the time machine! If Simon gets his hands on it, he'll start the whole thing all over again!"

"Calm down, Leo. It's going to be all right, I promise."

"But what is Simon *doing* here?"

"I thought it was pretty harsh that we killed him off—"

"We didn't kill him!"

"Made him not exist. Whatever. It wasn't fair. I mean, what he did was pretty bad, but not bad enough to justify annihilating him. So I took the time machine back to right after we left, and I talked Mark Twain into letting Mr. Smith go so he could catch his boat. That way Simon still got to be born, but it was perfectly safe because he never had the death ray. The models and all the plans burned up in the fire. While I was at it, I stopped off in 1937 and hid the quartz rod from the 1937 copy of the time machine in the geology collection."

"But Mr. Smith was there in the lab and saw the death ray being built! He could have built his own, from memory!"

Jaya shook her head. "He's not that smart. It would have taken a genius to build a death ray without the plans or models or research notes. Even Tesla never built it again."

"So does that mean Simon didn't try to threaten us in this timeline? Or that he did, but he was just bluffing?"

"I'm not sure," said Jaya. "I think he was about to tell me just now, when you interrupted us. But it doesn't really matter, does it? Either way, he couldn't destroy New York."

I thought of something. "But Jaya, can't you see how dangerous that was? If he never threatened us in this timeline, we might never have taken the time machine back to 1895. Then when we came back from our old timeline into this one, we would have found copies of ourselves here in the present—the ones who never left! You could have created doubles of us!"

"Would that be so bad? Two Leos would be twice as fun as one!"

"Jaya, be serious! That would have created an inexplicable anomaly! Two of me in one timeline isn't like splitting off a new universe with a separate one in each. Everybody would have noticed if there were two of me here! It would have been big trouble!"

She shook her head. "Come on, Leo. Do you seriously think there's any universe—even one single universe in the universe of universes—where you captured a time machine and we didn't *use* it?"

She was right. I had to smile despite myself. "But still," I said, "now that Simon's back and the model time machine's going to the Burton, he'll have access to it! He can change everything and stop himself from cheating Francis, and then you won't realize what a boson he is, and then—"

Jaya interrupted. "If you'll just let me finish what I was doing with Simon, you'll see you're worrying about nothing," she said. She took me by the arm again and marched me back into the Main Exam Room.

"Please, Jaya!" said Simon, as if I wasn't there. "I came all this way from London to apologize. You have to forgive me! If you'd forgiven me, none of this would ever have happened."

"Oh, so it's my fault?" said Jaya. "This is your idea of an apology?"

"I didn't say that. But I did it for you! Please, won't you forgive me?"

"All right, all right, I forgive you. I already forgave you. That's not the point."

"You do? Then you'll give me another chance?" Simon flung his arms around her. "I know long-distance relationships can be hard, but with the resources of the Burton and—"

She pushed him away—which was a good thing because I was about to do it myself. "Get off me, Simon. I said I forgave you, not that I liked you. I have a boyfriend already. Not that I would ever go out with you even if I didn't."

I felt dizzy. Could she really mean *me*?

Simon looked like he was about to leap over all the teapots and tear out my throat.

Jaya took a little box out of her pocket. "Hold on, Simon. Stand still a second, will you?" she said. She opened the box, took out the green mouse machine, and put it down on the table next to a teapot. Then she pressed a little lever.

A tentacle uncoiled, reaching toward Simon.

Crack! The tip of the tentacle sparked blue. "There," Jaya said. "That should fix things."

The door to the Main Exam Room opened behind Simon and a girl walked in. She was pretty, with shiny brown hair and an unpleasant face. "Excuse me," she said. "Those are my tea-pots. I was still using them."

Simon spun around. He gasped. His eyes darkened to a deeper blue, and two spots of pink flashed across his pale cheeks. Even his hair looked blonder, as if a ray of sun had hit it.

The girl stared back at him. She was blushing too.

"I'm Simon," he said, holding out his hand. "Simon FitzHenry."

"Campaspe Castle." The girl took his hand and held it.

Jaya put the green mouse machine back in its case and snapped it shut. "See, Leo? It looks like things are going to work out. Come on."

We walked away to the stacks, hand in hand.

I spent most of my spare time for the next few weeks working on my robot project. Jaya helped me, when she wasn't dragging me off to ice-skate or meet her sister or hunt for anti-gravity machines at the weekend flea market in my neighborhood.

I won the science fair blue ribbon in the History of Science category. I built an automaton based some sketches in Leonardo's notebooks for improving his knight's arm motion. Jaya jumped up and down and hugged me, knocking me over. Ms. Kang beamed at me, and my family all banged me on the back, even Dmitri. They were relieved that I was finally acting like a Novikov. I didn't tell them that there were only two other entries in the category.

Mom approves of Jaya. She says she's entrepreneurial.

Jake complained so much about how sucky I'd gotten at Gravity Force III that I built a robot to play it with him. Half the time, it beats him. The other half, it just draws bubbles around all the ships. "This thing is as bad as you are," he tells me.

Jaya keeps talking about visiting the past or the future, but for now we're living in the present.

"You know what the trouble with you is, Cubby?" Sofia said to me the other day. "You're too happy."

Note to Readers

Nikola Tesla really existed in our world. He really did have a laboratory at 33–35 South Fifth Avenue, which really did burn to the ground in a fire that started around 3 a.m. on March 13, 1895. The next morning, Tesla told a reporter from the *New York Times,* "I am in too much grief to talk. What can I say? The work of half my lifetime, very nearly; all my mechanical instruments and scientific apparatus, that it has taken years to perfect, swept away in a fire that lasted only an hour or two. How can I estimate the loss in mere dollars and cents? Everything is gone. I must begin over again."

Tesla really was great friends with Mark Twain (Samuel Clemens), who really did write the books and stories mentioned. He's a wonderful writer; you should read them.

Tesla was also friends with the actress Lillie Langtry and other celebrities of the time. His relationship with Thomas Edison was more complicated. The older inventor was Tesla's mentor and boss, but the relationship soured after Edison promised Tesla $50,000—a fortune at the time—for improving

Edison's inefficient dynamo. Tesla worked on the problem for nearly a year and solved it, but when he asked Edison for the money, Edison refused, saying, "Tesla, you don't understand our American humor."

Louis Latimer really existed, and all his inventions mentioned are real. I don't know whether he was a member of the Electric Club or whether he and Tesla were friends, but they certainly moved in the same circles.

H. G. Wells and Jules Verne were real people too, and they really did write the famous books mentioned. Their books are very exciting; you might like them.

Robert W. Chambers's novel *The Green Mouse* is also a real book. The New York Public Library had a copy on Stack 7 in their Central Research Division when I worked there as a page in high school. My supervisor knew I loved the books on Stack 7, mostly popular fiction from the late nineteenth and early twentieth centuries, and he would put me there on slow days so I could read them. I don't exactly recommend *The Green Mouse*—it's pretty racist—but I would love to get my hands on that machine!

The Czech playwright Karel Čapek coined the term *robot* in a play called *R.U.R.*, which stands for Rossum's Universal Robots.

The Electric Club really existed, with a clubhouse as described at 17 East 22nd Street, just east of where the Flatiron Building is now. However, in our universe the club went bankrupt in 1893 and was forced to auction off the clubhouse and its fixtures. (Electric chandeliers sold for a fraction of what they had cost the club because not many homes or businesses were wired for electric lighting back then.) I imagine that in Leo and

Jaya's universe, a wealthy backer—perhaps Edison or Westinghouse—was able to keep the club in its East 22nd Street home for at least a few more years.

There is no record in our universe of Tesla giving a lecture on March 12, 1895, but he did lecture on other occasions and he insisted that women be allowed to attend, even at venues that usually excluded them. All the views and inventions that he describes in his lecture are taken from his published writings, interviews with him, and contemporary descriptions of his work. However, some are from later in his career.

He really did claim to be working on a death ray. Nobody knows whether he ever succeeded in building one in our universe.

In 1895, New York City really did have elevated steam railroads, horse-drawn stagecoaches, and many other forms of transportation, including steam-powered cable cars.

Readers of *The Grimm Legacy* often ask me whether the New-York Circulating Material Repository really exists. Not in our universe, as far as I know. If any of you ever find one where it does exist, I hope you will tell me.

Librarian's Note

When Polly Shulman asked me to create call numbers for the objects in *The Grimm Legacy* and *The Wells Bequest,* I was excited but a bit nervous. As a librarian, I had created plenty of call numbers for books, DVDs, and the other things you normally find in libraries, but I had never tried doing it for objects before.

How do you assign a call number to magic slippers or to a time machine?!

Because Polly wanted the repository to work just like a real library, I thought the best approach would be to examine the objects the same way I examine books.

When my library gets a new book, I enter the author, title, and other basic information into a database called a catalog. Then I skim the book to figure out what it's about. It isn't always easy to do this quickly, especially if the book is really interesting! After that, I enter three to five subjects—standardized words that describe the topics of the book—into the database.

Finally, I have to decide where the book belongs and assign it a call number. This process, called classification, is the most difficult step. While a book can have many topics, it can only be put in one place in the library. For example, when dealing with a guidebook to London, a librarian has to decide whether to put it with other guidebooks or with books about London. Fortunately, there are systems that help librarians do this. For the repository, we decided to use Dewey decimal classification, the system used in most public libraries.

Dewey decimal classification divides all knowledge into topics and then gives those topics numbers. To determine the right call number for a book, the librarian just has to consider the book's main topic and then find the number most closely associated with that topic. (For example, in most libraries, a London guidebook's main topic would be travel and not London, putting it with other guidebooks.)

The problem in the repository is that objects don't have topics! I dealt with this by giving the objects the same call numbers that a book about those objects would have. Thus, I gave the niddy noddy (I had to look that up in a dictionary) on page 67 the same number Dewey gives to books about spinning yarn (746.12).

The niddy noddy also has a Cutter number (S53). Cutter numbers are based on the name of the book's author and make sure that two books never have the same call number. I had to play with this too. Here *S53* stands for "Shaker" since I decided that this was a Shaker niddy noddy.

The time machine was a big challenge because Dewey decimal classification doesn't provide a call number for books about time machines. In the end, I decided to use the number for relativity theory (530.11). I don't know how the Wells time machine works, but I figured it must have something to do with Einstein's theory of relativity! The Cutter number for the time machine (Z8485) is a code that tells the pages and librarians in the repository that machine is in the oversize collection (indicated by *Z*) and comes from Wells's *Time Machine* (84 = We; 85 = Ti).

If you want to create call numbers for the important objects in your life, check out a book on the Dewey decimal classification in your local library.

I had a great time working with Polly on *The Grimm Legacy* and *The Wells Bequest,* and I hope I will get to assign call numbers to all the great objects in future books about the repository.

—*Cyril Emery*
JULY 2012

Acknowledgments

Time travel is full of pitfalls, many more of which I would have fallen into if not for the generous, painstaking, hilarious help I had from friends, family, colleagues, and strangers, who variously read drafts, uncovered paradoxes, coined terms, corrected my British, provided counsel, poked fun, and helped hunt for the Time Traveller's house: Abby Amsterdam, Robert Butler, Mark Caldwell, Catherine Clarke, Liz Cross, Peter Derrick, Lisa Dierbeck, Stefanie Gerke, Erin Harris, John Hart, Katherine Keenum, Dick Kerr, Sara Kreger, Ruth Landé, Anne Malcolm, Shanti Menon, Miriam Miller, Laurie Muchnick, Alice Naude, Sharyn November, David Prentiss, Lisa Randall, Maggie Robbins, Andrew Scott, Alix Kates Shulman, Teddy Shulman, Andrew Solomon, Greg Sorkin, Owen Thomas, Richard Tuck, Sophy Tuck, Chelsea Wald, Howard Waldman, Jaime Wolf, and Scott York.

I'm especially grateful to David Bacon, who suggested a visit to Tesla's lab; to Anna Christina Büchmann, who kept me going through thick and thin; to Cyril Emery, who conducted me safely through Verne novels and Dewey decimal numbers alike; to Tom Goodwillie, who read endless drafts and suggested a mathematical solution to the problem of oversize storage; to Dee Smith, who bought colored pencils to sketch the death ray; and to my wise and patient editor, Nancy Paulsen; my endlessly supportive agent, Irene Skolnick; and my dear, funny, beloved husband, Andrew Nahem.

TURN THE PAGE TO READ THE
FIRST CHAPTER OF

THE GRIMM LEGACY

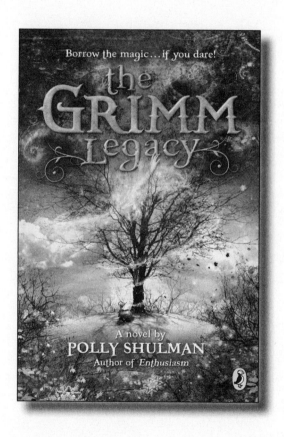

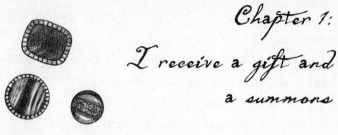

Chapter 1:
I receive a gift and
a summons

Snow fell hard: big, sticky flakes that got under my coat collar where the top button was missing. The weather had delayed my subway, and I was worried I would be late for class.

In front of school, a homeless woman was struggling with a shopping cart. A passing taxi sent out a freezing wave of gray slush, causing the woman and cart to topple over into the gutter.

I had to help. Her hands were icy claws as I pulled her to her feet. She felt much lighter than she looked in her bulky rags. "Thank you," she said, shaking snow off the blanket that had covered her shoulders. Underneath she wore a T-shirt stuffed with newspaper. And on her feet, to my horror, I saw sandals.

The late bell was about to sound, but I couldn't abandon someone wearing sandals in the middle of a snowstorm—not when I had a spare pair of shoes with me. I helped her set the cart back on its wheels, then took my gym sneakers out of my bag. "Here," I said. "Can you use these?" They probably wouldn't fit—I have embarrassingly large feet. But at least they would be better than sandals.

The woman took them and turned them over, studying the soles. She held the right sneaker close to her face and peered inside, seeming to sniff at it. The left she held to her ear like a telephone.

At last she looked at me. Her eyes were surprisingly bright, a pale, luminous gray like storm clouds.

"Thanks," she said.

"You want my socks too? Probably not, they need to be washed." As soon as I'd said it, I realized it was a pretty insensitive thing to say—people with nowhere to live don't have much opportunity to do laundry. Probably they're used to dirty socks.

"Thanks," said the woman again, starting to smell the socks but evidently thinking better of it. "Wait," she said as I turned toward school. She rummaged through the bags in the cart as the snow continued to tumble down and melt in my collar. I was getting impatient, but I waited till the woman found what she was looking for and held it out to me. "Keep it safe."

"Um, thanks."

It was a number 2 pencil—the ordinary yellow kind, with a pink eraser, like you use for the SATs. I put it in my book bag, pulled my scarf tighter, and turned toward the school door.

"Hurry, Elizabeth, you're late," said a grim voice. My social studies teacher, Mr. Mauskopf, was holding the door open for me. He was my favorite teacher, despite his intimidating sternness.

The homeless woman gave him a little wave, and Mr. Mauskopf nodded back as the door swung shut behind us. I thanked him and hurried to my locker, hearing the late bell chime.

The day went downhill from there. Ms. Sandoz made me play volleyball barefoot when she saw I didn't have my sneakers, and charming Sadie Cane and Jessica Farmer spent the period playing Accidentally Stomp on the New Girl's Toes. Then in social studies Mr. Mauskopf announced a research paper due right after New Year's, effectively eliminating the vacation.

"Choose wisely, Elizabeth," he said as he handed me the list of possible topics.

My stepsister Hannah called me that evening to ask me to mail her her black lace top. She'd handed it down to me when she left for college, but with Hannah, gifts rarely stayed given for long.

"What are you up to?" she asked.

"Working on ideas for my social studies research paper. European history, with Mr. Mauskopf."

"I remember Mauskopf—what a weirdo! Does he still wear that green bow tie? And give out demerits if he catches you looking at the clock?"

"Yup." I quoted him: "'Time will pass—but will you?'"

Hannah laughed. "What are you writing about?"

"The Brothers Grimm."

"The fairy-tale guys? For Mauskopf? Are you crazy?"

"It was on his list of suggested topics."

"Don't be a little goose. I bet he just put it on there as a test, to see who would be dumb enough to think fairy tales are history. Hey, I probably still have my term paper from that class. You can use it if you like. I'll trade it for—hm—your good headphones."

"No, thanks," I said.

"You sure? It's about the Paris Commune."

"That's cheating. Anyway, Mr. Mauskopf would notice."

"Suit yourself. Send me that lace top tomorrow, okay? I need it by Saturday." She hung up.

I chewed at the end of my pencil—the one the homeless woman had given me—and stared at the topic I'd circled, wondering whether to follow Hannah's advice about switching topics. Mr. Mauskopf took history very seriously, and fairy tales don't sound that serious. But if he didn't want us writing about the Brothers Grimm, why put them on the topic list?

Fairy tales were a big part of my childhood. I used to sit in my mother's lap while she read them out loud and pretend I could read along—until, after a while, I found I actually could. Later, in the hospital when Mom was too sick to hold a book, it was my turn to read our favorites out loud.

The stories all had happy endings. But they didn't keep Mom from dying.

If she were alive now, I thought, she would definitely approve of my learning more about the men who wrote them. I decided to stick to my choice.

Strange as it sounds, once I decided I found myself actually looking forward to the term paper—it would give me something interesting to do. Vacation was going to be lonely since my best friend, Nicole, had moved to California. I hadn't made any new friends in the four months I'd been at my new school, Fisher, and the girls I used to hang out with were too busy with ballet to pay much attention to me anymore.

I missed my ballet classes, but Dad said we couldn't afford them now that he had to pay for my stepsisters' college tuition, and I was never going to be a professional dancer anyway—I wasn't obsessed enough, and my feet were too big.

• • •

Fairy tales might not be history, but as I learned in the hours I spent in the library over Christmas break, Wilhelm and Jacob Grimm were historians. They didn't invent their fairy tales— they collected them, writing down the folk tales and stories they heard from friends and servants, aristocrats and innkeepers' daughters.

Their first collection of stories was meant for grown-ups and I could see why—they're way too bloody and creepy for children. Even the heroes go around boiling people in oil and feeding them red-hot coals. Imagine Disney making a musical version of "The Girl Without Hands," a story about a girl whose widowed father chops off her hands when she refuses to marry him!

I thought I'd done a pretty good job when I finished the paper, but I still felt nervous when I handed it in. Mr. Mauskopf is a tough grader.

A few days after we returned from vacation, Mr. Mauskopf stopped me in the hall, pointing a long forefinger at the end of an outstretched arm. He always seemed to have twice as many elbows and knuckles as other people. "Elizabeth! Come see me at lunch," he said. "My office."

Was I in trouble? Had my paper creeped him out? Was Hannah right—had I failed some kind of test?

The door to the social studies department office was open, so I knocked on the door frame. Mr. Mauskopf waved me in. "Sit down," he said.

I perched on the edge of a chair.

He handed me my paper, folded in half along the vertical

axis. Comments in his signature brown ink twined across the back. I took a breath and willed myself to look at the grade.

"Nice work, Elizabeth," he said. Was that a smile on his face? Almost.

I opened the paper. He had given me an A. I leaned back, my heart pounding with relief. "Thank you."

"What made you choose this topic?"

"I don't know—I always loved fairy tales. They seem so—so realistic."

"Realistic? That's quite an unusual view," said Mr. Mauskopf with a hint of a smile.

"You're right." I felt dumb. "What I mean is, all the terrible things that happen in fairy tales seem real. Or not real, but genuine. Life is unfair, and the bad guys keep winning and good people die. But I like how that's not always the end of it. Like when the mother dies and turns into a tree and keeps helping her daughter, or when the boy who everybody thinks is an idiot figures out how to outwit the giant. Evil is real, but so is good. They always say fairy tales are simplistic, black and white, but I don't think so. I think they're *complicated*. That's what I love about them."

"I see." Mr. Mauskopf consulted his planner. "You're new this year, aren't you?"

I nodded. "I used to go to Chase, but both my stepsisters are in college now, so the tuition . . ." I stopped, a little embarrassed to be discussing my family finances.

"Ah, so you have stepsisters," Mr. Mauskopf said. "I hope they aren't the evil Grimm kind?"

"A little," I replied. Veronica's a lot older, and Hannah—

Hannah hated sharing her room with me after my father and I moved in. Hannah liked having someone to boss around the way Veronica bossed her. Hannah was always taking my things and never letting me use hers. But I couldn't say any of that—it seemed too disloyal. "My stepsister Hannah was in your class—Hannah Vane," I said instead.

"Say no more," said Mr. Mauskopf. He gave me the ghost of a smile, as if we were sharing a joke. Then he asked, "Did you ever replace your sneakers?"

"My sneakers?"

"I recall seeing you give away your sneakers—very generous of you."

"I haven't had a chance," I told him. I didn't want to get into our embarrassing financial situation again.

"I see." He cleared his throat. "Well, Elizabeth, this is all very satisfactory. Would you like a job?"

"A job? What kind of a job?"

"An after-school job. A friend of mine at the New-York Circulating Material Repository tells me they have an opening. It's a great place. I worked there myself when I was your age."

I tried to imagine him at my age, but the bow tie got in the way. "Is that like a library?"

" 'Like a library.' Exactly. Well put."

"Yeah—yes, please. I'd like that," I said. A job meant money for things like new gym shoes, and it wasn't like I had a crammed social schedule.

Everybody at Fisher had known each other for aeons. It was already taking them a long time to warm up to me, the new girl. Then I made the mistake of sticking up for Mallory Mason when some of the cool girls were making up songs about her weight and her braces. Worst of all, Ms. Stanhope, the assistant principal, overheard me and used me as an example of "compassionate leadership" in her next "class chat." After that, nobody wanted to have anything to do with me except Mallory herself. But I didn't actually like her.

Who knows? Maybe if I took the library job, I would make friends there.

Plucking his fountain pen from his breast pocket, Mr. Mauskopf wrote a number on a slip of paper, folded it vertically, and handed it to me pinched between his index and middle fingers. "Call and ask for Dr. Rust," he said.

"Thank you, Mr. Mauskopf." The bell rang, and I hurried to my next class.

That afternoon when I got home, I went straight to my room, avoiding the living room so Cathy, my stepmother, wouldn't rope me into doing errands or force me to listen to her bragging about my stepsisters.

I wished my father were home so I could tell him about my new job. Not that he listened to me much these days.

Instead, I told Francie, my doll. I know it sounds babyish, but she was my mom's doll, and sometimes talking to her makes me feel a tiny bit like I'm talking to Mom.

Francie smiled at me encouragingly. Of course, she always smiles since her smile is sewn on—but I still took it as a good sign.

Francie is the only one of Mom's doll collection that Cathy let me keep after Hannah chipped Lieselotte's nose. Lieselotte was the crown of Mom's collection. She's a bisque doll, made in Germany over one hundred and fifty years ago and worth a lot of money.

"I'll just put these away until you're old enough to take care of them properly," Cathy had said when she packed the dolls away.

I knew back then it wasn't worth protesting. Cathy always sided with her own daughters. At first I used to complain to my father, but he would just say, "I need you to get along with your stepsisters. I know you can. You're my little peacemaker. You have a big, generous heart, just like your mother." So I told Cathy I didn't break Lieselotte, but I didn't say who did.

"If you're not old enough to take responsibility, you're certainly not old enough to play with dolls this valuable," said Cathy. "Now, don't start crying—here, you can keep this one; it's not worth anything. Even *you* can't do much damage to a rag doll. You'll thank me when you're older." She handed me Francie and shut the lid on Lieselotte's look of faint, aristocratic surprise.

"Time to make a phone call, Francie?" I asked.

She smiled a yes.

I called the number on the slip of paper.

"Lee Rust," said the person who answered.

"Hi, Dr. Rust? I—this is Elizabeth Rew, and my social studies teacher, Mr. Mauskopf, said to call you about a job?"

"Ah, yes, Elizabeth. Stan said you would be calling. I'm glad to hear from you."

Stan? So Mr. Mauskopf had a first name?

"Can you come in for an interview next Thursday after school?"

"All right. Where do I go?" I asked.

Dr. Rust gave me an address not far from my school, east of Central Park. "Ask for me at the front desk; they'll send you up."

The discreet brass plaque beside the door said *The New-York Circulating Material Repository*. From the outside, it looked like a standard Manhattan brownstone, the last in a long row. Next door was a big old mansion, the kind that are now mostly consulates or museums. That place would have made an impressive library, I thought as I walked up the steps to the repository and pulled open the heavy doors. It was just the sort of place I used to go to with my father, before he met Cathy. We used to spend every rainy weekend in museums and libraries. Especially the less famous ones, like the Museum of the City of New York and the New-York Historical Society, with their odd collections of things—old china and tinsmiths' tools and models of what the city looked like before the Revolution. We would play a game: pick out which painting (or clock, or chair, or photograph, or whatever) would have been Mom's favorite.

I hadn't been to a museum with my dad in years, but when I opened the doors, the slightly dusty smell brought it all flooding back. I felt as if I'd stepped back through time into a place that was once my home.

Through some trick of geometry, the entrance opened out into a large rectangular room apparently wider than the building that held it. At the far end was a massive desk, elaborately carved in dark wood.

A guy my age was sitting behind it.

But not just any guy—Marc Merritt, the tallest, coolest, best

forward our basketball team had ever known. I had once seen
him sink an apple core into the wastebasket in the teachers'
lounge from his seat across the corridor in study hall, with both
doors partly closed. He looked like a taller, African American
version of Jet Li, and he moved like him too, with the same
acrobatic quickness. He was in Mr. Mauskopf's other social studies section, and we had health ed together. Most of the girls at
Fisher had crushes on him. I would too, if I didn't think it would
be presumptuous . . . Well, to be honest, I did anyway. I was
pretty sure he had no idea who I was.

"Hi, I'm here to see Dr. Rust?" I said.

"All right. Who should I say is here?"

"Elizabeth Rew."

Marc Merritt picked up the receiver of an old-fashioned
telephone, the kind with a dial. "Elizabeth Rew here to see you,
Doc. . . . Sure. . . . No, till six today. . . . All right." He pointed a
long arm—longer than Mr. Mauskopf's, even—toward a fancy
brass elevator door. "Fifth floor, take a left, through the arch.
You'll see it."

When I stepped out of the elevator, corridors branched away
in three directions. I couldn't imagine how they fit it all in one
narrow brownstone. I went down three steps through an arch to
a small, book-lined room.

Dr. Rust was slight and wiry, with thick, shaggy hair just on
the brown side of red and a billion freckles.

"Elizabeth. I'm glad to meet you." We shook hands. "Please,
have a seat. How is Stan?"

Strict but fair. Stern-looking, but with an underlying twinkle
in his eye. Oddly dressed. "Fine," I said.

"Still keeping that great beast in that tiny apartment, is he?"

"I guess? I've never been to his apartment."

"Well. Let's see, you're in Stan's European history class, yes?"

"That's right."

"Good, good. Stan's never sent us a bad page. He says you're hardworking and warmhearted, with an independent mind—which is high praise from Stan, believe me. So this is really a formality, but just to be thorough, do you do the dishes at home?"

What kind of a question was that? "Yes, most of the time." One more bad thing about my stepsisters going away to college—I was the only kid left to do chores.

"About how often?"

"Most days. Five or six times a week, probably."

"And how many have you broken this year?"

"Dishes?"

"Yes, dishes, glasses, that sort of thing."

"None. Why?"

"Oh, we can never be too careful. When was the last time you lost your keys?"

"I never lose my keys."

"Excellent. All right, sort these, please." Dr. Rust handed me a box of buttons.

"Sort them? Sort them how?"

"Well, that's up to you, isn't it?"

This had to be the strangest interview I'd ever heard of. Was I going to lose the job because Dr. Rust didn't like the way I sorted buttons?

I poured them out on the desk and turned them all faceup.

There were large wooden disks and tiny pearls, shiny square buttons made of red or blue or yellow plastic, sparkly star-shaped ones with rhinestones that looked as if they would shred their buttonholes, little knots of rope, a set of silver buttons each engraved with a different flower, tiny rabbits carved from coral, plain transparent plastic buttons for inside waistbands, big glass things like mini doorknobs, a heavy gold button studded with what looked like real diamonds.

I grouped them by material: metal; wood and other plant products; bone, shell, and other animal parts; stone; plastic and other man-made materials, including glass. Then I divided each category into subgroups, also by material. Within the subgroups, I ranked them by weight.

"I see. Where would you put this?" Dr. Rust handed me a metal button, the kind with a loop on the back rather than holes. The front part had a piece of woven cloth of some sort, set behind glass.

I hesitated. Should it go in metals, in man-made materials for the glass, or in plants for the cloth? Maybe the cloth was wool, though, which would put it in animal parts. "Am I allowed to ask a question?" I said.

"Of course. Always ask questions. As the Akan proverb says, 'The one who asks questions does not lose his way.'"

"Where's Akan?"

"The Akan people are from west Africa. They have a remarkably rich proverb tradition. Perhaps because they believe in asking questions."

"Oh. Okay—what's the button made of?"

"Excellent question. Gold, rock crystal, and human hair."

Not man-made materials, then; maybe stone. Other than that, the answer didn't help me much. By weight, the button was mostly gold, so maybe it should go in with the metals? But I had put the diamond-looking one in stone, not metal. I decided to classify the new button by its weirdest component and put it in the animal pile.

"Interesting," said Dr. Rust. "Sort them again."

I scrambled them and resorted, making an elaborate grid of size and color. It started with red at the top and ran through the rainbow down to violet at the bottom, with extra rows for black and white. From left to right, it started with tiny collar buttons and finished with vast badges.

"Where would you put this?" Dr. Rust handed me a zipper.

A zipper! "Why didn't you give me this the last time?" I said in dismay. "I could have put it with the metals."

Was it my imagination, or had Dr. Rust's freckles moved? Hadn't the large one over the left eye been over the right eye earlier?

I scrambled the buttons again and started over. This time I sorted them by shape. I put the zipper with the toggles and a rectangular button carved with zigzags. I didn't like that solution, but it was better than nothing.

Dr. Rust raised an eyebrow (no large freckle anywhere near now) and asked, "Which do you think is the most valuable?"

I considered the diamond one but picked an enameled peacock with blue gems in its tail. Dr. Rust seemed pleased.

"The oldest?"

I had no idea. I picked one of the silver ones.

"The most beautiful?"

I was getting a little impatient with all this. I picked one of the plastic ones, in a lovely shade of green. Dr. Rust didn't seem quite to believe me. "The most powerful?"

"How can a button be powerful?"

"Oh, I think you'll find over time that every object here has its own unique qualities. You'll find that the materials in our collections speak to you."

Did that mean I'd gotten the job?

Still, some of the buttons did seem to draw me more than others. I chose a black glass button with a disturbing geometry. Dr. Rust picked it up and examined it closely for a long time while I watched the freckles, trying to catch them moving. Wasn't that butterfly shape of freckles on the left side just a minute ago?

"Well, Elizabeth, this has been most illuminating, but we both have a lot of work waiting," said Dr. Rust at last, as if *I* had been the one staring endlessly at a button. "Can you start next week? Here, I think you'd better have this."

Someone opened the door just as Dr. Rust handed me one last button. It matched the buttons on my coat—it might have been my missing top button.

"And here's Marc, right on time."

READ POLLY SHULMAN'S

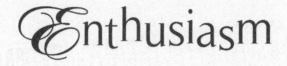

Enthusiasm

"Whenever someone asks for a reading suggestion,
Enthusiasm is the first word off my tongue."
   —Stephenie Meyer, author of the Twilight Saga